UNCRASHABLE
DAKOTA

ANDY MARINO

UNCRASHABLE DAKOTA

HENRY HOLT AND COMPANY ∫ NEW YORK

Henry Holt and Company, LLC
Publishers since 1866
175 Fifth Avenue
New York, New York 10010
macteenbooks.com

Henry Holt books may be purchased for business or promotional use.
For information on bulk purchases, please contact the Macmillan Corporate
and Premium Sales Department at (800) 221-7945 x5442 or
by e-mail at specialmarkets@macmillan.com.

Library of Congress Cataloging-in-Publication Data
Marino, Andy.
Uncrashable Dakota / Andy Marino. — First edition.
pages   cm
Summary: In 1912, an airship on its maiden flight is hijacked and young Hollis Dakota,
heir to the Dakota Aeronautics empire, his friend Delia, and stepbrother Rob, become
embroiled in a family feud that could send the ship—and them—crashing from the sky.
ISBN 978-0-8050-9630-9 (hardback) — ISBN 978-0-8050-9958-4 (e-book)
[1. Airships—Fiction. 2. Hijacking of aircraft—Fiction. 3. Vendetta—Fiction. 4. Social
classes—Fiction. 5. Stepbrothers—Fiction. 6. Adventure and adventurers—Fiction.] I. Title.
PZ7.M33877Umt 2013   [Fic]—dc23   2013018845

First Edition—2013 / Designed by April Ward

Printed in the United States of America

1 3 5 7 9 10 8 6 4 2

FOR TONY

HOLLIS DAKOTA was ten years old when his parents took him to the shipyard that sprawled like a spilled bucket of ash across the river from New York City. His family owned the shipyard, but Hollis had never been there, because he lived in the sky.

The Dakota family business was airships. The yard was their clattering, smoky birthplace. Hollis had seen it from above: a gated compound the size of a city, gridded with factories and littered with the skeletal husks of unfinished ships. He pictured it this way, spread out in his mind like a full-color map, as he followed his parents along a wide gravel road between two hangars. The sulfurous smoke that hung about the yard slithered into his nose. His eyes began to water. He stumbled dizzily behind his parents with rubbery legs and hesitant steps.

He was getting groundsick.

"Whoa!" his father said after a while, as if Hollis and his mother were horses. They stopped walking. They were somewhere in the center of the yard, past the hangars, standing in a vast expanse of packed dirt. Hollis didn't know why they were here. The whole trip had the winking, secretive air of Christmas morning. His father cleared his throat with a phlegmy rasp and swallowed with a pained grimace.

"You are free to spit in front of me if you must, Wendell," his mother said. "I've seen worse."

"That was more dust than spit, I'm afraid." His father used the tip of his finger to balance loose, smudgy spectacles on the bridge of his nose. "Well. Here we are."

Hollis rubbed the grit from his eyes, and the hazy confusion of his surroundings sharpened into a magnificent scene. He had been led into the heart of a grand excavation: the remains of some prehistoric monster whose rib cage alone would dwarf a whale. Unearthed silver bones curved up to challenge the tall buildings of Manhattan rising out of the fog to the east.

"You see," his father said, "I want you both to experience firsthand the not-so-humble origins of what will one day be the flagship of the Dakota Aeronautics fleet."

Not monster bones, Hollis thought. The steel frame of a new airship big enough to carry a Hawaiian island in its belly. He tried not to look disappointed that he wasn't touring a city-sized fossil.

"Hot rivet!"

Hollis tracked the insistent shout to a scaffold embracing the nearest steel rib. Fifty feet above the ground, a man flung a tiny piece of metal from a steaming brazier. There was an arcing flash, and his partner caught it in a wooden bowl. In a single practiced motion, he extracted it with a pair of tongs, held it against the framework, and answered with a "*hot riv-ETT*" of his own. Two diminutive figures bearing mallets emerged from a shadowy part of the scaffold, and a quick, brutal bashing took place to drive the rivet in.

"What you're witnessing up there is the hull in its infancy," his father said.

Hollis was entranced by the loose-limbed courage of the workers. In less than a minute, they secured four rivets. Their voices rang out in a call-and-answer that harmonized with others up and down the row. Some of the voices sounded like they belonged to women.

Not women, he realized, squinting. *Children*.

"She's going to be a real cloud splitter," his father said. "The perfect combination of luxury and practicality, relaxation and exploration, comfort and luxury. Brought to life by all this productive sweat you can feel in the air."

Hollis tried to detect moisture.

"I'm just not sure it's going to be *big* enough, dear," his mother said.

His father failed to catch the gentle sarcasm. He unclasped his hands from behind his back and stretched them out straight to either side.

"Darling, I assure you, you're standing inside the framework of the world's first metropolis in the sky, with all the familiar diversions and entertainments of Manhattan and space to accommodate enough passengers to rival the population of a modest northeastern town. And the first airship to be positively"—he paused to nod at a gang of passing workmen shouldering long wooden boards, then lowered his voice to a whisper—"*uncrashable*."

His mother snorted a single quick *hmmph*. "Uncrashable?" She shook her head. "That's a bit cavalier, don't you think?"

"But, Lucy, you have to remember . . . ," his father said, trailing off before he could tell her what it was she had to remember. Hollis considered the word *cavalier*. It conjured images of charging cavalry horses and puffs of pistol smoke.

"Don't you *but, Lucy*, me," she said. "You know as well as I do where that kind of headstrong attitude landed your father."

"My father never landed anywhere."

She put her hands on her hips. "Exactly."

O**N A CLEAR,** bright morning in April of 1912, Hollis helped his mother cut the ribbon that hung across the first-class entrance to the *Wendell Dakota*. It was a two-person job, because the scissors, like the airship, were enormous. One of the silver blades caught the sun and beamed it across the faces of the crowd gathered at the Newark Sky-dock; everybody blinked at once. The blades snapped together. There was a momentary hush as the halves of the ribbon whipped and fluttered in the wind. Then the crowd erupted into cheers. Tall black hats tumbled up into the air along with short-brimmed bowlers and floppy caps.

A pair of earnest young crewmen hopped up on the platform with Hollis and his mother. They took the giant scissors and disappeared, leaving the two Dakotas to wave and grin and bask in the hoots and hollers of the exhilarated crowd. Hollis felt a gentle hand on his shoulder and glanced up at his mother. Without unfreezing her smile, she fanned her face with a few up-and-down waves of her hand and rolled her eyes. Hollis gave a quick nod in agreement. He was sweating right through the fabric of his custom-tailored suit, giving some of the richest people in the world—not to mention their servants, biographers, music instructors, translators, masseuses, and governesses—a fine view of the spreading stains that had already claimed his armpits. And he thought it must be ten times worse for his mother, who was wearing a complicated dress topped with a lace collar that crept up her neck and presented her head to the world like a blossoming rose.

Hollis let his gaze drift across the jostling landscape of passengers waiting to board, their faces flushed and shiny in the heat. Uniformed stewards assigned to each prominent family were scattered about to ensure that no first-class feathers were ruffled by line-cutting or a lack of decorum. Red-capped porters dotted the crowd like cherries on a rich dessert. As high as the roof of a midtown office building, the top of the sky-dock was the first-class rallying point, where the wide gangway transferred passengers to their expansive staterooms in the upper third of the airship. Below them, second-class travelers looked forward to their own well-appointed rooms, while third class would make for shared bunks (men to starboard, women to port). At the bottom of the towering sky-dock, steerage passengers were bound for the holds that surrounded the coal bunkers and boiler rooms.

"I suppose I'll take a hot day over a stormy one," Hollis's mother said, blowing a kiss to some ancient specimen whose pince-nez flashed as he bowed.

"I have to get out of this suit," Hollis said, resisting the urge to loosen his tie. Using his hand to block the sun, he observed the far edge of the platform where the last passengers were gathered. Beyond them, the blue sky hung empty, and he imagined the clouds had been driven away at his father's command.

BESIDES THE CREW MEMBERS readying the ship for launch, Hollis was the first person to climb aboard. It was part of his belated birthday present: he'd turned thirteen last month. He clanked up the ramp from the snipped ribbon to the first-class promenade deck in heavy, steel-lined boots. Every passenger wore them for boarding a Dakota Aeronautics ship so as not to get blown out into the sky by a vicious gust of high-altitude wind. Accidents happened, but the boots kept the blow-away rate to a minimum.

Hollis was greeted at the top of the ramp by Marius Rogers, one of the laborers at the fringes of any given airship's crew—assisting the chief second-class purser, performing minor plumbing repairs, helping the ship's librarian stay organized. The joke was that Marius had a secret twin; he always seemed to be in two places at once.

"Morning, Mr. Dakota." Marius tipped a nonexistent cap by tugging on a lock of his hair. Hollis held out his hand, and they shook. Marius made a face. "You stick that in water?"

"It's hot out."

"Oh, come on, now. We're in New Jersey, not New Guinea. And it's not even summer." He dropped Hollis's hand with exaggerated disgust. Then he stood a little straighter and added a crisp, "Sir."

"Not you, too," Hollis said. Lately, crewmen had begun to treat him with an alarming level of professional respect. "Marius, you don't have to *sir* me."

"Better get used to it."

"Don't—"

"Sir."

Hollis sighed. "When did you slink aboard, anyway?"

"Been here three days."

"Shoveling coal?"

Marius laughed. "I doubt the stokers want me anywhere near a furnace."

Hollis eyed the screw top of a hip flask peeking out of the crewman's uniform pocket. "I'm glad you caught this assignment."

"Honest truth, I would've booked passage anyway, just for the ride."

"Maybe next time you'll get to," Hollis said. Marius smiled weakly. Concerned that the man had taken this as a threat to his job, Hollis pointed at the screw top. "I don't care about that."

Marius shifted his weight, and the flask dropped out of sight. "You know, Mr. Dakota," he said, "I never seen anything like this ship. Every hair in place. They could load the passengers, give it a shove, and let it fly itself across the Atlantic."

"It would have to be a pretty big shove."

Hollis stepped out onto the flat expanse of the first-class promenade deck. The fresh-cut pine planks had been sanded, waxed, and buffed to a glossy sheen. Straight ahead, the over-hang of the topmost recreational area—the sundeck (steel-lined boots required at all times)—sheltered fifty reclining chairs bolted down in a perfect row. In the enticing shade behind them, a hundred round black stools squatted next to a mahogany bar as long as a city block. Unopened bottles of clear and amber liquor, including his grandfather Samuel Dakota's patented Moonshine Whiskey, were stocked ten feet high along the back of the bar, the small print of their labels reflected in gilded mirrors. Bright little dots of light slid up and down the bottles in time with the gentle bobbing of the docked airship.

Above the bar was the row of glass that defined the star-board edge of Il Bambino's Restaurant. Its chef had abandoned a thriving career in Florence to create a first-class menu for the *Wendell Dakota*'s maiden voyage. On his birthday, Hollis had been treated to Il Bambino's signature dish—braised rab-bit on a bed of prunes in a white wine reduction—which he suspected was a punishment disguised as a gift. Skewering the center of the restaurant was the false smokestack, an exact replica of its two functional sisters that loomed over the back half of the sundeck. Each funnel was emblazoned with a black beetle, the logo of Dakota Aeronautics.

Hollis leaned against the rail and craned his neck in the other direction, toward the bow. Both the promenade and sundecks continued unimpeded for a few hundred feet, then began to slope upward, gently at first, then severely, until Hollis's eyes were following a vertical wall up into the sky, as high as the smokestacks. This was the forward prop tower, built above the nose of the ship to house the turbine that spun the main propeller—the biggest in the world, and *Propulsion Weekly*'s current centerfold. Only three of the eight steel blades were visible from his vantage point, each the size of a freight-train car.

"I think Mr. Castor is trying to get your attention," Marius said, pointing toward the dock.

Hollis tore his gaze from the tower. His mother waved up at him. A tall man had joined her on the platform. He put his arms out at his sides, palms up, and cocked his head—the universal gesture for *quit messing around and get on with it*.

Hollis gave his stepfather a brusque professional nod. He pulled a glass vial from the breast pocket of his suit and dangled it out over the rail. The crowd hushed and watched him expectantly. The christening ritual for a new airship's maiden voyage was usually performed by one of the company's board members, but earlier this morning, Hollis had unwrapped a surprise present to find the vial of dirt. He could still hear his mother's low, serious voice:

Send her off, Hollis. Your father would have wanted you to.

Down on the dock, photographers hid behind black curtains, thumbs crooked over the triggers of their silver flashbulbs. Hollis glanced up at Marius, who said softly, "If you'd like, I can give you a nudge when the wind's just right."

Hollis took a deep breath. "Thanks, but I think I'm supposed to do it myself."

A proper airship christening was performed by spilling the dirt out into the sky at the precise moment the wind shifted, scattering it *away* from the ship. It was bad luck for the dirt to blow back onto the deck, which was why the more experienced members of the aeronautical community generally performed christenings.

Hollis uncorked the vial and closed his eyes against the blinding pops of a few premature flashbulbs. He felt the wind swirl around him. He concentrated, listening hard, trying to plot its meandering course. The glass vial was getting slippery in his sweaty hand.

Don't rush it, Hollis.

All at once, the wind began to cool the back of his neck. He pictured the dirt scattering above the crowd. He could practically trace the journey of each little particle through the air. It was now or never.

He tipped the vial.

The crowd cheered. He opened his eyes in time to see the dirt float down in a loose spiral away from the side of the airship before vanishing into the sky. He exhaled. Flashbulbs popped. Frantic photographers rushed to pull glass slides from their cameras as assistants replaced the bulbs. His stepfather beamed. Leaping up onto the platform, his stepbrother, Rob Castor, whistled shrilly between two fingers jammed in the corners of his mouth, then doffed his hat to let hair the color of sun-bleached straw whip in the wind.

Marius saluted and returned to his post at the top of the ramp. Hollis put the empty vial back in his pocket, a souvenir of his first christening. When he glanced down to shield his eyes from the extra-bright glare of a flashbulb surrounded by a white reflecting umbrella, his breath caught in his throat.

A tiny pile of dirt sat atop the otherwise spotless railing, a smudge that hadn't been carried out into the sky.

He told himself that it could have come from somewhere else. A bit of debris that fell from the prop tower. Ash from a crewman's cigarette. But he knew that every inch of the ship had been scrubbed, spit-shined, and polished for today's maiden send-off.

It had to be dirt from the vial.

Hollis leaned his elbows casually against the rail as if he were taking one last look across the dock and nudged the dirt with his sleeve to brush it over the edge. He strained his eyes to make sure every last speck blew away, but such a tiny bit was lost as soon as it hit the swirling air.

"**H**EY, DAKOTA!"

When Rob Castor yelled his name, Hollis had already been at the entrance with his mother for an hour, greeting the first-class passengers as they clanked on deck. To distract himself from the secret little smudge of dirt that darkened his thoughts, Hollis was keeping a tally of the old society ladies who insisted upon treating him like the cutest baby in the world. So far he'd endured eleven head pats, seven cheek pinches, and three nightmarish kisses. Now, instead of merely being damp, his clothes were infused with the clashing odors of mothballs and lavender.

"Rob," he said with relief as the two Castors appeared beside him. At fourteen, Rob stood an inch or two taller than Hollis. Since the day they met nearly three years ago, Rob had always been the heavier one, until a bout of influenza that kept him bedridden on their last voyage aboard the airship *Secret Wish* had left him gaunt and hollow-eyed. Although he'd been fully recovered for several weeks, his former stockiness seemed to have deserted him for good. Equal parts dapper and shabby, he wore a finely tailored pinstripe suit like his father and a beat-up peaked cap that he hid when he slept so Hollis's mother couldn't dispose of it.

"How are the celebrities?" Rob leaned in close. "Pungent, it seems."

"And never ending. The Countess of Rothes tried to peck off my face."

"How terrible for you. Heavy lies the crown, eh?"

"I wouldn't know."

A pair of yelping Pekingese bounced daintily onboard, their leashes attached to the gloved fist of a fierce-looking old maid trailed by a coterie of pursers bearing luggage. With maniacal insistence, the animals demanded the attention of Hollis's mother and stepfather.

"Did you hear about our class schedule?" Rob asked.

"I assumed it would be the usual."

"It is. Except it starts today."

Hollis's plastered-on smile wavered. "What do you mean, today?"

"I mean today as in these waking hours we're currently occupying."

"We've never had classes on launch day before."

"The Pea's exercising her authority to hit us where it hurts. She's been cozying up to Captain Quincy."

The Pea was Miss Betzengraf, who favored green wool dresses too tight for her short, plump figure. She traveled with the aeronautical families, charged with maintaining a normal schedule of lessons amidst the constant chaos of embarking and disembarking, sky-docking and sky-crossing. A few of their classmates insisted that she was a gypsy from Romania who was constantly placing ancient curses upon her two least favorite students, Hollis Dakota and Rob Castor.

"You know," Hollis said, his mother's most recent lecture fresh in his mind, "I think we should try a little harder. Go to *some* of the classes, at least."

Rob shot him a squinty sidelong glance, then nodded solemnly. He removed his cap—first undoing the chin strap that kept it from blowing off his head—and held it across his heart. "You speak the sky's honest truth, Dakota. We haven't been fair to Miss Betzengraf. We haven't been fair to our parents. And most of all—"

"I'm not joking. People are starting to take stock of my behavior."

Now Hollis was quoting his mother directly. Rob arranged his face into a droopy mask of sadness and regret, wiped an invisible tear from his eye, and flung it down to the deck with a dramatic flourish. "We haven't been fair to *ourselves.*"

There was a riot of blue and gold as an army of porters rushed past with luggage carts and began dismantling a teetering pile of trunks and boxes dragged aboard by five weary attendants. The dogs transferred their affections to a peacock-feathered handbag. Hollis's mother and stepfather stiffened their postures. She straightened her dress while he smoothed his necktie.

"Behold," Rob whispered. "His lordship and the lady Sir Edmund Juniper!"

The Junipers appeared in the shadow of their suitcase mountain. Edmund Juniper was the fourth-richest man in the world and was dressed, as always, like the avid golfer he most certainly was not. (He simply preferred the "fashions of the links.") Hollis had seen him decked out in plaid shorts for stuffy, unbearable dinners where all the other men wore tuxedos. He also refused to wear sky-boots on the exposed decks, which used to make Hollis's father agitated, forcing him to fix his spectacles several times a minute. Edmund hailed from an old New York real estate family (the lordship was Rob's invention) and, as far as Hollis could tell, didn't do anything except spend his family's money. According to Rob, this money was very old and arranged in piles.

Edmund strutted over to Jefferson Castor and gave him a vigorous handshake. Then he pulled the cigarette from his mouth and handed it to an attendant who had materialized beside him at just the right moment.

"My whole damn body's shaking like a leaf!" Edmund said happily, stamping his foot on the deck and visibly unnerving Hollis's mother and stepfather.

"On behalf of Dakota Aeronautics," his mother began, "I'd like to welcome you—"

"A ship like this gives off electrical vapors," Edmund

explained, taking her hand, "which I can feel in my toes. Have you met my wife?" He groped the air behind him.

Hollis tried to imitate his mother's professionalism and held his vacant smile. The newest Mrs. Juniper wore a simple dress that looked light and comfortable, unlike the dense, showy garment Hollis's mother wore. He figured that when you were as rich as the Junipers, you didn't have anybody left to impress. Maybe that was why Edmund didn't seem to care what anyone thought of his domestic arrangement. His divorce had been frowned upon, but high-class reputations had survived worse. It was marrying a nineteen-year-old governess that gave his social circle a case of the horrified gasps.

"And you must be young Master Dakota."

Mrs. Juniper was standing before him, offering an alarmingly pale hand which dangled at the end of her arm, palm down. Was he supposed to kiss it? She smelled like honeysuckle and had very white teeth. It occurred to Hollis that she was only six years his senior. And married to a stout old man.

"I am the . . . young master," he agreed—at the same time wanting desperately to kick himself. *Young master, Hollis? Really?*

He could sense Rob's internal quiver as his stepbrother stifled laughter. And suddenly Rob's hand was holding Mrs. Juniper's as he brought it to his lips and kissed it gently.

"Clarissa Juniper," she said. When Edmund turned to collect her, she gave Hollis a small bow. "We are very much looking forward to spending time on your uncrashable ship.

It's all anyone is talking about." The newlyweds walked off, arm in arm.

"I hadn't realized it was *your* ship," Rob said.

"Oh, shut up."

"Whatever the young master wishes."

Rob nodded at a hawklike patrician thudding his cane along the deck with every step. Hollis scoured his brain for the man's identity. His mother gave him little pop quizzes from time to time, as it would soon be his job to know every important passenger by his or her face.

"Colonel something-or-other," Hollis said.

"General," Rob corrected. "Swallowtail Ovaltine the Fourth."

Making up first-class names was a reliable source of launch-day entertainment, but right now Hollis was vaguely annoyed that he couldn't think of the man's actual title. Behind the colonel/general with the percussive cane, a plump little boy was showing a sweat-drenched steward a card trick. The steward pulled a card from a fanned-out deck. The boy screwed up his face, bit his lip, and closed his eyes. Finally he exclaimed, "Three of diamonds!"

The steward reluctantly turned the card toward the boy and said, "*So* close, sir—king of hearts. I'm sure that was your next guess."

"It was!" the boy said, snatching the card. "You threw me off, that's all."

"You are a wonderful and mysterious magician, sir," the steward said wearily.

"I know." The boy handed the steward the pile of cards in his hand. "Please arrange these carefully on my night table."

"Yes, sir." The steward sighed and clicked his heels together before pocketing the cards and rushing off to attend to the boy's parents.

"He really does seem like a *wonderful* magician, that one," Rob said.

"The true young master of this voyage," Hollis agreed. "So what time's our first class supposed to be?"

"Dakota, you can't be serious."

"I am serious. Except . . ."

"Ah. I knew you'd come around."

"We do have to meet up with Delia."

"*Delia!*" Rob exclaimed, as if he'd just now remembered the name of their friend. "So I'm not worth it, but when Delia enters the picture, you've once again conveniently forgotten the location of the classroom."

"I have that stuff she wanted me to bring her," Hollis said.

"What stuff?"

"Electrics. Wires. Junk. I don't know."

"For a bomb."

"Not for a bomb, Rob."

"She's an anarchist. I always suspected."

"She is not. She's just, you know, Delia."

"Either way," Rob said. "It's *yes sir, no sir* until after lunch, right? All *P*s and *Q*s. Then we accidentally get lost on the way to lessons."

An immaculately groomed hound sniffed its way across the deck, clearing the lane for a young couple and their twin daughters. *Dr. and Mrs. Jacob Wellspring.* Hollis was proud of himself for the speed of his face-to-name association. *And their children . . .* but before he could think of the girls' names, his mother was calling out, "Junie! Jessie! How wonderful of you to join us!"

One of the girls ran over and curtsied. Hollis watched his mother *oooh* and *ahhh* at the stupid bow in Junie or Jessie's hair, air-kiss her pudgy cheeks, and make a theatrical fuss over how pretty and grown-up she looked. Jefferson Castor beamed, placing a hand on his wife's waist. Their eyes met. Hollis was struck by something he had never considered: his mother could be planning to have a child with Castor. A new baby to unite their fractured families. His collar suddenly felt like it was choking him. He took a deep breath and tried to reassure himself. *She's still Lucy Dakota. She kept my father's name.*

The other twin hung back, making some kind of inscrutable face.

"She looks like a little schemer," Rob said.

The girl pulled a toy pig from her pocket and twisted its curlicue tail until a tinny melody filled the air: "Pop Goes the Weasel."

Hollis shuddered inwardly. He didn't like that toy one bit, although he would have been hard-pressed to explain why. Voices of the boarding passengers seemed to rise in pitch, an onslaught of nonsense syllables grating against his nerves.

"You ever seen a mulberry bush?" Rob asked.

Hollis and the little girl locked eyes for a moment.

"I wish she'd quit it with that pig."

LATER, AS THE SUN crept past its highest point, the boarding ramps were withdrawn into the empty sky-dock. Hollis watched the last of the first-class passengers—a group of single men who'd made a big show of waiting until women, elderly folks, and families were aboard—cross the deck and disappear down the Grand Staircase beyond the bar. From there, they would disperse into a labyrinth of thickly carpeted corridors and funnel into their staterooms, where they would remain until the ship had safely launched.

Hollis and Rob followed their parents through the shade of the overhanging sundeck in time to see the final passenger make his way down, ushered by a patient steward. They rested for a moment, silently basking in the splendor of the Grand Staircase, which had been designed to evoke the sumptuous interior of an Italian prince's villa. *De'Medici*, Hollis thought. *Or maybe da Vinci.* His brain was scrambled from the day's forced chatter. It was a prince who favored solid gold, at any rate—the railings alone looked as if they weighed several tons. Hollis wiped his forehead with his sleeve. Jefferson Castor mopped his with a monogrammed handkerchief.

"One of these days, I'm going to hire a substitute family

to stand in for us as the welcoming committee," Jefferson said. "We'll put out an advertisement for look-alikes, or some such. One more clammy handshake from a perfect stranger, and I'll abandon ship."

Hollis almost chimed in—*same here!*—but caught himself before he could give his stepfather the satisfaction of a shared moment.

"You were positively charming, Jeff," Hollis's mother said as she collapsed into a bulky, overstuffed sofa that reminded Hollis of Miss Betzengraf. "The passengers value the personal touch." She nodded at Hollis. "On the other hand, *you* looked like you were ready to stick your head in the propeller."

Jefferson knelt and helped his wife pull off her steel-lined boots. He placed them in a cubbyhole beneath the sofa and retrieved a pair of soft white slippers, then waited until she'd curled and cracked her toes before sliding them onto her feet.

"Thank you kindly."

Jefferson stood and rested his long fingers on his son's shoulder. "Rob, give me a hand with a bit of last-minute scheduling, and we can watch the launch from my office."

"Top flight," Rob said without much enthusiasm.

"Or the prop tower," Jefferson offered.

Rob shrugged. His father was chief operating officer, which mostly seemed to involve writing letters, reading contracts for supply shipments, and handing envelopes to people. To Hollis and Rob, this was scarcely more exciting than one of the Pea's droning lectures.

"Catch up later," Rob said. Hollis joined him in studying the frescoed walls that lined the staircase while their parents kissed good-bye. Then he watched Rob and Jefferson get smaller as they crossed the deck.

Hollis's mother took him by the elbow. "Now you may join the lady on the bridge."

Hollis was speechless. No one but his mother, the captain, and the navigational officers were allowed on the bridge. Supposedly not even Jefferson Castor, although Hollis didn't know of a crewman who would stop him. The bridge was crammed with the sensitive machinery that stabilized the ship, along with the eighty-phone switchboard that connected the flight crew with the propeller technicians in the tower and the lift engineers belowdecks.

Hollis tried to make words come out of his mouth. "Bridge . . . ," he managed. "Here? The *ship's* bridge?"

"Well I'm not referring to the architectural marvel in Brooklyn," his mother said. "Unless you'd rather spend the afternoon in the stateroom, helping the maid dust the drapery."

"The bridge," Hollis said one more time. He'd just bungled the simple act of tilting a vial of dirt. Maybe the delicate nerve center of the ship wasn't the best place for him to be. But his mother laughed and handed him a pair of shiny black shoes. Of course he was going to the bridge. She'd have him examined by some Austrian head doctor if he refused. And despite his nerves, Hollis wanted more than anything else in the world to see the bridge of the *Wendell Dakota*.

He yanked off his boots so fast he almost removed his feet at the ankles, then laced up his shoes with trembling fingers.

"There's something I want to make very clear first," his mother said. "You have Miss Betzengraf at three. If I find out that you've skipped lessons again, I'll hire her as your personal tutor, and you'll spend all day in her stateroom, conjugating Latin verbs until we dock in Southampton. I don't care what Rob Castor does—you're a Dakota. You have to think for yourself sometimes, you know."

THE GREAT BELLY of the *Wendell Dakota* hung in the sky like the scoop of a pelican's beak, and the bridge was its glass-walled smile. This long mouth spanned the entire bow—two hundred feet, according to the blueprints tacked up in Hollis's mother's office—and curved around the port and starboard sides, where it became an indoor observation deck.

The center of the bridge was devoted to the ship's wheel, which looked just like the wooden wheel of a sailing ship but was—much to Hollis's amusement—purely decorative. Radiating out from the wheel was a maze of blackboards and easels displaying bumpy topographical maps and blue sky-charts with names like ATLANTIC CORRIDOR and ARCTIC PASSAGE. Beyond them, aisles of sprawling, rattling machines exhaled smoke through a web of metal pipes that pierced the ceiling like an overgrown church organ. Sky Captain Quincy, a gruff, white-haired man whose nose was perpetually crimson and whose mouth was frozen in a scowl, barked orders to officers scrambling back and forth between machines.

The black sheep of a New England whaling family who took to the skies in a fit of youthful rebellion, Arthur Quincy had a reputation for getting his airships to their destinations ahead of schedule. Besides his formidable glower, decades of pipe smoking had turned his voice into a combustion engine. Hollis had never seen him have to repeat an order.

Two of the captain's attendants lowered shades to cover the floor-to-ceiling windows. Hollis supposed that harsh, unfiltered sunlight wasn't conducive to reading gauges and instrument panels. Out of courtesy, the attendants left the window near Hollis and his mother unblocked. He lost himself in the view. The vastness of the sky made even the most terrible problem seem unimportant. He imagined the stubborn pile of dirt scattering into tiny grains, skimming the curved surface of the earth on the horizon, disappearing from the back of his mind forever.

A patch of wispy fog drifted up past the window.

"First cloud I've seen today," Hollis said.

His mother shook her head. "It's smoke from the shipyard." She nudged Hollis closer to the glass, which broadened his view to include more of the earth. With his nose pressed against the window, Hollis looked down across the grid of factories leaking dark streams of smoke. Long hangars pointed like splayed fingers across the New Jersey lowlands toward hazy Manhattan. Here and there, the skeleton of an unfinished airship poked halfway out of a hangar or rested in the dirt.

It was an ugly stretch of landscape that reminded Hollis of the other shipyards sprawled outside Philadelphia and Boston. He couldn't help but picture the day they would grow together, forming a single, massive blob of soot-stained architecture. He wondered if it would be in his lifetime. His mother seemed to read his thoughts.

"Hollis, everything you see down there is what makes this flight possible." She gestured toward the empty sky. "We take what we need from the earth because one day—a day that maybe you will get to see—we won't need her anymore. Your father used to say that the skies were the end of one kind of manifest destiny and the beginning of another."

"I remember."

Sky Captain Quincy stopped giving directions to his men, and the sudden absence of his gravelly baritone was jarring. Hollis watched as the captain huddled with two senior officers beside a chart labeled GULL MIGRATIONS. Quincy's right hand pressed the receiving piece of a telephone into his ear. A long cord snaked across the floor to join the nest of coiled wire at the base of the switchboard.

His mother lowered her voice. "Have you heard Jefferson's imitation of Captain Quincy? The inflection isn't quite there, but the scowl . . ."

At the mention of his stepfather, Hollis's mind drifted.

He pursued a thought that had been torturing him for days. It was the stuff of funny-books: a world much like this one, except Hollis was with both his mother and father on the bridge of the most magnificent airship in the world, the *Lucy Dakota*—its original name, restored. A life in which events had taken their proper course instead of a detour into something dismal and strange.

"I hope the daydream you're having is spectacular, Hollis."

"What?"

"Is something the matter?"

Caught off guard, he tripped over several answers at once—*no, I don't know, I'm fine*—and ended up saying nothing at all.

"Mrs. Dakota!" Quincy beckoned with a single quick wave. Hollis's mother joined the men in front of the chart and placed the telephone receiver against her ear. Quincy dismissed the two officers, and they disappeared behind a row of tall metal cylinders that vibrated and sputtered like water boilers. Hollis's mother drew herself up until her back was as straight as Quincy's. Her face was blank as she listened. Something about his mother's stillness made Hollis feel prickly and uncomfortable. When she spoke into the mouthpiece, which she held in her hand like a tall candle, Hollis strained to hear, but the bridge had become noisy with chatter as operators coordinated phone lines.

And we're off, thought Hollis. A lifetime of launches had

given him a sixth sense for that final tethered moment before an airship freed itself from the sky-dock.

The *Wendell Dakota* heaved a great shrug. Hollis staggered two steps back but didn't fall. Several officers rushed to the stabilization gauge, an immense maze of delicate glass tubes in which ball bearings the size of musket shot were suspended in pure argon gas.

An officer yelled, "Sir! Permission to spin props two and three!"

"Spin 'em," Captain Quincy growled, without taking his eyes off Hollis's mother, who looked pale and slightly sick, as if this were her very first ride on an airship. She handed the telephone back to the captain, who passed it to an operator. Hollis left his post in front of the window and joined them.

"Would you like to give the order to spin number one, Mrs. Dakota?" the captain asked.

But Hollis's mother was lost in thought. She stared back at Captain Quincy as if she didn't recognize him. Up close, she didn't look sick after all—she looked disconnected from reality, as if she'd just awakened from a bad dream. Finally, she took a deep breath and let it out.

"I leave that to you, sir."

The captain turned to an officer who'd been watching him expectantly.

"Spin number one, Mr. Fitzroy."

The officer repeated the order to an operator. Hollis

imagined the words streaming through the long wires and bursting out into the ears of the men in the prop tower.

"We'll find out who it is," Quincy assured Hollis's mother, who smiled weakly.

"I have no doubt that you will."

Hollis said, "Find out who *who* is?"

"One of the stokers deserted," Quincy said. "Nothing to worry about."

The captain was right: a runaway stoker was a minor annoyance. Hollis gave his mother a curious look, but she had already composed herself.

The *Wendell Dakota* shuddered again as the turbines that drove the propellers began their coal-fired churn. A rumble from deep within the ship clacked Hollis's teeth. His mother grabbed his shoulder.

"Watch with me," she said.

In a cloudless blue sky, with nothing but empty space zooming past the windows, it was sometimes hard to tell if you were moving or just hanging in the air. But when Hollis pressed his nose to the glass and looked down, he could see the shipyard disappearing beneath the ship. It was easy to imagine the *Wendell Dakota* as a mouth swallowing the earth, house by house and tree by tree, leaving a blank path of emptiness in its wake.

At the far edge of the factory grid, two spire-topped office buildings poked out above the smog.

"Eat them," Hollis said to himself.

"Hmm?" His mother started, as if a switch had flicked her to life. "Are you hungry, Hollis?"

"No, I was just . . . never mind. Rob isn't going to believe this when I tell him."

"Suppose not," his mother mumbled distractedly. She pressed her palms against the glass as if she were trying to urge the ship onward, faster and faster, with the strength of her bare hands.

PART

ONE

THE HISTORY OF FLIGHT IN AMERICA

ON THE DAY he discovered the secret of flight, Hollis's grandfather Samuel Dakota woke from yet another dream about food to find himself aching and soaked in sweat. He licked his dry lips and kept his eyes closed, trying to sink back into sleep to finish the strawberry-rhubarb pie his dream self had been enjoying. But in the distance, a trumpet bleated the call to march. The daily reality of war—stinking, humid, and dreary—snuffed out thoughts of flaky crust and gooey sweetness.

Samuel creaked up off the hard ground, his mind raging and boiling with curses against enemy Confederates, his fellow Union soldiers, this endless march through scorching Virginia countryside, Abe Lincoln, Jeff Davis, and most of all, the poisonous muck and stale hardtack that passed for food in the army. With furious resignation, he coiled his sleeping roll and rummaged in his knapsack for his itchy blue uniform shirt. Then, sliding his arms through the long sleeves, he managed to knock an uncorked whiskey bottle off the rock where he had set it the night before.

"Mighty fine work there, Dakota," chided a pale, freckly soldier from the long column of men snaking wearily past. "Looks like you're in for a thirsty march!" The soldier nudged the man next to him, who lit a droopy cigarette and chuckled, exhaling smoke.

Samuel stared dejectedly into the dirt as the last drops of his moonshine whiskey pooled between the gnarled roots of an ancient maple tree. He picked up the empty bottle. It wasn't broken. He reckoned that maybe he could skim some whiskey from the top of the little pool, and it wouldn't be too full of Virginia grit. He knelt and prepared to scoop, only to find that the whiskey had mixed with a sticky pile of sap that had been dripping from a knothole in the tree. Samuel's heart sank as he watched the formation of a slimy amber sludge that looked about as appealing and thirst-quenching as the foam around a horse's mouth. He set the bottle next to the puddle and sighed. It was time to finish packing and join his regiment, which would leave him behind in enemy country if he didn't hurry. But then he noticed something peculiar: a black beetle about the size of his thumbnail had emerged from one of the maple tree's huge, twisted roots. It was soon joined by several more, until the entire pool was ringed with beetles. Samuel peered in for a better look. The beetles were slurping the whiskey-drenched sap with tiny pincers that Samuel supposed were their ugly little mouths. Their stomach parts seemed to be inflating.

"Yick," he said.

Then he gagged. A pungent stench that Samuel later described as "the rottenest egg rotting inside the rottenest onion on earth" wafted up from the thirsty beetles and into his nostrils. He jumped to his feet, coughing and sputtering, just in time to see the empty whiskey bottle float up past his face and clank hollowly against the underside of a branch.

He turned to see if any of his fellow soldiers were staring in disbelief, but the end of the blue column was headed away from camp. Samuel Dakota was alone. He looked up at the bottle, trapped in the branches. A single beetle—fat and round, full of sludgy whiskey-sap—was stuck in the center of its thick glass base. Samuel took a deep breath, pinched his nose shut, and stood on his tiptoes to study the insect.

No wings. The stinky little thing shouldn't have been able to fly. But it had not only shot straight up into the branches of the tree, it had carried a big glass bottle with it. Maybe the whiskey-sap feast gave it a special brand of buoyant gas?

Samuel stepped back and thought about his situation. He didn't know much about the customs and traditions of Southern people, and he knew less about the habits of Southern bugs. But he figured he was witnessing some kind of unusual spectacle nonetheless. He reached up and flicked the fat beetle away, catching the bottle as it fell. The smell was becoming unbearable.

Suddenly he felt a rumble beneath his feet. A massive root ripped itself up out of the ground, dripping whiskey-sap and shedding clumps of earth. All around him, the ancient roots of the maple tree were flinging themselves out of the dirt like angry tentacles. He scrambled back against his knapsack, scraping his elbow on the rock where the bottle had spent the night.

The gaseous beetles were lifting the entire tree.

He glanced behind him again, up and down the trampled dirt path. His regiment had moved on.

The maple tree hung suspended three feet off the ground, attached to the earth by a single stubborn root, until a few more fat beetles popped it free. As he watched the ancient maple float up into the sky, borne on the backs of drunken, flatulent beetles, he thought of the strawberry-rhubarb pie.

Fate had suddenly given him the chance to rid himself of army life—and army *food*—forever.

With a plan still forming in his mind, Samuel grabbed the empty bottle, filled it with whiskey-sap, and placed it carefully inside his knapsack. Then he rummaged until he found a round tin of hardtack bread, which he happily dumped out. Using the empty tin, he scooped up about two dozen beetles that hadn't yet slurped the sludge and weren't capable of floating away. He stowed the tin next to the bottle, shouldered his pack, and headed north, in the opposite direction from his regiment.

SAMUEL TRAVELED mostly at night, eating the rest of his meager army rations and then existing on a wild pig he was lucky enough to catch. As a deserter, *all* territory was enemy territory. He was fair game for both enemy soldiers and Union military justice.

After a week of this tense and lonely journey, during which every distant shout and muffled report of cannon fire sent him diving into the bushes for cover, Samuel reached the outskirts of Washington, D.C. He had long since stripped off his blue coat, and before he entered the city, he smeared mud on his blue pants. Looking like a filthy vagabond was better than facing a firing squad.

He made his way down Pennsylvania Avenue, ignoring his gnawing hunger, until he reached the iron fence that surrounded the White House. He sauntered up to the gate and cleared his throat. The guard eyed Samuel with a distaste usually reserved for lepers and rebel prisoners. He looked at the mud caked on Samuel's shoes, pants, shirt, arms, neck, and face. He sniffed the ripe odor that hung in the air between them. Then he simply glared without saying a word.

Samuel smiled. His grand scheme was the one thing that had sustained him throughout the wanderings of the past week.

"Greetings. I'm here to show President Lincoln how to win the war in a fraction of the time at a fraction of the cost. So if you'll kindly send word inside, or just let me through . . ."

The guard maintained his glare.

Samuel gave a friendly nod. "No doubt he's a very busy man. I would also accept an audience with the secretary of war."

Silence.

"The undersecretary of war."

The guard spat on the ground between them.

Samuel's smile faltered. "The assistant to the undersecretary? The press secretary?" He thought quickly. "Mrs. Lincoln, perhaps?"

The guard raised his revolver. Samuel put up his hands.

"I see. Well then, if you could kindly get word to Mr. Lincoln that I stopped by. Name's Dakota, like the territory."

The guard cocked the hammer. Samuel backed away.

"Once again, I've got the answer to the Confederate problem, and I only need a minute or two for a *very* convincing demonstration." He nodded professionally, as if this encounter had been a civilized exchange of ideas. "Thank you for your time."

Samuel carried himself proudly through the bustling crowd until he was out of the guard's sight. Then he turned to look back at the fence that surrounded the White House. It wasn't very high. A new plan formed in his mind. He gazed beyond the fence at the upper floor of the White House, then sat on a bench to wait until dark.

THE NEXT DAY, page twelve of the *Washington Evening Star* carried the brief mention of a curious incident: several pedestrians on a street near the White House reported a disturbance in the air above their heads.

"Man-shaped," insisted a sober insurance clerk. "Flailing and yelling."

"Tumbling about the sky like a monstrous idiot bird who forgot how to fly," his wife elaborated.

"Rebel spies," warned an old gentlemen. "Assassins. A secret weapon catapulted into the White House."

The Metropolitan Police officer who took their statements saw no reason to trouble the White House guards with such a bizarre story. Even the witnesses themselves reluctantly admitted that they had no proof. The thing in the air had somersaulted into the night sky and disappeared.

Years later, they would all claim to have been present at the very first Dakota flight.

"**YOU'RE LYING** through your low-born teeth," Rob said as he and Hollis sauntered down the wide corridor that delivered passengers to the largest and most elegantly appointed staterooms. This part of the ship's interior was pleasantly hushed, lined with thick Egyptian carpet and oak paneling to muffle the whooshing bass hum of the propellers.

"No friends or family allowed on the bridge," Rob continued, repeating the rule that Hollis's father had established and that they both knew by heart. "Not even for a little peek."

"Late birthday present," Hollis said. "Sky Captain Quincy didn't seem too happy, though."

He decided not to mention the phone call. Ever since he'd changed out of his wilted suit in favor of crisp new slacks and a button-down shirt, he felt lighter and more carefree, and he wasn't keen to ruin a bout of good feelings with some trivial bit of anxiety that wasn't any of his business. Even his cumbersome schoolbooks were hardly an irritation, carried in a new leather satchel slung across his shoulder, along with the odds and ends that Delia had requested on their last day aboard the *Secret Wish*.

"Old Quincy doesn't know *how* to be happy," Rob said. "It's all that whale meat he grew up eating. It thickens the blood."

"What does that have to do with being happy?"

"Practically everything, Dakota. So if I assume you're telling me the truth, then you got to see the stabilizer?"

"Big time. And the ship's wheel. It's fake."

"Good lord," Rob said, eyes wide in mock horror. "You mean there's no way to steer this monstrosity?"

As they passed room 12B, the door swung open. Out popped a little boy struggling to balance a formidable stack of textbooks, followed by his older sister. The Reynolds siblings—Arthur and Annabel—were the grandchildren of a Dakota board member who'd been steadily increasing his company shares since Hollis's father was a teenager. Hollis was supposed to treat them with the utmost courtesy.

Without skipping a step, Rob slid the two books he'd been carrying against his hip onto Arthur's pile.

"Hey!" The boy teetered dangerously.

"Give my regards to the Pea," Rob said as he sprinted down the hall, shirttail flapping. Annabel turned her eyes accusingly to Hollis. This wasn't the plan—they were still too close to their own stateroom, where the risk of running into a family steward was high. They had agreed to wait until they'd moved farther aft, past the first-class smoking lounge, before making their move.

"Really, Hollis," Annabel said, pulling the two books from her little brother's collection and steadying the boy with a gentle hand on his head. She regarded the lurid covers with disapproval. "These aren't even for school."

Hollis took Rob's books—*Air Pirates!* and *All-True Pinkerton Files*—with a twinge of embarrassment that caught him by surprise. "They're not mine," he mumbled, stuffing them in his satchel.

"Why don't you offer to help Arthur with his books until we get to class," Annabel suggested slowly, as if English wasn't his strong suit.

Arthur peered up at Hollis, eager eyes magnified by thick glasses.

"Maybe next time, Arthur."

Annabel shook her head. "You used to be decent." She turned to lead her brother away, and Hollis was gone, careening around corners and bounding down stairs, chasing Rob deep into the belly of the airship.

DELIA COSGROVE was apprenticed to Big Benny Owens, Dakota Aeronautics' chief beetle keeper. Beetle keeping took a long time to learn because it was such a precise skill: one mistake, and the *Wendell Dakota* could tilt dangerously in the air, even flip over. Release too many beetles at once, and the ship could share the infamous fate of Hollis's grandfather, although it was hard to imagine a ship as big as a city vanishing somewhere high above the charted sky.

Delia bunked in her own room in the keepers' dormitory, a warren of low-ceilinged cabins squashed between the third-class deck and the lift chambers. Aspects of a working airship that didn't seem to fit anywhere else were deposited here. Searching for the dormitory, a visitor might happen upon the steel siding of an auxiliary freshwater tank or the empty closet labeled DEAD LETTER DEPARTMENT. The passageways were dim, the sounds perpetually distant and hard to place. Reverberations seemed to come from within, bodily shiftings and inner clanks echoing from impossible corridors. There was no ornamentation. This was an eerie place on any ship, but on the *Wendell Dakota*, it had the added distinction of feeling endless. How long since they'd passed the cramped third-class bedrooms and smoky cafeterias already filled with men in their shirtsleeves? As they moved along, encountering no one, Hollis felt unmoored from the laws that governed hallways and footsteps. It was as if he'd been relocated onto another ship entirely—perhaps the *Lucy Dakota*. By the time they reached Delia's door, their conversation had long since evaporated into irregular gulps of air.

Rob knocked. The door swung open.

"Gosh sakes," Delia said, making a show of peering out into the empty hall. "You two getting chased by a Sumatran rat?" Her dark hair was swept back beneath a crocheted headband. Instead of the heavy dungarees and work shirt typical of a beetle keeper, Delia wore a blue dress that hung below her knees and curved inward at her calves.

"You live at the absolute"—Hollis paused to catch his breath—"*South Pole* of the airship."

"Lucky for you."

All three of them knew that Delia's distance from the prying eyes of first class made their friendship possible. After a few days in flight, airships became hermetically sealed gossip factories. It wouldn't do for the sons of the company's ruling family to be seen escorting an apprentice beetle keeper around the promenade.

Delia stepped aside to let the boys in and closed the door behind them. Hollis watched her slide a heavy bolt into place, shake her head, slide the bolt back the other way, and rattle the lock's casing. She paused for a moment, muttering to herself, and raised her wrist to the lock. On her wrist was a bracelet—the only piece of jewelry Hollis had ever seen her wear—and dangling from the bracelet was a coin-sized charm. Her slender fingers fit the edge of the charm into a tiny screw, and she began to tighten the casing.

"Don't you have a screwdriver?" Hollis asked.

"I do—I just haven't seen it in a while."

Delia's living quarters were cluttered with miniature versions of the machinery that sprawled around the bridge. Her table was a junkyard of dismantled radio parts: coils of thin copper wire, cloth speaker covers, disconnected black and silver dials. The bookshelf sagged under the weight of impossibly thick tomes filled with esoteric drawings and the smallest print known to man. They had titles like *A Compendium of Popular Beetle Myths & Legends*, *The Gentle Keeper's Guide to Maintaining Cordial Interspecies Relations*, and *An Occult History of Samuel Dakota*. A messy collection of broadsheets and pamphlets were wedged between the books. Rob pulled out a single sheet of paper, dense with badly lettered type.

"This one's called 'Ethical Beetle Treatment Now' exclamation point," he announced. Clearing his throat, he began to read. " 'It is a national disgrace that nature's most wondrous and holy creatures are bred for servitude and toil. They must be freed from this cruel bondage to prepare the way for man's salvation. The soul of the beetle is a blessed and ageless thing. . . .' " Rob's eyes scanned the rest of the page. "It just keeps going like that." He looked up. "You know, I thought this was going to be some boring science report. But it's actually the rambling of an insane person."

Hollis shrugged. "It takes all kinds."

Rob opened his hand and let the paper drift down to the floor. "I guess."

"That's actually a direct quote." Hollis said. "Back when all those new religions started popping up—just crazy people, praying to beetles and making up beetle gods and forming cults and who knows what else—somebody started mailing these funny little wooden beetle statues to the shipyard foremen. A reporter from the *Herald* interviewed some Dakota people about it, and my father talked about how the cult members were harmless and everybody needed a hobby."

Hollis smiled at the memory. "Anyway. He went on forever, but that was the only thing they printed in the article. 'It takes all kinds.'"

"Delia," Rob said gravely, just as she slammed the bolt triumphantly into place and turned to face her visitors, "tell us the truth—are you in a cult?"

She frowned at the discarded broadsheet page. "It's research." Hollis picked up the paper and returned it to the shelf. "Chief Owens encourages us to be open-minded."

Rob pointed at Hollis's head. "Incoming."

Hollis ducked to avoid a cigar box as it floated past, thumping along the ceiling.

"Excuse me." Delia reached up and plucked a single beetle from the underside of the box, which fell into Hollis's waiting palm. He watched in fascination as Delia began murmuring softly to the smelly little creature, cupping it gently in her hand.

"Right," Hollis said. "That's new."

Quickly, before it could float away, she gripped it between her thumb and forefinger and began to massage its shiny, bulbous abdomen. A stream of liquid the color of a brackish puddle ran down her forearm. Satisfied the beetle had been rendered flightless, Delia placed it in a jar on her table and wiped her hands on a stained rag.

"Huh," Rob said.

Hollis had heard of beetle keepers using all manner of coercion and trickery to wrangle their charges, but the intimacy of Delia's process was shocking. It was as if he'd witnessed something deeply private—something vulgar—and he was relieved to see her move on to the next item in her daily menu of projects and experiments. She eyed the leather satchel. "That what I think it is, HD?"

Hollis opened the flap, tossed his schoolbooks on Delia's cot, and dumped the rest of the contents on a bare patch of table. Silently, she examined each curious little treasure.

"This is exactly what I asked for," she said at last, as if she'd doubted Hollis's ability to follow her instructions. "I owe you one."

"Just tell me what in the blue sky you're doing with this junk, and we'll call it even."

"Oh!" Rob said, reaching inside his suit jacket. "Almost forgot. I got you something too." He held out a medicine bottle. "Spirit of hartshorn," he said proudly. "I borrowed it from the infirmary on the *Secret Wish* and now I'm extending those borrowing privileges to you."

"Spirit of *what*?" Hollis asked.

Delia took the bottle and examined the neat block-letter type on the label. "Smelling salts."

"Strong stuff," Rob said. "Trust me."

"I wanted to see what would happen if I interrupted a few of the beetles' sleep cycles."

"They sleep?" Rob asked. This had never occurred to Hollis either.

"Sort of," she said, setting the bottle on the table. "Anyway, HD." She held up a small black cube with two barrel-shaped silver diodes sticking out of the top like miniature smoke-stacks. "This is a battery."

Rob sniffed and slid a finger under his nose, then wiped the finger absently on his pants. "This may surprise you, but we know that."

Next, Delia presented a metal switching device mounted on a block of wood. "Telegraph key."

"Uh-huh," Rob said.

Delia raised an eyebrow at Rob, then gave Hollis a sly grin. Their customary standoff began, with Hollis having no idea what he was supposed to say and Delia acting like what she was doing was the most obvious thing in the world. After a few long seconds of silence, Delia sighed dramatically.

"Doesn't that fancy Austrian tutor teach you any electri-cal science?"

Hollis shrugged. "I thought she was Romanian."

"Our attendance has been kind of poor lately," Rob said.

"Well, okay, but you've seen telephones, right? So what if I told you I had an idea for a telephone that didn't need a wire? And what if I told you that telephone could transmit from the ship to the sky-dock, or even to the ground as we were in flight?"

"I would say you've been breathing the fumes from my grandfather's moonshine for too long," Hollis said.

"Beetle Keeper's Madness," Rob intoned, crossing his eyes.

Delia slid her headband forward and pressed it on the

left side, near her temple. A gold-rimmed magnifying glass slipped down in front of her eye. She examined the battery and wrinkled her nose.

"Here we go," Hollis said.

Delia turned the battery over in her hand and moved her lips in wordless communication with herself.

"Permission to contact the Republic of Delia," Hollis said.

Rob fidgeted with a piece of scrap metal on the table, then stepped over to the room's single window, a porthole the size of a dinner plate. "This is just like the beginning of *Brice Blank and the Lightning Genie.* You shouldn't play around with this kind of energy." He looked at Hollis for backup. "That's the moral of the story."

Hollis ignored his stepbrother. He hadn't learned anything from that particular tale, because he hadn't read it. There were hundreds of Brice Blank funny-book adventures—maybe thousands—and unlike Rob, Hollis had only read a few of them. The artwork bothered him. The perspective was just a little off, the faces hasty and underdrawn. He always wanted to give the books a good, hard shake, as if that would knock Brice's ink-rendered world into a more believable plane of existence.

He raised his voice. "*Delia!*"

"Hmm?" She looked up absently, then flicked the magnifying lens back up into her headband. "Right. Sorry, HD. What I was saying was that I think it might be possible to transmit signals without a wire. Simple ones, I mean. Mr.

Morse's code at first, like a telegraph someday the human voice. My theory the right kind of sparks and tune th the frequency . . . Anyway, that's w

Rob prodded beneath his cap, scratc.

"Okay, Delia," Hollis said, "I'll bite. Let's say you to actually send a message through the air. How far can it go before it just . . . um . . ." Hollis didn't know how frequencies worked, but he pictured the scattering dirt from the morning's failed christening. "Disappears?"

"Not far enough," Delia admitted. "That's where the beetles come in. It's a pretty big series of *ifs*, but I think *if* we can set up floating relay stations, and *if* we can—"

A long, deafening *CREEAAAAK* rattled the floorboards, followed by a sharp, decisive *SNAP*. The clouds outside the window seemed to swirl into one another like whipping cream as the airship fluttered from port to starboard and back. Rob and Delia managed to grab the edge of the bolted-down table. Hollis's fingers missed, and he lost his footing.

He had time to think, *I hope I land on the bed*, before a blinding light popped like a flashbulb behind his eyelids as he slammed against the wall. Gently, he rubbed the back of his head: slight tenderness, no blood. He sat on the floor and endured a woozy spell. A glance up at the window once again revealed steady clouds, blue sky, and natural forward progress.

Rob helped him to his feet. "Should've aimed for the bed, Dakota."

at was quite the shake-up."

Rob scoffed. "For you, maybe. First time on an airship?"

Hollis shot his stepbrother a mildly exasperated look and, with a downward glance, drew Rob's attention to the floor. Or, as he knew Rob would understand, *through* the floor to the lift chambers that lined the hull.

"Very alarming," Rob suddenly agreed. "I say we go confirm with Chief Owens that everything's in proper working order. Since we're all the way down here, anyway."

"It was just turbulence," Delia said. "That's when the air—"

"We know what it is, Delia," Hollis groaned. He tamped down a wave of nausea—genuine, despite his impromptu ploy. "But Rob is right. We came all this way. It would be a shame to pass up an opportunity to perform a routine inspection."

"It's our responsibility," Rob agreed.

"No," Delia said, "it is not your responsibility. You've never performed an inspection in your life, either of you." She crossed her arms. The charm wiggled beneath her wrist. Hollis wondered what someone like Annabel Reynolds would make of an apprentice beetle keeper talking to him this way. "We're not on some old bucket like the *Secret Wish*, making its hundredth crossing. I can't just take you on a grand tour of the lift chambers whenever you feel like it and expect Benny to turn a blind eye. The mood down there is all business on this one."

If the bridge was Captain Quincy's exclusive domain,

the lift chambers were Benny's to rule like a petty despot. All nonessential personnel were forbidden—*especially* Hollis and Rob, whose reputation for being anywhere but the place they were supposed to be seemed to grow with every voyage.

"You don't have to give us a tour," Hollis said.

"Hollis's mom made us memorize the blueprints." Rob tapped the side of his head. "I could take this ship apart and put it back together. So you just stay here and get on with your science. We'll show ourselves around."

"Want to know the quickest way to all eleven of the second-class shoeshine booths?" Hollis said. "Quiz me."

Delia stepped in front of the door.

"We're not going to foul anything up," Rob assured her.

With tingling dread, Hollis thought of his secret smudge of dirt. Rob nibbled at a fingernail and then studied the soggy nail up close.

"Haven't you already seen the lift chambers?" Delia asked.

"Sure," Hollis said. "Way back when they were being built. When they were empty."

"Very boring," Rob said.

She looked past them, studying something on her bookshelf.

"*Republic of Delia*," Hollis whispered.

"All right," Delia said, her attention snapping back into place. "Fine. But you go where I go and do what I tell you."

Hollis grinned.

"It's not funny!"

"No, it's just that sometimes your accent comes out."

The single fact that Delia had ever let slip about her past was that she was from Hell's Kitchen, which made Hollis imagine a pocket of blazing furnace heat that kept a few blocks of Manhattan perpetually scorched, even in the dead of winter.

"You can take a little peek, and then we're gone. We're not doing anything to attract the attention of Chief Owens. Getting grounded for good isn't high on my to-do list."

"Benny won't touch your apprenticeship," Hollis said. "The company's gonna need you one day. I'll make sure nothing happens."

Delia uncrossed her arms and used her thumb and forefinger to worry at her bracelet.

"At thirteen years old," Rob said, affecting the nasally tone of a radio announcer, "Hollis Dakota became chief personnel manager, operating magically without the approval of any adult in the company."

"That reminds me," Hollis said, waving a hand dismissively at his stepbrother. "You're fired."

"I rehire myself."

"You don't have the authority."

Delia sighed as a tin of biscuits rose unsteadily off her table and bumped gently against the bookshelf.

"**M**IGHT WANT TO hold your noses," Delia suggested as they lowered themselves down the ladder.

"Some kind of scented handkerchief would be good," Hollis said. The dizzying odor of millions of inflated beetles had begun to assault his nostrils. He thought of his grandfather's famous description of the stench.

"You say that every time, HD."

"And you always tell us that we can't come down to the lift chambers, not a chance, and then every time we do."

"That just proves you should be more prepared."

Hollis buried his face in the crook of his elbow. Rob struggled to pinch his nose without losing his grip on the smooth metal rungs. "How you beetle keepers stand this is beyond me."

Delia took a deep breath and let it out with a contented

sigh—she always seemed to take perverse pride in her ability to withstand the smell.

The ladder deposited them with three echoing clanks onto a steel catwalk that stretched high above the floor of the lift chamber, a cavernous hollow at the very bottom of the airship, where the pelican's beak scooped down from the bow, leveled off, then scooped up toward the stern. A sign at the base of the ladder was imprinted with the company insignia, the number 2 painted in red on the beetle's back. This was the secondary chamber—not a bad place for some incognito tourism, as Big Benny Owens supervised his crew from the primary.

There were sixteen chambers in all. The next-largest airship in the Dakota fleet, the *Windy City*, had twelve. While the abundance of chambers kept the *Wendell Dakota* aloft, they didn't make it uncrashable. (That single word, so bound up with his father, always gave Hollis a melancholy shiver.) What made it that way—what they had come here to see— was the revolutionary new system of automation. In the past, beetle keepers obeyed a set of basic, well-worn procedures. They fed whiskey-sap to the insects and applied them to the hull under the guidance of Benny and his officers. But the mechanical chambers on the *Wendell Dakota* offered a more efficient way to harness the beetles' abilities, compensate for the natural tilts of an airship in flight, and cut down on the most stubborn of problems—human error.

Hollis went to the rail of the catwalk and peered down

through the gloomy space. He caught the vaguest sense of rhythmic, nonhuman movement. "I can't see anything."

Rob elbowed up alongside him. "We're too high."

The view afforded them nothing but glimpses of the lower catwalks, crisscrossed in such a way that they blocked the floor. Every so often, a pair of keepers or technicians would scurry along one of the walkways, sending a hint of conversation up to their perch at the top of the chamber.

"Listen," Delia said.

Hollis cupped his hands behind his ears and closed his eyes. Even down here, with miles of oak and carpet between them, Hollis felt the spin of the great propeller in his chest like a heartbeat. But there was another sound, very faint, unique to the chamber: a thousand wooden drawers sliding open and closed in precise time, the cataloging of some infernal librarian. Hollis couldn't help but picture a giant armor-plated squid wearing thick glasses sorting through a mazelike cabinet, tentacles clanking, steam issuing from its beak. (He'd just seen the cover of *Brice Blank and the Aluminum Kraken* on Rob's dresser.)

The look on Rob's face told Hollis that he'd also heard it. As if to tantalize them further, there was a network of pipes creeping up the side of the chamber, silver vines on a three-story trellis, delivering exhaust to the main funnels. Hollis remembered that five hundred extra tons of coal had been earmarked to produce electricity for the chambers— never before had an airship needed such a resource.

"Absolutely not," Delia said, reading the look that passed between them. "This is as far as we go."

Rob seemed poised to leap over the railing and hop his way from catwalk to catwalk until he reached the Sorter/Picker/Dispenser machine—"spider" for short—that sprawled along the floor, disseminating beetles. Hollis felt like a little boy being denied some coveted plaything he'd seen in a friend's stateroom.

"You there!" A sudden shout reached them from across the platform. A crewman hailed them with a wave. "Don't move!"

Delia turned to head back to the ladder, muttering curses, but Hollis stopped her.

"He already saw us—just say your shift is about to start."

Once he'd been spotted somewhere he wasn't supposed to be, Hollis had found that it was best to be cursory and polite, and keep his lies within the bounds of reason. The same tension he felt with crewmen like Marius, who didn't know whether to treat him like a friend or a boss-in-training, could also work to his advantage.

"Ahoy!" Rob lifted his cap in a jaunty greeting.

"Don't move!" the man yelled, striding fiercely to intercept them as if they were fleeing madly instead of holding still. Right away, Hollis noticed the man's unkempt hair shoved hastily beneath a uniform cap. His features floated within a doughy, indistinct face. And he was dressed like a porter, without even a single gold bar on his shoulder to identify him as the type of petty officer assigned to patrol the lift chambers. But the strangest thing by far was the holstered pistol slung across his hip.

Since when did porters walk around *armed*?

"Afternoon," Hollis said.

The man stared at him uncomprehendingly. "You kids can't be here," he said. "Clear the air."

"We were just leaving." Hollis flashed Delia a quick smile. *See how easy it is?*

Then Rob stepped forward, toe-to-toe with the armed porter, and Hollis sensed that something about the man had provoked his stepbrother into going off script.

"I'm not sure you understand. We have security clearance from up top, for every corner of the ship from bow to stern."

That was hardly true, but Hollis kept his mouth shut. What was Rob trying to prove?

The porter thwacked Rob hard on the chest with a single finger. "I said clear the air, boy."

"Hey!" Delia bristled. "You can't talk to him like that."

The porter's hand hovered above his holster. "Who says I can't, cupcake? You're not allowed here, and that's the high and low of it."

For a moment, Hollis had the sickening notion that they were about to be shot by some rogue psychotic porter. Then he dismissed the thought and tried to sound like his father at his most serious and puffed up.

"What's your name and position with this company?"

The man looked genuinely taken aback by the question.

His hand drifted down to rest on the pistol's ivory grip. "That's none of your business, kid."

Hollis was about to inform the man that, as he was Lucy Dakota's only son, it was the definition of his business, when Rob began to yell and wave.

"Hey! Dad!"

Jefferson Castor emerged from a small office at the far end of the catwalk. He looked up at the little group, startled.

Hollis waved too, relieved that this misunderstanding was about to be peacefully resolved. Whatever severe and unpleasant discipline his stepfather was about to impose was preferable to being riddled with bullets by some high-strung new recruit of a porter. But instead of hurrying over to take charge, Jefferson Castor stayed frozen in place. The funny way he stood, motionless and trapped, long arms caught midswing, reminded Hollis of the time Miss Betzengraf caught Rob stealing the answers to a history test. It seemed like his stepfather was going to duck back into the office, but then he unfroze and walked toward them, regaining his usual confidence with each step.

"Sir," Hollis said.

"Dad." Rob jerked his thumb toward the porter. "Tell this rookie where to stick it."

Jefferson Castor walked right past the man and took Rob roughly by the shoulder.

"Why aren't you in class?" he asked. The porter snickered.

"The Pea—Miss Betzengraf's sick," Rob said quickly.

Hollis cleared his throat, desperate to shift attention from Rob's lie. "Is something wrong with the stabilizer?"

"What?" Castor said sharply, taking his hand off his son. "Oh." His tone softened. "That was nothing, Hollis. Routine turbulence. And you should be in class, too."

Hollis bowed his head, thinking of his mother's threat to have the Pea tutor him personally. Getting caught skipping on the first day was pathetic. Castor fixed his stony gaze on the porter. His lip twitched once, then he flicked his chin toward the office and the man slunk away.

"I'll deal with him. You get to class." He smiled warmly, an entirely different person from the angry father he'd been a moment ago.

"Yessir," Rob said.

"I'll be working late tonight, boys. But I'll be receiving a full report about your behavior, and you've already dug yourselves a hole." He paused to scowl at Delia, who lowered her eyes. "So do your best to fly straight." Even this threat had a softened edge. It sounded like a casual suggestion.

"Yessir," Rob said again. Hollis kept quiet. He'd made up a secret rule on the very day Jefferson Castor became his mother's new husband: his stepfather couldn't tell him what to do or how to act until Hollis started calling him Dad. Behavioral corrections were for Rob alone. They had never discussed this rule, but for reasons that Hollis didn't quite understand, his stepfather seemed to agree.

Castor spun on his heel and strode back toward the

office. Through the half-open door, Hollis saw the porter talking to two other men.

"All due respect," Delia said as Castor shut the door, "but did he seem strange to you?"

"All the time," Rob said.

"Listen," Hollis said. "There's something else." The incident seemed like his cue to share another peculiar moment, so as they walked back to the ladder he told them about the phone call just before the launch, how it had darkened his mother's mood, how the captain had explained it away.

"That settles it," Rob said with a single clap. "This sightseeing trip has officially become an investigation. If we're gonna get to the bottom of this, we need a plan."

Hollis was wary of the excitement in his stepbrother's voice. They had already pushed their luck. His head throbbed where it had smacked the dormitory wall, and his right temple began to pulsate in time with the echoes of the chamber. The feather bed in his blessedly nonreeking stateroom loomed soft and inviting in his mind. The mere idea of crawling beneath its covers and closing his eyes seemed to bring a measure of relief.

"Name one time you've ever made a plan that worked, Rob. Or done anything besides get us in trouble."

"Come on, Hollis, this is different," Delia said. "This is something."

Hollis rubbed his temple gingerly and winced. "Everything's something with you."

L UCY DAKOTA called her chronic headaches *tiger claws*
because they dug in and roared and didn't let go for days.
She had always seemed terrified of passing along this afflic-
tion to Hollis and used to warn him of "auras" so often that
every innocent action in his peripheral vision—the normal
interplay of light and shadow—became a harbinger of
doom. Fully aware that talk of a headache would result in
being surrounded by doctors, Hollis explained his early
bedtime simply by saying he was tired from launch day, the
vaguest excuse he could think of that wouldn't invite a concerned examination of his pupils.

Willing himself to sleep so early proved impossible, but
curling up to watch the sky darken outside his window
soothed his aching head. Voices drifted through his bedroom
door: his mother was holding court in the sitting room

while Jefferson Castor, true to his word, was working late, and Rob was hatching plots with Delia.

Hollis heard Elizabeth Quincy, the captain's wife, steer the conversation toward rumored cargo. The Reynolds' dead Shetland pony had been stuffed and mounted on a pedestal, and was traveling in a private storage hold along with two automobiles and a dozen gilt-framed portraits of itself. Several first-class ladies were happy to use this tidbit as a prompt.

"You know our maid Francine?" one asked. "Darling girl. Not from Paris, from some provincial town—country girls simply know how to clean in a way that city girls will never master, they encounter more varieties of dirt—well, anyhow. Our Francine says that Heddie—that's Juniper's new governess, now that the old one's been, how shall I say this, *promoted*—well, Heddie swears that Edmund just bought a prehistoric fossilized *man* from some Canadian explorers, some beastly thing that had been frozen solid in a cave for who knows how many thousands of years, which of course he's taken aboard with him and stashed in a hold."

"Left it there to thaw? I should think it would smell after a while, don't you?"

"Well, of course he's not letting it thaw."

"You're saying they've got the man encased in ice? For the duration of the crossing?"

Hollis imagined a leather-skinned specimen stashed away among the spoils of high-class life. What if the caveman woke up and found himself in Edmund Juniper's private storage hold? What would it be like to track a mammoth through an ice field, fall into some crevasse, and open your eyes a few thousand years later aboard an airship high above the Atlantic?

"Perhaps he's lodging in the meat locker at Il Bambino's. I thought the steak tasted a bit *ancient*."

Peals of laughter barreled through Hollis's bedroom door and reignited his headache, giving a queasy backdrop to his thoughts. Who was the armed porter? Why hadn't his stepfather disciplined the man? Hollis couldn't shake the guilty feeling that his failed christening had released some kind of slow-acting poison into the corridors and offices and engine rooms of the ship, changing the very nature of the voyage. It was a long time before he slipped into a shallow, disturbed sleep.

In his dream, Hollis found himself alone on the main deck at night, surrounded by the high stone battlements of a castle. *Terrible airship design*, he thought. Above the castle-deck, a yellow moon dangled from two long cords like a stage prop. He climbed a narrow staircase up the side of the stone wall and studied the moon, which was only a few feet away. As he reached out to touch it—he'd always wondered what the moon felt like—he heard the unmistakable wet, raspy sound of his father clearing his throat. A gob of spit landed on the surface of the moon, and Hollis was suddenly afraid. His father had been dead for two years.

The spit on the moon was flecked with blood. Hollis turned. His father fixed his spectacles and frowned.

"Swear," he said.

Hollis backed against the stone wall. Dirt poured from his father's ear and gathered in a pile at his feet. Hollis cupped his hands to catch the dirt so he could fling it over the side.

"Swear," his father said again.

Hollis awoke with a jolt, damp sheets twisted around his legs and waist. His head felt much better, but his heart was pounding. The only light in his bedroom was a thin rectangle that outlined his door. Was his mother still entertaining? It felt like the small hours of the morning. He slid from his bed and fumbled into an old pair of pants and a long-sleeved shirt, then opened the door just enough to peek out with one eye.

Four men in Dakota uniforms were scattered about the room—two flanking the door, two sitting in leather armchairs across from his mother, whose nightdress trailed on the floor beneath the sofa. One man was speaking in a low voice, barely above a whisper. The other man was sipping from a cup and balancing a saucer in his lap.

"So y'see, Mrs. Dakota, the doc thinks it might've been the liver pâté. At least, that's what he's determined might be the cause of the . . . uh . . ."

"Speak freely," his mother said. She sounded amused.

"The cause of the bowel, uh, troubles."

"*Digestion issue,*" said the officer with the tea.

"And just so we're clear, he sent for all of us?"

The first man nodded. "He says to me, 'Everett,' he says, 'Go and fetch Lucy and Hollis.'"

The second man chimed in. "He kindly requested your presence in the infirmary, ma'am, along with your son. And Robert, too."

Hollis thought his mother was going to burst out laughing. "Should I wake Father Cairns for last rites? This sounds like a very serious episode of indigestion."

"I'm sure he's not in that kind of mortal danger, ma'am."

"We're just obeying orders."

"Of course you are." Hollis's mother slapped her hands against her knees and rose to her feet. "But I see the rest of you haven't touched your tea. How rude, to make poor Steward Bailey cart it here for nothing."

It was then that Hollis noticed the tray, upon which rested three identical and untouched teas. What was going on? Why would his mother spend so much time entertaining Castor's errand boys at such an hour?

"Wasn't necessary," said one of the burly men by the door.

The man's barrel-chested partner rumbled in agreement. "Shouldn't have bothered."

Hollis's mother hesitated for a moment, eyes fixed upon the door as if she were waiting for another guest to arrive. Then she threw up her hands in resignation. "Well, I suppose I'll go attempt to lift his spirits. But I'm not waking the boys for this."

The men looked at each other as if they were unsure of how to proceed. Hollis wondered if they'd forgotten whose name was on the ship. He stepped out into the sitting room.

"It's okay, I'll go with you. Let Rob sleep." He was already anticipating the look on Castor's face, crippled by stomach pains, his orders almost—but not quite—obeyed.

"Morning, Hollis." His mother smiled.

"Is it?" He locked his fingers together and stretched his arms above his head.

"Half past four."

"Ungodly."

It occurred to him that an even more satisfying facial expression might be derived from Castor's orders being completely ignored. He could try and talk his mother out of going altogether. But then he wouldn't be able to see his stepfather's face, which was the whole point. He decided to stall while he figured out how best to play his hand.

"What's this about liver pâté?"

"It's rendered your stepfather's bowels inoperable, apparently." She cast a quizzical eye at the man draining his teacup. "Or have they become *too* operable?"

Flustered, the man placed the cup and saucer carefully on the table. "Much obliged for the refreshment."

A hurried knock on the door proved to be a formality, since it swung right open. Hollis recognized the dim shape of Steward Bailey, a modest crewman with whisper-smooth movements, well suited to darting about airship passageways and bustling kitchens.

"Mr. Castor is not in the infirmary, ma'am. I checked myself, and then I confirmed with Dr. Mapplethorpe on night admittance duty."

"Thank you, Mr. Bailey. I thought not." She turned to the man who'd enjoyed his tea. His face attempted an apologetic smile. "Where is my husband?" His smile didn't waver. Her next statement was an accusation. "You're the one who's been phoning me."

He laughed nervously. "Phoning you, ma'am?"

So the call on the bridge wasn't the first one, Hollis thought. This was too much to process so early in the morning, when everything still had the churning, not-quite-correct feel of a dream. Hollis half expected his father to stroll into the room, ear leaking dirt.

His mother beckoned to the steward. "Mr. Bailey, please join us while these men explain what kind of game they're playing and who put them up to it."

Steward Bailey stepped forward into the room. One crewman quietly shut the door while the other whipped the back of the steward's skull with a leather sap. The first man caught him beneath the armpits and lowered him into the corner, chin resting senselessly against his chest.

"See? You shouldn't have done that," said the man with the sap.

Hollis yelled for his stepbrother to wake up as he lunged for his mother's arm. The futility of the situation gave his movement a quick, desperate edge. If Rob would come bolting from his bed, they might have a fighting chance. Everyone in the sitting room seemed flung on a collision course with everyone else. His mother turned to him, arm outstretched, but was viciously bundled up by the two crewmen from the chairs. Her stockinged feet kicked heel-first at their shins. Hollis swiped nothing but air and tried, at the last second, to let his momentum slam him into the man on the left, who sidestepped him neatly and sent him sprawling against the legs of the sofa.

"Rob!" he screamed again, twisting away from the burly man with the sap.

"Keep him quiet," growled the fourth man, who had remained by the stateroom door. Hollis wriggled beneath the sofa and sprang up on the other side. He was near the open set of French doors that led to the dining room. Beyond that, a kitchenette with a servants' entrance led to the access corridor that ran behind the largest staterooms so that food could be delivered without disturbing the occupants. If it was unguarded, it would be his only escape route.

But he wasn't thinking of escape. The man with the sap advanced on him. Hollis's eyes searched for a weapon— like the deadly looking poker in the wrought-iron fireplace set. He'd never reach it in time. A strange calm settled over him. He was no match for these men, but he knew how to throw a punch. Sort of. Maybe, if he got one good shot on the big guy—

"Run," said his mother, right before they clamped a soaking wet rag over her nose and mouth.

Hollis willed Rob's doorway to burst open. Why wasn't he getting up? His mother's eyes bored into him. Then her body drooped like a deflated balloon. The big man swung the sap, and Hollis ducked. Leather whisked his hair. In the corner, Steward Bailey groaned, head lolling from one side to the other. The crewman by the door planted a boot in his ribs, and he slumped forward.

Hollis was faced with a decision that he had no time to ponder: lunge at the big man's legs and try to catch him off balance or scramble through the dining room and out the servants' door?

Take him down.

Already his body was obeying a more reasonable and insistent command, hurtling through the kitchenette, past a wooden block of razor-sharp steak knives, handles facing out.

Go back and fight.

The knives were behind him. He crashed through the door and out into the empty, undecorated hallway, where he did what his mother had told him to do.

THE HISTORY OF FLIGHT IN AMERICA

PART

TWO

UP ON THE ROOF of the White House, Samuel Dakota brushed himself off, took a long look at the gas lamps of Washington, and began poking around in the darkness until he stumbled against a wide chimney. He climbed over the top and wedged his back against the bricks, knees bent, feet pressed against the opposite side. Reassuring himself that there was little chance of falling into a roaring fire in the middle of summer, he eased into a halting descent, breathing slowly to silence the pounding of his heart. After scraping his way down the narrow shaft for a few torturous minutes, he began to wonder if the presidential bodyguards were instructed to shoot intruders on sight. Perhaps he should have formulated a better plan.

When he reached the bottom, he paused, listening, just above the pool of light seeping in from the room. Empty and quiet, as far as he could tell. He put a hesitant foot down, expecting a pile of ash but finding smooth brick, and unwedged himself from the chimney. It smelled vaguely charred, but otherwise the fireplace was free of soot. *Well, this is the White House*, he thought. *Of course it's clean.*

He crawled out and was surprised—again—to find himself in a hallway rather than a room. Scowling portraits lined the walls. He smelled the rich, lingering odor of savory, slow-roasted meat, and his stomach gurgled and growled. It had been months since he'd eaten a decent meal. He placed his hand over his belly and willed it into silence.

He wondered what President Lincoln was in the habit of doing after supper. With the war still raging, Samuel guessed the man would be in his study, poring over battlefield assessments and reports, absorbed in his work. He had always heard that Lincoln was a melancholy loner.

Just ahead, the hallway split, forming a T-shaped corridor. To the right, the delicious smell of the presidential dinner seemed stronger. He guessed that the offices were separate from the living and dining rooms, so he took a left.

Suddenly the strident, overlapping voices of two men drifted toward him. He froze for a second, then darted beneath a sofa that was not quite long enough to shelter his tall frame. Wedged once again in a narrow space, he hugged his knees as best he could and peered out between the polished maple legs as the two men strolled past.

"I commend General Sherman's single-mindedness," one halting voice said. "His zeal is not the issue, Mr. Stanton."

The second voice, much fiercer: "Then what *is* your issue, sir?"

"It has more to do with— Ah! These drafty halls strike again."

A stovepipe hat tumbled to the floor and rolled to a stop in front of the sofa, inches from Samuel's face. He pressed himself back against the wall, but it was no use. He felt a sudden tense stillness in the air as the two men froze in surprise at the sight of a filthy vagabond stuffed beneath a sofa in the hallway of the White House.

The fiercer voice spoke first.

"Come out of there at once and identify yourself, soldier. And bear in mind that we are most inclined to have you shot for trespassing, so move slowly and carefully."

Samuel crawled out on his belly and picked up the fallen top hat. He struggled self-consciously to his feet and extended the hat to its owner, President Abraham Lincoln himself, who accepted it with a mystified smile.

Samuel bowed his head. His mouth was suddenly very dry.

"Well?" the other man asked. In nursery-rhyme contrast with the gaunt, lanky president, this man was short and fat, with spectacles pressed into his round face and a bushy gray beard covering his thick neck. He looked upon Samuel with revulsion. Samuel wished he had spent the afternoon taking a bath and scrubbing his uniform instead of sitting on a bench in the heat.

"Shall we hear the explanation for your desertion and this unwelcome trespass, or shall we summon the guards?"

Samuel thought of the unsmiling man at the front gate who had shooed him away at the end of a gun. If sent for, that man would certainly not hesitate to shoot him on principle.

Samuel cleared his raw throat and drew himself upright. He ignored the fierce little man and addressed the president directly.

"My name is Samuel Dakota, and I request a brief audience with you, sir, in order to demonstrate a top-secret new method to achieve total victory over the rebel secessionists in a matter of months, if not weeks."

Lincoln's smile remained. The other man tried to speak but instead began to cough.

"Mr. Dakota," the president said, "please allow me to introduce Edwin Stanton, my secretary of war, who seems a bit taken aback by your offer. As for me, I had assumed you were an assassin and am quite overjoyed to find that you are not."

Cheered and emboldened by the president's oddly genteel manner, Samuel began to speak with greater confidence as Mr. Stanton looked on in disbelief.

"What I can offer you," Samuel said, "is the means to conquer the cities of the South—"

Stanton interrupted, "General Sherman currently has that task well in hand, and may I remind you that you're speaking with the president of the United States—"

Samuel held up a finger for silence. Stanton sputtered.

"As I was saying," Samuel continued, "the means to

conquer the cities of the South *and* demolish her armies, all the while keeping our soldiers completely out of harm's way."

Lincoln replied, "I confess, I don't see how you can demonstrate something so outlandishly large in scope and ambition to me inside these walls."

Samuel could have hugged the president. Quickly, with a pounding heart, he sat down on the sofa and removed the bottle of whiskey-sap and the tin of beetles from his knapsack.

"May I please have your hat once again, Mr. President?"

Stanton rolled his eyes. "This is ridiculous. We're indulging the whims of a madman."

The president shrugged and removed his hat. "Perhaps." He handed the hat to Samuel. It was worn and frayed; clearly the president's favorite. Samuel took a deep breath, opened the bottle, and smeared the brim of the hat with amber sludge.

The president winced. Mr. Stanton said, "He mocks you, sir."

Samuel, savoring the moment despite his fear, said, "In a moment, I promise you will forget all about the minimal damage to your hat." From the tin he selected two beetles, which he placed along the brim.

Almost instantly, they set about ravenously consuming the whiskey-sap. Within seconds, their pungent flatulence filled the air.

Mr. Stanton pinched his nose. "And now he poisons us with this stench!"

President Lincoln's accommodating smile wrinkled into a sour grimace. He opened his mouth to speak, then widened his eyes in astonishment as the hat leaped into the air, banged against the ceiling, floated down the hall, and disappeared around the corner.

"A parlor trick!" Stanton yelled, unclasping his nose. The president regarded Samuel warily, as if weighing the extent of the intruder's madness.

Working quickly, Samuel knelt on the carpet, smeared more whiskey-sap on the legs of the sofa, and released four beetles. The two men watched in disbelief as the sofa sprang effortlessly into the air without so much as a jolt of hesitation, crashed through the ceiling, and vanished into the night sky.

The rest of the evening was spent on the roof of the White House, where Samuel Dakota, President Lincoln, and Secretary Stanton dragged five more sofas, two guest beds, an oak desk, and a grandfather clock that had belonged to John Quincy Adams. One by one, Samuel sent them soaring over the hushed Washington streets.

When they had exhausted their supply of furniture, the president turned to Samuel.

"Mr. Dakota, this has truly been an extraordinary evening."

Secretary Stanton's permanently weary, sunken eyes had achieved a new, childlike gleam. "We'll destroy them from the air," he said in wonderment. Then he stepped to the edge of the roof and mimed shooting a rifle down at the lawn below—"Pop! Pop! Pop!"—his imaginary bullets picking off imaginary rebel soldiers.

The president stared grimly at his secretary of war. Samuel noted the shadow that passed across the president's face before he blinked it away and said, "The question, Mr. Dakota, is how you would like to proceed."

Samuel grinned. "Well, Mr. President, if I may, I'd like to propose a deal."

HOLLIS KNOCKED QUIETLY on Delia's door with the tip of his
fingernail, keeping an eye on the dormitory hall. To his
surprise, it opened immediately. Delia was wearing the same
dress as the day before, and her eyes were ringed with dark
raccoon circles.

"I didn't expect you so early." Her voice was cracked and
weary, struggling out through a bone-dry throat. "How's
your head?"

"Fine." He'd actually forgotten about his headache, and
now he was nostalgic for yesterday, when that had been his
biggest concern. "I have to come inside."

"Wait," Delia protested, but he'd already brushed past
her and shut the door.

"Interesting choice of shoes, Dakota."

Rob Castor was stretched out on Delia's bed, wearing

his pinstripe suit. With his head propped against two pillows and a funny-book balanced on his thigh, Rob looked thoroughly at home.

"You're here," Hollis said.

"So are you."

"No, I mean you're *here*. They didn't get you."

With an exaggerated sigh, Rob closed the funny-book and sat up, swiveling so that his feet rested on the floor. His hair was matted against the side of his head.

"Okay, you win. I'll bite. Who didn't get me, exactly? And also . . ." Rob pointed at Hollis's shoes. Hollis looked down at the Italian loafers. Leather tassels dangled from the tongues like tiny brooms.

"I stole them from a second-class sky-boot exchange on the way down. When I ran away from the stateroom, I was barefoot, so I had to grab the first pair of anything that fit."

The funny-book drifted up behind Rob's head and floated toward the window, where a hesitant glow was just beginning to hint at the dawn.

"Don't get gunk all over that," Rob said to Delia as she went after the airborne book. "Wait," he said, turning to Hollis, "why were you running away?"

Hollis told them the whole story in a feverish torrent. At several different points, they had to urge him to relax and take a breath, with Delia finally pressing him forcefully into her lone chair. That was fine with him. The loafers felt as if they should come with a warning: NOT TO BE WORN AS

SHOES. When he got to the ambush of Steward Bailey, Rob's face darkened and he got up to pace the tiny room. Delia sat on the bed while Hollis related the end.

"She told me to run. I didn't have a choice."

As Delia reached out to rest a hand upon his knee, Hollis knew he'd told a lie. He'd had a choice, and he'd opted to save his own skin rather than stand and fight. His mother always said that misfortune traveled in packs of threes. One more to go.

Rob's pacing slowed, then stopped as he drummed his fingers against the edge of the table. He was lost in thought, chewing on the inside of his cheek, contorting his face. Hollis recognized this kind of jumpy stillness from when they'd organized big games of Haunted Ship or Capture the Steerage Rat.

"Binoculars," Rob muttered. "Rope." He ticked off each word with a finger. "Mustaches."

Hollis was too weary to remind his stepbrother that this was no game.

"Whoever they are, Rob, they probably have your father, too. They made up that infirmary story."

"I realize that," he said. "I'm thinking." He turned to look at Hollis. "Question: why did you come here? Why not go straight to Captain Quincy or get Marius to round up some people or—"

"Because the crew was in on it," Delia said.

"Or at least they were dressed like crewmen," Hollis said. "But either way, how do I know who to trust?"

Rob shook his head in wonder. "You think this goes all the way to the top?"

It sounded as if he wanted Hollis to say yes, so they could play at being Pinkertons unraveling a grand conspiracy.

"*Rob*," Delia said. She gave Hollis's knee a little squeeze.

"All I know right now," Hollis said, "is that this whole trip has been wrong from the start. I keep getting these little glimpses into stuff I'm not supposed to see." He rubbed his face. "Like my dreams last night," Hollis continued, running on fumes, slipping into a welcome delirium. "The airship was a castle. The moon was fake. My father told me to swear to something, I'm not sure what, and then when I woke up, they took my mother away. I feel like I should have known, somehow."

Delia moved her hand from his knee to her lap and began to fuss with her bracelet. "It's not your fault, Hollis." She was looking at him so deeply, it brought him back to how everyone had treated him in the wake of his father's accident. As if it were a contest to pick out the most sympathetic and understanding person. He turned away and watched Rob's aggressive thinking, fingertips playing at invisible typewriter keys. Over his shoulder, the sky had brightened. Golden rays sliced through the dorm room, illuminating dust. Suddenly Rob stopped moving. He was looking outside.

"Hey," he said, "I think something's wrong."

"Oh, now you do?" Hollis glared at Rob. His stepbrother always had to be the one to figure things out in front of

Delia. "Were you listening to a word I just said? We have to . . ."

What did they have to do, exactly? Tell someone powerful but unconnected to the crew, a first-class lawyer or doctor? Appeal to the second- and third-class passengers for help? Or was he just being paranoid, and he really should have gone to find Captain Quincy or another high-ranking officer?

"I know—just get over here." Rob beckoned, peering outside. They joined him at the window. The dawn had given way to a wispy morning, and the ship's forward progress was measured by the clouds drifting past.

"Tell me what you see," Rob said.

The view put Hollis in a trance. He felt like he could push open the window and dive out into fluffy white softness, buoyed along on a pillow of air.

"What are we looking for?" Delia asked.

Then the clouds parted unexpectedly, exposing a patch of earth below, and Hollis felt a little shiver of understanding.

"We're not over the ocean," he said, pointing at the horizon. "That's New York City over there." Just before the clouds gathered to block the view, Delia and Hollis crowded the window to peer at the office towers of Manhattan, toy blocks in the distance.

"Right," Rob said. "We shouldn't be able to see it. Which means sometime in the night, we turned. We're flying due south." He looked at Hollis. "Does that make any kind of sense?"

"Okay," Hollis said, not wanting to give Rob the satisfaction of discovery. "So we're not following the flight plan *exactly*, but—"

Rob snorted. "We seem to have completely ignored it."

The *Wendell Dakota* should have been headed east over New York, before flying straight across the Atlantic to the sky-dock in Southampton, on England's southern coast. Captains filed their flight plans weeks in advance and obeyed them with strict precision. Hollis was certain that Quincy was not the type of man to test the uncrashability of the *Wendell Dakota* by violating a sacred flight plan.

"Maybe there's a good explanation," Hollis said.

Rob snorted again.

Hollis sensed they had reached the moment when a true leader would step up to propose a sensible course of action. He looked down at his tasseled shoes and tried to think.

"Here." Delia handed Hollis a thick leather-bound book, at least a thousand pages long. He studied the embossed lettering on the cover.

"A dictionary?"

"The room across the hall is empty," she said. "Go open it in there."

Hollis hesitated, imagining some ingeniously accordioned homemade critter springing forth from the pages, making him shriek as Delia and Rob doubled over in laughter.

"I'm not falling for this again. And now's really not the time."

"It's not *that*," Delia said. "Trust me."

Hollis didn't, but he retreated to the empty room anyway and sat on the bed with the book in his lap. He felt trapped in a highly suggestible state—happy to let Delia and Rob move him around, seat him in chairs, give him little tasks. This only made him more ashamed: there was no room at the top of Dakota Aeronautics for someone who lacked initiative in critical situations. Hollis had recently come to realize that thinking about thinking only led deeper into anxiety and hand-wringing. And yet he often found himself powerless to break the habit.

Slowly, he lifted the dictionary's cover to reveal a meticulously razored-out hollow the size of a large brick. It contained the telegraph key, two coils of wire, the battery, and two curious metal rods separated by a tiny gap. Carefully soldered wires snaked through the hollow, connecting each instrument in a circuit except for the telegraph sounder—a spool connected to a weighted lever—alone in the corner.

"Um . . . ," Hollis said, examining the unfamiliar machine up close. It looked like a bomb. Maybe Rob was right: maybe Delia *was* an anarchist.

Suddenly, the sounder began to click. Hollis almost flung the book onto the floor in surprise. From the other room, a series of loud, crispy sparks matched the clicks from the sounder bolted to his machine. He looked through the open door across the hall, where Delia was clicking the telegraph key on an identical contraption in her lap.

Hollis looked for the hidden telegraph cable, something Delia was surely using to connect her transmitter to the sounder in Hollis's. But there was nothing: the two dictionaries were talking through the air. He listened carefully, trying to decipher Samuel Morse's code in his head. It had been some time since he'd been forced to learn the alphabet of dots and dashes, and at first the sounds were meaningless. But the basics were fairly well ingrained—his father had seen to that—and after a little while, the taps arranged themselves into words:

GREETNGS HOLLS

He might have missed "I," but the other letters were clear enough. Hollis worked frantically at his own key. Each tap closed the circuit and sent a sparkling charge of miniature lightning across the gap between the metal rods. His body quivered in awe, like the first time he watched the launch of an airship, an impossibly bulky tub of wood and steel lifting gracefully into the sky.

YOU ARE A GENIUS

After a brief pause, his sounder clicked again.

THNKS

He heard Rob's voice from the other room: "I think you just sparked us into the history books, Delia." Hollis clicked two short *dits*, one long *daaahhhh*, and three more *dits*. He added an emphatic *dit dit daaahhh daaahhh dit dit* as punctuation.

US?

Rob again: "Obviously we're equal partners in this endeavor." Hollis listened to Delia's indignant taps.

DISCUSS LATER

Hollis pictured the future in a supersonic flash: communication towers on every airship; wireless transmissions to control centers on earth; advance weather reports. A greater *sense* of things, the vast world made smaller by little blips of electricity.

He brought his wireless telegraph book out of the empty room to join its counterpart on Delia's table. "This," he said, "is exactly what we need."

"Hope so," Delia said. "I was up all night." This wasn't a boast disguised as sly understatement—it was merely a fact that when she was obsessing over a project, she tended to go without sleep. "So listen, I know they're heavy, but I have these two satchels . . ." She rummaged through the mess on the table until she produced two leather shoulder bags. "They should be big enough to hold a book, one for each of you." She gave one bag to Hollis and the other to Rob.

"Right, so we can stay in contact," Hollis said, as if he'd been close to formulating the perfect plan, and this was the finishing touch he'd been waiting for. "While we—"

"Split up," Rob finished his thought. "Cover more ground. Every inch of the ship, fine-tooth comb, nose to the floor."

"That's pretty much the long and the short of it," Delia said. "My shift is about to start. That'll give me a reason to poke around the chambers some more."

"I'll see if I can pick up my old man's trail," Rob said. "Maybe he'll know why we turned south."

"And I'll do whatever I have to do," Hollis said. He tried to sound upbeat and hopeful, but the sheer size of the *Wendell Dakota*—miles of corridors, thousands of rooms, acres of deck space—put them at an obvious disadvantage.

"You'll find your mother," Rob said.

"I know that."

"I just want to hear you say it. Brice Blank always sets specific mission objectives."

Hollis wanted to remind him, in the most forceful way possible, that *this was actually happening*. Both their parents could be shoved into some dank crawl space. Maybe now wasn't the time to be taking their cues from a funny-book.

These thoughts came out as a mumbled "guess we should get going."

Rob slapped the satchel. "Stay in touch."

"We'll meet up after my shift," Delia said. "Four o'clock."

Hollis shouldered his transmitter bag. "I don't think we should come back here. We should meet somewhere they can't find us."

Nobody wondered out loud who, exactly, *they* might be. *They* had turned the ship southward. *They* were taking people away. Maybe *they* were even responsible for the wind that had swirled the dirt back onto the deck at the christening.

"The steerage quarters," Delia suggested.

Hollis's heart quickened. He'd never actually been to a steerage-class section on any of his family's airships and had been sternly instructed never to go there. Unlike the other rules imposed by his mother, which were breakable to varying degrees, the no-steerage rule was an ironclad warning. And unlike the rest of her ironclad warnings, which he had defied, this one had always been sacrosanct.

"What's wrong with that?" Delia asked, seeing the boys' expressions.

Rob cleared his throat. "Nothing. Four o'clock's good. Just zap directions to us if anything changes."

"I only had the parts for two transmitters."

"So how will we know where to find you?" Hollis asked. "Isn't it crowded down there?"

"Get to the message drop in the center of the hold," Delia said, as if this were everyone's favorite meeting spot. Hollis felt like he might as well be wearing a monocle and clutching a stylish cane in a white-gloved hand. He tried to shrug casually.

"Steerage it is."

HOLLIS TRAVELED THROUGH the dormitory, a bundle of exposed nerves, aware of every little twitch in the faces of the beetle keepers. Most were returning from long shifts and didn't give him a second look. The clothes he'd thrown on in the dark were drab enough not to betray his status at a glance.

He walked briskly up a staircase that led to a gymnasium where medieval-looking exercise equipment was flanked by a pair of mechanical horses (only a penny to ride). A trio of bullish men were lifting dumbbells, their shirts heavy with sweat. He lingered just outside the doorway, tolerating body odor, and tried to recall if the door at the other end of the gym was a storage closet or an exit to the third-class berths. His memory of this part of the ship on the blueprints was sketchy. He decided it was a closet: third-class passengers wouldn't have access to the gymnasium.

He was headed for the bridge. His paranoia had cooled just a bit. Hollis didn't really believe that Captain Quincy could be involved. The man who had forsaken the sea would set things right.

The passage beyond the gymnasium brought him to one of the cold-storage lockers. On the other side of the frosty window, great hunks of butchered cattle swung gently back and forth, wreathed in icy mist that was somehow more unsettling than the carcasses. Was his mother in a place like this? He shuddered.

Now he was faced with a choice: up another set of stairs lined with framed covers from *Turbines Illustrated* and *Crossings*, or through a door marked BINS. Since he had no idea what BINS meant—garbage bins? Laundry bins? Some acronym beginning with the word *beetle*?—he went for the stairs. A lifetime spent aboard airships meant he could improvise a route when the map in his mind failed him. Like any neighborhood in New York or Philadelphia, the *Wendell Dakota* had back alleys and shortcuts. You just had to know where to look.

Hollis pressed against the wall to make way for half a dozen stokers, their sleeveless shirts stained with ash. The words COAL TOWN were burned into a piece of cedar and nailed above the archway at the top of the stairs. The men disappeared beneath the sign while Hollis clutched the heavy satchel close to his chest. The heft of Delia's invention was comforting. It was as if Rob were at his side, the two of them walking together down the corridor between the bunk rooms that housed the furnace men. And yet, Hollis found that he was relieved to be away from the sound of his stepbrother's voice. In this way, the transmitter was perfect. They could be allies without having to deal with the odd currents of their friendship, which had been ebbing and flowing since before their broken families were joined.

IN NOVEMBER OF 1909—six months after his visit to the shipyard with his parents—Hollis met Rob at a stuffy aeronautical gala, where the completion of the *Lucy Dakota*'s hull had inspired a record-breaking airship cake. The length of three long tables pushed end to end, the cake was a cross-section cutaway of the ship, a preview of the interior. Each deck was a layer of a different kind: the promenade was dark chocolate; second class was fluffy angel food; lower decks a jumble of red velvet, peanut butter, vanilla. When the cutting began, it was more careful than he'd anticipated; caterers on short ladders, surgically removing perfect little cubes of cake and frosting, working their way down through the first-class decks. They were an efficient crew. Hollis wondered if they'd built a sister cake in their baking headquarters and run strict cutting-and-serving drills. Part of him thought it was a bad idea to build a replica of the ship just to gleefully destroy it.

For most of the evening, Hollis scarcely noticed the

people at his table. There was a new face: Jefferson Castor, a rising star in the company who had just been promoted to deputy operating officer. Castor's son was seated next to Hollis. During the meal, Hollis looked up from his filet mignon and noticed that Rob Castor had eaten the center of his steak while preserving the edges. The empty space was filled with mashed potatoes and topped with a pillar of green beans. Rob was frowning at his sculpture, as if it hadn't quite come out the way he'd hoped. Hollis, who had very politely and neatly finished his dinner, wiped his mouth, and transferred his refolded napkin from his lap to the table, was waiting for Jefferson Castor to notice. The children of employees were always on their best behavior around Hollis and his parents. But Castor was preoccupied, speaking with Hollis's father. He was gesturing with his fork, which clicked against his empty plate. It wasn't until the cake was half carved that Rob said his first words to Hollis.

Chocolate propeller molds.

Excuse me?

You see that giant cake shaped like an airship?

Uh . . . yes.

The propellers are made out of chocolate, so they must have had to make a mold.

So?

So somebody had to make a chocolate propeller mold. You ever think about how many funny jobs like that there are in the world?

The orchestra launched into a lively piece, with a violinist sawing out a furious solo over the top. This made the cake-cutting take on a madcap feel. Hollis thought about Rob's question. There *were* a lot of strange jobs in the world, when you took a moment to think about where things actually came from.

A caterer with his back to Hollis sliced into a virgin section of C Deck, almost perfectly amidships, and plopped the luscious red slice onto a plate brandished aloft by an assistant.

ON THE *WENDELL DAKOTA*, Hollis imagined the silver blade of that caterer's knife blocking his passage, stabbing through the hull and bisecting the hallway as he moved past the office where the chief steam engineer presided over his schedules. He scurried away from Coal Town by slipping into a closet full of mops and brooms and out the back into one of the crew-only passages. These access hallways were designed to take as little of the ship's square footage as possible away from the staterooms and restaurants. If he ran into someone traveling in the opposite direction, they would have to turn sideways and slide past each other—if the other person happened to be overweight, one of them would have to back all the way up to the last closet. To avoid a time-wasting detour every time this happened, passing lanes were placed at convenient intervals, bulges in the hallway that provided space for one person to slide into and wait for the other to pass, which Hollis did at the sound of footsteps and the squeak of an ungreased wheel. He pressed himself against the back of the alcove, making way for a steward pushing a cart laden with sandwiches and pickles. The steward moved farther down the hall, whistling tunelessly, and Hollis was about to resume his journey when he realized he was standing among sheaves of discarded papers. He picked one up. It was a notice, neatly typed on Dakota Aeronautics letterhead.

 **DAKOTA AERONAUTICS**

WEATHER ALERT
All Passengers Please Be Advised

The flight plan has been altered to avoid a major storm over the Atlantic Ocean. We apologize for the inconvenience. The following establishments will be serving complimentary food and drink as a gesture of gratitude for your patience.

- FIRST CLASS: Il Bambino's, La Coquette Parisienne, Samuel's Steakhouse
- SECOND CLASS: The Delmonico Grill, Café Pembroke
- THIRD CLASS: Dining Hall B

Cordially,

LuD

To save herself from painful wrist cramps that contributed to tiger claws, his mother used a special rubber stamp molded into the shape of her signature (stately *L*, looping *D*, scribble in between). This symbol of his mother's decision to keep the name Dakota instead of adopting Castor—a salacious bit of gossip in the weeks following the wedding— usually gave Hollis a quick jolt of good cheer. But here it only meant that her captors had broken into her office to steal the stamp, or the ship was taking a detour around a genuine Atlantic storm. It was hard not to lean toward the more sinister option.

Hollis was drawn onward by the sound of an exuberant melody from the other side of the wall. A similar tune had provided the backdrop to Rob Castor's very first ridiculous plan.

THE GALA ORCHESTRA had pushed the pace of the cake-cutting, encouraging people to dance. Edmund Juniper was swinging his arms like a skier trapped in one spot, two empty glasses in his hands. Rob had turned to Hollis.

> *I'm going to steal it.*
> *How do you know where they keep the mold?*
> *Forget the mold. I'm talking about the propeller.*
> *You can't do that!*
> *Why not?*
> *It's too big.*
> *Okay then, not the main. One of the smaller ones. You in?*

Hollis glanced back across the table. His father was scrubbing his spectacles with a linen napkin while Castor bent his ear. His mother appeared to be listening more intently to Castor. Lucy and Wendell Dakota often worked as a secret team at functions like this. Hollis could get his mother's attention and rat out the chocolate thief to his left. That was the proper way to handle this. He was always very proper. He turned to Rob.

I'm in.

INSIDE A SECOND janitor's closet, Hollis listened to the plucking of the violin. He could trace the course of his present life back to those two words. He and Rob were the reason his father and Jefferson Castor became friends rather than business acquaintances; the reason the Castors and the Dakotas spent so much time together both before and after his father's death. If he could somehow go back in time and unglue the two families, Castor would be just another ambitious company man in a pinstripe suit.

Hollis nudged open the door, letting in a sliver of bright light and amplifying the merry-go-round music. He had reached the Automat, putting him in the middle of the second-class promenade on the starboard side. He was perfectly dressed for a casual morning among moderately well-to-do military officers, bank managers, and theater directors. Devoid of a jacket and tie but not slovenly, Hollis could keep his head down and pass as a doctor's son, out for a stroll and a bite to eat. He slipped out and joined the throng.

The Automat was a cheerful floor-to-ceiling display case that ran for hundreds of feet along the promenade, sectioned off into panels for hot meals, savory pies, sweet cakes, pastries, and coffee. Each panel consisted of countless windows; behind each window sat a plate; upon each plate was a piece of food that could be claimed by inserting coins into a slot and pushing a button.

"What do you mean it doesn't apply to the Automat?"

A passenger with a spotty beard was badgering a crewman who was posting the weather alerts. Behind him skulked an embarrassed woman, studying her feet. The crewman had his back to Hollis, and as he reached up to fasten a notice to the wall opposite the pies, his unbuttoned cuff slid down his forearm. Black ink covered the bare skin.

"Well?" the passenger demanded.

When the crewman turned to reply, Hollis realized it was Marius and ducked behind a tall bistro table. If the ship had been cruising steadily in the proper direction, if his mother had been safely going about her morning, if his launch-day christening had been a great success, perhaps he would have crossed the promenade and revealed himself. But today he stayed put.

"The restaurants listed on this piece of paper *here*"— Marius slammed his palm against a tacked-up notice—"are the ones with free food." His voice was much too loud, his syllables thick and woolly. Hollis wondered how many times Marius's pocket flask had been guzzled and refilled.

"I don't want to eat at one of those," the passenger said. "I want to eat something from the Automat."

"Be my guest."

"No. You're missing the point. What I would like is for

that machine to serve me a piece of Key lime pie, and I would like it to be free of charge. I do not believe one single slice of Key lime pie constitutes an unreasonable demand, considering that we will now be arriving late to Southampton!"

Passersby, many of them walking and eating at the same time, couldn't decide if they should stop to gawk or quicken their pace. Hollis felt like he was watching a performance and half expected Marius and the angry man to grin, join hands, and take a bow.

"Allow me to recommend the Key lime pie from Delmonico's, *sir*."

"I don't want the Key lime pie from Delmonico's."

"It's the same damn thing!" shouted Marius. Hollis flinched, along with a few nearby passengers. The man's mouth dropped open as his red-faced wife, who could barely raise her eyes, took him by the elbow. Marius went back to posting notices. Hollis hadn't planned on turning to Marius for help in the first place, but witnessing the crewman's outburst swamped him with a new kind of dejection.

At the same time, Marius's final retort had given him an idea. The trick of the Automat was that, besides the mechanism that opened the windows, there was really nothing *automatic* about it. Food wasn't replenished all day and all night by some kind of wondrous engine or conveyer belt; it was cooked in a kitchen and delivered to the back of the display by runners from the Delmonico Grill at the end of the promenade. Since this ruined the mystique of the heavenly food windows, it wasn't common knowledge.

Moving swiftly, keeping his head down, Hollis located a door between SANDWICHES and FRUIT. He snatched a filthy apron from a hamper just inside, and a cap spattered with what he hoped was gravy. The neat passenger-facing side of the Automat was all perky music and radiant lights, but the loading area involved a bewildering choreography. Runners moved up and down paths marked off by lines on the floor. Lights flashed above windows. Team leaders called out numbers. It was like the floor of the New York Stock Exchange, where Hollis had once gone with his father to ring the closing bell. Except the stock exchange didn't smell like roast chicken and cherry pie.

At the far end of the bustling line, he found that in addition to the kitchen annex on this level, runners were also receiving trays from dumbwaiters sent down from the deck above. Nico's Café—Delmonico's first-class cousin—was used for Automat supply at peak hours. He began to rethink his situation. He'd planned on slipping behind the scenes, grabbing a tray or two to complete his delivery boy disguise, and heading back out among the passengers. But if he could hitch a ride up and sneak out the back of Nico's, he'd be practically at the entrance to the bridge.

A rough hand on his shoulder nearly made him strike out blindly. He caught himself in time and tried to act like he belonged, averting his eyes as a team leader barked an order and handed him a tub full of food-smeared plates to be washed. The man, whose apron was splashed with a single dot of tomato sauce in the area of his belly button, began rattling off numbers to Hollis's new coworkers as they hurried past. Hollis struggled to see over the top of the enormous tub. When he reached the end of the line, a pair of hands took it away. Hollis raised the brim of his cap for a better look around.

"These are dishes," said the runner who'd taken his tub, as if dishes were the last thing he was expecting.

Hollis ignored him and scanned the row of elevators.

"Don't you turn your back on me. What the hell am I supposed to do with these? Hey!"

Hollis had to stop the runner from doing whatever the Automat crew did when somebody screwed up the chain of dish command.

"Shhh, it's okay. I'm sorry. Give them back, please." Hollis extended his arms, trying to stay meek and apologetic behind his hat.

"No, it ain't okay. Wait a minute." The runner, who had a few years and about fifty pounds on Hollis, narrowed an eye while the other spiraled lazily. That gave it away—he'd been a busboy at Nico's on the *Secret Wish*, where Hollis had eaten lemon meringue almost every night.

"I'll be damned! Hollis Dakota, bringin' me the dishes. I know somebody who's looking for you."

"**S***HHH*," **HOLLIS WHISPERED**, glancing around. The runner didn't seem to care about the bosses seeing him idle. He just cradled the tub and shifted his weight. The dishes clinked. Behind them, a dumbwaiter slid open, revealing a steaming tray of pot pies balanced in a pyramid. Hollis grabbed the tray and held it out to someone passing by.

"Fifty-two," he said, and the tray was taken away. "Who's looking for me?"

"Your mama," the runner said.

"Oh . . . she is?"

"This fella who popped back here earlier to give us the story with the weather, he also said that you'd gone missing and Mrs. Dakota was worried sick, and if we spotted you, we were supposed to tell a boss, who's supposed to report it.

And also we gotta have you stay put. Did you run away or something?"

Hollis wondered how far the alert had spread. It was probably for the best that he hadn't known about it until right now, or he'd still be hiding out in Delia's room. A wave of indecision made him want to climb into the tub with the dirty dishes and curl up.

"What's your name?"

"George."

"Okay, George. I need your help."

"So." The nonlazy eye was searing into him in a way that made him deeply uncomfortable. "You left her all alone, huh?"

Hollis was speechless. How did George know that he'd abandoned his mother?

"I get it," George said. "I ran away myself. That's how I know about you, because I can read it on your face. This one eye has the power of two. It *sees* things better."

"Please don't tell anyone I was here."

George looked from side to side and lowered his voice to an absurd stage whisper. "You were never here."

"I need to get up to Nico's without anyone seeing me— think you can help me with that?"

Without another word, George opened a dumbwaiter and traded his dishes for a heaping plate of croissants. Then he led Hollis down the row to another dumbwaiter with a scrawled note stuck on its door: OUT OF ORDER. Without even checking to see if anyone was looking, he slid the square door up and ushered Hollis and the croissants inside the cramped space.

"Isn't this one broken?" Hollis protested as the door slammed shut and he was engulfed in darkness. After a surprisingly smooth rail-and-pulley ascension, he thumped to a stop and emerged. His plate was two croissants lighter. He had to will himself not to devour a third, or else the "delivery" would be awfully meager. Now the OUT OF ORDER sign made sense: this was Nico's wine cellar. Every available inch of space was filled. To get to the door, he would have to wade through a cityscape of corked tops. This was a bad omen: the last time he'd been in such a room, it had been a disaster.

I THINK WE LOST 'EM!

Rob struggled with the door handle. They were in a passageway beneath the ballroom. Sounds of the gala reverberated through the floor, but the footsteps pounding at their heels had gotten farther away. Hollis's shoulder, which had supported the flat end of the propeller blade during their mad dash, was covered in thick smears of chocolate.

Come on, come on!

Finally, the knob turned and Rob slammed his hip against the door, dragging Hollis inside. But he moved too quickly. All four feet six inches of chocolate slipped from Hollis's shoulder, leaving a melted trail along his ear and cheek. Struggling to hold on, Rob fumbled the propeller into the edge of a wine rack. Hollis realized with mounting terror that they were surrounded by hundreds of bottles with French labels.

He closed his eyes to avoid seeing them shatter—the noise was bad enough.

Time to go!

Rob grabbed his arm. Hollis didn't open his eyes until they were out in the hall, just in time to see the irate pastry chef and two ballroom ushers skid around the corner— followed by a new pursuer. Hollis's heart sank. It was his father. He looked to be in a state of total disbelief, as if Hollis had just been caught robbing a bank in an evening gown.

NOW, AS HOLLIS crept past the bottles in Nico's wine cellar, he ate a third croissant just to distract himself from the memory. With one hand on the door handle, he couldn't keep from begging his father to please be there waiting for him when he opened it.

But of course there was only a kitchen full of chefs and runners, all gleaming steel countertops and quiet precision. The nearest cook had his broad back to Hollis and was hacking at a mound of skinned flesh with a cleaver. Hollis shut the door soundlessly behind him and hoisted the plate as if he were a waiter, keeping the brim of his hat low and the croissants in front of his face.

"Twelve-nineteen!" called a chef from across the kitchen. Two delivery boys entered through a set of swinging doors, received a pair of dome-topped platters, and moved fluidly back out before the doors had even stopped flapping.

Room twelve-nineteen, thought Hollis. Now that he was back in familiar territory, his mind was practically a passenger manifest. *Julius Germain: spiritualist, author, publisher.* Croissants held aloft, Hollis marched across the tiled floor.

"Where you headed with those?"

"Seventy-four eleven." Hollis mumbled, giving the delivery door a businesslike shove with his free hand. At the end of the hall, he was greeted by an enormous portrait of twin girls holding cats. He took a left and found himself awash in humid air—someone had left the door to the first-class steam room ajar. A bright green tropical vine had unfurled itself out into the hallway as if it were mounting an escape. Hollis nudged it back inside to join the rest of the transplanted Brazilian foliage.

When he reached the end of a long corridor decorated with Louis XIV wall sconces, he had the urge to fire off a message to Rob—*made it to the bridge!*—but didn't want to break their silence until he had something better to report. Then he peeked around the corner and suddenly felt like a little boy playing a grown-up game.

The bridge was guarded by a pair of mismatched crewmen. One had scraggly hair tucked back beneath his cap, a wrinkled uniform, and two pistols in low-slung holsters. The other was well-groomed, with the square-jawed face of an actor and a perfectly round eye patch. He pulled a cigarette from his front pocket, placed it between his lips, and smacked his partner on the shoulder. The unkempt man fumbled with a match, striking it against the side of his pant leg until it caught on the third try.

Hollis hid behind a credenza full of sky-boots arranged behind glass doors—an Automat for shoes. He shoved a final croissant into his mouth, pulled off the apron and cap, and stuffed the disguise into an empty cabinet, along with the plate. The smoking crewman had given him a better, simpler idea. He fumbled in the satchel. Delia always had long-forgotten knickknacks stuffed in every closet, pocket, and knapsack she had used. This particular bag was no exception. Hollis retrieved a ragged handful and spread it out on the carpet.

A hardened piece of spruce chewing gum.

Several faded picture cards with images of holy men and women smiling benevolently; the back of each card said KNOW YOUR SAINTS—Property of St. Theresa's Industrial School for Girls.

Two stick figures made of twisted wire that reminded him eerily of voodoo dolls.

A bone-white business card, upon which was printed a single black beetle that resembled the Dakota logo without being quite the same.

And finally, just what he needed: a book of matches labeled *Secret Wish*, leftovers from their last voyage. There was no better diversion than smoke. He flipped open the paper lid.

Empty.

Suddenly his transmitter began to click, sounding like pistol shots in the silence of the hallway. He hugged the satchel to his chest and slid beneath the credenza. Heavy footsteps approached. His heart pounded almost as loud as the sounder, which clicked a message:

CAREFUL SHIP CRAWLING WITH FAKES

Thanks for the warning, he thought.

From his hiding spot, Hollis peered out at one pair of scuffed boots, followed by a second. The long piece of furniture creaked as one of the men leaned against it.

"What the heck was that?"

"Wasn't nothin'. Noise of the ship, is all."

"Let's get back."

"Well, lemme finish this."

"Those things *stink*, Jasper. Anybody ever tell you that?"

"Anybody ever tell you *you* stink, Bill? How 'bout you let me smoke in peace for once. You're like a complaint factory runnin' overtime."

From his hiding spot, Hollis had to agree with Bill: Jasper's acrid smoke had begun to fill the hallway and was burning his eyes. A sharp and insistent tickle scraped the back of his throat. He stifled a cough. His whole head felt itchy. It would be such sweet, instant relief to sneeze. . . .

He pinched his nose and clamped a palm over his mouth until the urge subsided.

"I'm tellin' you," said Bill. "Soon as this is over, I'm buying me a bona fide ranch. Montana, maybe. Or Wyoming."

"You Yankees don't know the first thing about the life of a rancher."

"I'll hire some good old country boys to do the work while I enjoy a never-ending river of fine spirits from my porch swing."

"I truly cannot believe how many of you Yanks signed up for this here ride."

"Not for the ride, Jasper. We ain't aboard this death trap for our health."

"What about the cause, then? You with us on that?"

"Sure, sure. South will rise, and all that. Long as I get my cut of the ransom, South can rise all day and all night till the end of time, for all I care."

Hollis wanted desperately to continue eavesdropping— were they holding his mother for *ransom*?—but this might be his only chance to travel undetected. He scuttled backward beneath the credenza, silently begging Rob not to transmit another message. The shuffle of his knees and toes against the carpet was drowned out by the escalating pitch of the men's argument. He wiggled around the corner as Bill said, "What's my *sister* got to do with any of this?"

Jasper erupted into a fit of hacking coughs, while Hollis found himself in front of the unguarded door to the bridge. He pulled it open a crack and peeked straight down the central walkway to the windows, where the sky had turned as gray and flat as a stage backdrop. Strange crewmen glided back and forth across the aisle, emerging from one great chugging machine only to disappear behind another. Hollis slipped inside the door and darted behind the stabilization gauge. Entranced despite the circumstances, he reached up and slid his hand along one of the smooth glass tubes. Inside, the suspended silver ball hovered slightly left of center: the *Wendell Dakota* was tilting starboard. The other tubes curved around him like a rib cage, measuring the invisible axis that stretched from bow to stern. He crept forward to the front of the gauge, where a switchboard arranged a coiled mess of wires into rows that fed a bank of telephones marked PROP TOWER 1, LIFT CHAMBER, TURBINE 3, and a dozen more onboard locations.

He eased around the edge of the machine and hugged the wall, running toward the front windows with his knees bent and his upper body in a low slant. When he was almost there, he squeezed sideways down a narrow, dusty space between the backs of two long chalkboards that weren't quite pushed together. He wiped away the sudden mess of dust and cobwebs that coated his sweaty face. At the end of the chalkboard tunnel, he managed to contort himself so that he could peek out into the center of the bridge.

Ten feet away, a man wearing a crisp uniform with gold trim around the cuffs and collar sat in a chair with his back to Hollis. His hands were tied behind him. His hair was as white as a blank sheet of Miss Betzengraf's writing paper.

Captain Quincy.

The *Wendell Dakota* had officially been hijacked.

HOLLIS COUNTED two dozen armed men on the bridge—porters, stewards, low-ranking officers, and telephone operators. And according to Rob's transmission, more were swarming the corridors of the ship like the deadly viruses in *Journey to the Center of a Human Being*, the only Julius Germain book he'd ever managed to slog through.

Captain Quincy flexed his gnarled fingers and struggled in vain to free his wrists. Hollis couldn't help but picture his mother's hands scraped raw against a tightening twist of rope.

Suddenly, Jefferson Castor appeared, hands also clasped behind his back, but *comfortably*, like he was out for a stroll. Hollis rubbed his eyes, convinced the stress of the last few hours was playing tricks on him. Castor stopped in front of Captain Quincy, regarding him as if he were a tedious chore to be avoided until it absolutely had to be dealt with. Hollis looked from one man to the other. This was no hallucination, and yet he couldn't quite grasp the meaning of what he was seeing.

Beneath the chalkboard to his left, several pairs of black boots gathered. Someone began tapping the board with a metal pointer. Hollis shrank back into the shadows.

Castor pulled a hand from behind his back and raised it across his body, letting it waver for a moment alongside his head. Then he brought it down in a vicious backhand across Quincy's face. The old man's head whipped to the side. The muted crack of knuckle on cheekbone gave the moment a sickening clarity, and Hollis knew exactly what he was seeing: his stepfather had taken the ship by force. Castor shook his wrist and winced.

Quincy spit blood and growled, "That all you got?"

Castor nodded at one of his men, who drew a pistol and pressed the barrel against the captain's temple. Rather than flinch away, Quincy seemed to push his head into the weapon, driving the hijacker's hand back a few inches and forcing him to apply even more pressure. Hollis pictured a braver version of himself running from his hiding spot, wrenching the gun from the man, taking control of the bridge. In a series of rapid-fire fantasies, he was freeing the captain, testifying at Castor's trial, getting his picture taken for the front page of—

Dit dit dit dit.

His transmitter crackled. The men on the other side of the chalkboard fell silent.

HEY DAKOTA ANY SIGN OF YOUR MOTHER?

Nope, he thought. *But I found your father.*

Hollis had started to edge back through the narrow gap when a head wreathed in a mane of hair appeared ahead of him.

"You there!" The crewman pointed straight at Hollis as if there were other kids sneaking around the bridge. The man turned to get Castor's attention.

Hollis's mind hurtled through several stupid ideas and came to rest on one sure thing: if he stayed in this chalkboard tunnel, he would certainly be trapped and caught. He changed direction and crawled toward the man, bursting out inches from his legs before scrambling to his feet. The man spun and swiped at him, missing the strap of the satchel by an inch as Hollis ducked sideways. Castor froze in the middle of buttoning his blazer.

"*Hollis!*"

The man holding the gun to Captain Quincy's temple transferred his aim.

My stepfather is about to have me shot, Hollis thought with an oddly calm inner voice. Jefferson Castor, the man who just last week took him on a sightseeing trip to the private sky-dock atop the Statue of Liberty's crown. Moving automatically, Hollis cut left past a table full of open books and maps, around which a few hijackers were gathered. One of them, he was surprised to see, was a tall, willowy lady wearing reading glasses. Another one managed to yell, "*Hold it!*"

Hollis clenched his teeth, waiting for the bullet to tear through the flesh of his back. He'd once overheard a sky-dock security guard say that being shot was like getting hit with a searing-hot sledgehammer, and he was fully prepared to be knocked off his feet by a fiery blow. Instead, Castor barked orders.

"Alive, I need him alive! He doesn't leave the bridge!"

Hollis heard the scrape of wood against the floor, followed by a clattering scuffle. He risked a glance over his shoulder. Captain Quincy had tripped Castor, and they were flailing together in a heap along with the chair.

Nice move, old man.

Up ahead, hijackers rushed to block the exit. Hollis slid around a boxy machine topped with a glass dome spitting ticker tape that heaped, unattended, in curlicues on the floor. He turned down a passage of archived sky-charts. Up ahead was an exit. For all he knew, it was locked or it dead-ended inside a closet, but he had no other choice.

With footsteps pounding behind him, he slammed into the door and spun the knob.

It swung open.

Hollis sprinted up a stairwell lined with hazard signs that warned of terrible danger to unauthorized personnel. He took the steps two at a time, trying to control his ragged breathing. If his mother wasn't being held alongside Captain

Quincy, where was she? Not that he'd be much use to her right now, even if he succeeded in discovering her location. The hijackers bounding up the steps behind him left only one open lane: a steel pathway that took him on a winding tour through the forest of pipes that delivered exhaust from the bridge machinery to the air outside. A sudden rancid smell almost knocked him flat. It wasn't until Hollis was almost on top of them that he became aware of the nests stuffed in the gaps between the pipe-work. At some point in the ship's construction, birds had colonized the ventilation chamber, and now their feathery remains seemed to be guarding the exit. Gagging, Hollis nudged the gristle out of the way and spun the wheel in the center of the door. He burst out onto the highest promenade deck, not far from where he had greeted passengers in what seemed like a previous life.

The sky was streaked with storm clouds. The wind whipped around him, sliding behind his back and curling between his arms and legs in wild figure-eight gusts. He wished for heavy sky-boots, but as soon as he heard the foot-steps behind him, he was glad for his loafers. He ran past the few passengers left on deck, who pressed their floppy hats to their heads and squinted against the wind as they made their way to the Grand Staircase. The only person at the long bar was Edmund Juniper, who was pouring his own moonshine julep and struggling to keep the sprig of mint from blowing off the surface of the overflowing drink. He seemed to be enjoying the weather and greeted Hollis with a friendly wave.

"Bracing day we're having!"

Hollis tried his best to indicate that he needed help, but the wind changed direction with a vicious about-face. He pumped his arms and lowered his head; the wind beat him back with such force that it stopped his forward progress and turned him into a flailing octopus struggling to run.

Sir Edmund was torn from his chair, moonshine julep in hand. He tumbled down the deck and slammed into one of the two hijackers who had managed to follow Hollis outside. The other man planted his feet in a wide stance and drew his revolver. Hollis grabbed one of the bolted-down barstools, hoisted himself over the top of the bar, and dropped behind it. Stray bottles and highball glasses rolled back and forth. The wind howled over his head, but the sturdy oak bar provided enough shelter to pull out the transmitter and send a message to Rob.

STEERAGE NOW

He packed the book away and crawled along behind the bar until he reached a dumbwaiter, which had very quickly become his preferred method of interdeck travel. With a swipe of his hand, he cleared the small metal cube of snack trays and clean glasses that were still warm and steaming from the dishwasher. Hollis stuffed himself inside, knees pressed against his chin. He released the brake lever and descended into darkness, the abrupt silence broken only by the hysterical pounding of his heart and the echo of Jefferson Castor's betrayal.

PRESIDENT LINCOLN agreed to pay Samuel Dakota fifty thousand dollars a month to build and test flying machines, with the United States government as his exclusive contractor. Treasury Secretary Salmon P. Chase balked at this exorbitant sum, which he called "a gross miscalculation" on the president's part.

"Would you care to provide me with an estimate of what you think each individual soldier's life is worth, then, Mr. Chase," the President responded, "so that when Mr. Dakota's secret weapon ends this terrible conflict in months rather than years, we can compensate him in a manner more to your liking?"

Secretary Chase signed the check.

Samuel Dakota promptly bought and consumed two strawberry-rhubarb pies from the best bakery in Washington.

Then he scoured the ranks of the Union Army engineer corps for smart, hardworking, trustworthy men. He assembled one team to harvest sap, another to hand-pick the proper beetles from the soil, and a third to distill vats of moonshine—reverse-engineering the precise recipe from the original bottle—to be mixed with the sap for beetle food. They traveled south under heavy guard to the spot where he had made his discovery, marked by the gaping hole and disturbed earth left by the tree that was probably still soaring up into the heavens, toward God or at least some other world unknown to man. In three weeks, they built an office, employee barracks, and the first of several warehouses. Samuel surrounded his compound with a high fence like a prisoner-of-war camp, keeping away the curious onlookers who never seemed to run out of questions for the men in the guardhouse. After that, a few persistent locals returned every day to peek through the fence. Samuel supposed the construction was free entertainment for them. While the sap was being harvested and the beetles transferred from the countryside to dirt farms within the compound, Samuel busied himself with the design of the very first airship.

Dakota Aeronautics was born.

ONE DAY, sitting at his drafting table alternately scribbling and chewing on his pencil, Samuel recalled a boyhood trip down the Susquehanna River. He began idly sketching the old, rickety boat his uncle had made for their journey. As he retraced his lines and shaded the edge of each chopped and sanded strip of bark, a thought began to buzz around in the back of his mind. By the time he finished sketching the thick braided rope that attached the boat to his uncle's dock, the nagging buzz had become a full-fledged idea. Samuel grabbed the drawing and ran outside to find Solomon Pembroke, his chief builder, who was sitting beneath a tree whittling a toy train out of a stick. Pembroke had been whittling every day since he'd been hired, waiting for Samuel to deliver the first design.

"Solly!"

The lanky engineer stood up to greet his boss, stooping to avoid a low-hanging branch.

"Sir."

Panting and out of breath, Samuel handed Pembroke his drawing. Pembroke handed Samuel his toy train, almost finished except for the back wheels, and squinted at the sketch. Samuel studied the toy train.

"Hmm," each man grunted at the same time.

"This is fine work," Samuel said once he'd caught his breath. He meant it: the train was a perfect scale model, right down to the impression of a tiny conductor's profile in the window.

"This is a canoe," Pembroke said, holding up the drawing and cocking his head, as if he had to explain to Samuel what he'd just drawn.

Samuel nodded. "Sure is."

The two men stared blankly at one another for a few seconds. Then Pembroke grunted again, snatched back his toy train, and wandered off with the sketch, shaking his head.

THE FIRST DAKOTA AERONAUTICS airship looked like a hollow, upside-down hedgehog. Pembroke had improved upon Samuel's design, adding square flaps that stuck out of the side like blunted wings. His idea was that once the whiskey-sap and beetles were applied along the bottom of the canoe, additional beetles could be added to the flaps for extra lift, or scraped off the bottom to begin descent. For this purpose, he built small, oarlike protrusions into the sides of the canoe that could be controlled by the pilot. Proud of his crafts-manship, Pembroke had to admit it just might work. And while he didn't exactly admire Samuel Dakota—not yet, anyway—there was no denying the man's crazy willingness to see things through to the end. The probable end, in this case, being his death from a high-speed plummet to the ground.

"Solly." Samuel clapped his chief builder on the back on the morning of the launch.

Pembroke nodded hello. "Sir."

"Tell me the truth." Samuel pulled on his new leather helmet with straps that flopped down over his ears. "I look okay in this?"

The three dozen employees gathered at the testing field eyed their boss with a mixture of amusement and the kind of frightened awe reserved for asylum inmates.

"Like a man on the verge of winning a war," Pembroke said.

Samuel climbed into the sky-canoe, which was resting three feet off the ground on wooden posts. He cleared his throat.

"Gentlemen," he began, launching into an impromptu speech, "for centuries mankind has dreamed—"

"Mr. Dakota, sir!" One of the compound guards came running up to hand him a glass bottle with a rolled-up paper inside. "Sorry to interrupt. Messenger said it was urgent."

Samuel held the bottle up to the light. Someone had scratched a crude letter *C* into the bottom with a knife.

"Who gave this to you?"

The guard fidgeted. "Like I said, sir, a messenger came to the guardhouse. Said you would know what it meant."

"You didn't see this," Samuel said.

"Y-yes sir. I mean, no sir. I didn't. See what, sir?" The guard, clearly puzzled at Samuel's tone, retreated down the steps.

"Dismissed," Samuel said. But the guard was already running back to his post.

Samuel stowed the bottle beneath his seat. His men were watching him curiously. Without another word, he nodded to his chief whiskey-sap mixer, who slid beneath the ship on a rolling board and smeared the mixture evenly across the underside with a paintbrush. When he rolled out, Samuel nodded to his chief beetle keeper, who slid beneath on the same board and carefully applied eight evenly spaced beetles.

The pungent flatulence wafted up. Samuel, who had grown to value, if not quite enjoy, the smell, flared his nostrils and sniffed it proudly.

The ship ascended with an abrupt, purposeful jolt that almost spilled him over the side. He began a mental checklist of improvements for the next test flight: *seat harnesses*. After shifting his weight to regain balance, he saluted Solomon Pembroke as his chief builder took on the size and demeanor of a surly ant. He took a deep breath and looked out across the flat expanse of Virginia countryside that had been fenced off into neat squares of brown soil for the beetle farms, dense rows of transplanted trees rich with sap, steel tanks full of moonshine, and half-finished factory hangars waiting to produce the Union Army fleet. His heart swelled with pride. It was amazing how far a man could come in a few weeks with the right combination of brains, hard work, and—

His foot brushed against the bottle beneath his seat. The little hairs on the back of his neck stood up, and he felt a chill that had nothing to do with altitude. He was floating alone in the empty sky, but suddenly felt as if he were being watched. Off to the right, his landing spot—the Shenandoah River—was a thin blue ribbon curling through the countryside. He grabbed hold of the little scraping-oars, prepared to swipe beetles from the undersides of the canoe to begin his descent. It had been a short flight, but he didn't want to push his luck; he just had to wait for the air current to carry him over the river. As he hung in the gentle sky for what seemed like an eternity, he added another item to his checklist: *steering sails.*

He stretched an arm over the side and opened his hand so that his palm caught the wind. He gazed out at the surrounding clouds and thought, *There will be more of us up here very soon.* Finally, when he couldn't put it off any longer, Samuel grabbed the bottle and slid the rolled-up paper out into his hand. The scrawled message read:

> TO MISTER SAM DIKOTA,
> YOU OWE ME.
> HEZEKIAH CASTOR
> PS: IM WASHING YOU.

Samuel tore the note into pieces. *What's done is done*, he thought as he scattered the flecks of paper into the gently swirling air that he had conquered on behalf of the United States of America.

STEERAGE BEGAN WITH A STRUCK MATCH.

Hollis had descended as fast as he could from the promenade bar to the depths of the pelican's belly—a straight vertical drop on a map, but maddeningly slow going within the physical reality of the ship. As a hunted fugitive, he had to stick to the back-alley network of the *Wendell Dakota*, seeking pools of shadow like a dog on a hot summer day. He skirted Coal Town by ducking into the third-class infirmary, where minding one's business was an art form. An all-out sprint through a rank tunnel that connected the lift chambers provided express service from aft to fore. Then a bad guess had gotten him lost in a place where even his own hands were difficult to see.

A smoker lit her pipe by scraping a match along the wall. Hollis would have blundered right into her, but now he followed the orange glow. If she noticed him, she didn't say, just kept going as if she were taking a stroll to clear her head. When the tunnel emptied out onto a gangway that overlooked the massive hold, the smoker vanished and Hollis was confronted by a potent blend of noise, heat, and stench. A mangy Labrador bounded past, trailing a viscous rope of saliva from its bared teeth. Something thudded against his shoe, and he looked down to see a little girl retrieving an errant marble. She grinned up at him and snatched it away, sliding back into the game circle while her companions laughed. At the edge of the gangway, a rickety catwalk connected two makeshift tent cities nestled among the rafters. Hollis found an empty spot next to the railing and peered over the side. Some families had staked out shelters with blankets strung from clotheslines, little checkered tents. Others simply camped out in the open. Groups of men gathered around overturned crates, playing cards and tossing dice. But most people just milled about, jostling endlessly for a sliver of space.

It was hard to believe they were all passengers on the same ship. He had always imagined steerage to be a slightly more cramped version of third class. But this was something else entirely—there didn't appear to be any bunks. It was as if the population of several tenement buildings had simply been transported en masse into the belly of the *Wendell Dakota*.

He was thankful not to be wearing a finely tailored suit, but still felt as though his outfit screamed *spoiled first-class dandy* to the passengers cradling babies swaddled in rags or herding wild-eyed, barefoot children. He had gone out on the catwalk in hopes of spotting the rendezvous point, when he realized—too late—that he was halfway inside the moist, dim closeness of someone's tent.

A gruff voice came out of the darkness.

"It's about time."

Hollis straightened up as a man stepped into view, old and gaunt, with thin wisps of hair that spilled across his forehead. He carried a cane, which he extended to thump Hollis in the center of his chest. Then he pressed the cane harder, forcing Hollis back into the creaky wooden railing.

"Sorry, sir," Hollis said quickly. "I'll be on my way."

"Now, hold on. Not so fast, boy." The man, still pressing his cane into Hollis's chest, leaned forward slowly, reminding Hollis of a medieval knight sliding down the length of his foe's sword. The man cocked his head to the side and said, "I could use some more soup."

"I'm sorry, but I don't . . . *soup?*"

The man pulled the cane back slightly and jabbed Hollis once again. "That's right." He thought for a moment. "More soup."

Another voice came from the darkness, an old woman. "Leave 'im alone, Sidney. Godsakes, you'll scare the poor boy to——" The woman blinked in surprise as she moved forward to lower the man's cane with a liver-spotted hand. "Oh," she said. The saggy skin of her face seemed to tighten as she regarded Hollis. Her mouth made a thin line. "You shouldn't be here."

"He's getting my soup!" protested the old man. The woman ignored him as she pointed back across the catwalk, the way Hollis had come.

"Get along, now," she said, not unkindly. "There's nothing but trouble for you here."

"I have to meet someone," Hollis said. "Can you help me find the message drop?"

The woman's face softened, as if an invisible mask had been removed from her skin. She studied him for a moment and shrugged. "Downstairs, smack in the middle."

"We're going to Ireland," explained the old man matter-of-factly as the woman melted back into darkness. "Where it's quiet and the dust don't settle in the soup."

Hollis felt ashamed of something he couldn't quite put his finger on. "Safe journey, sir."

The old man's mouth stretched into a toothless grin. He broke into hideous peals of wheezing laughter. Hollis ducked away from the cane, backed out of the tent, and took the first set of stairs down to the floor of the hold. Rattled and out of breath, he leaned against a stack of crates and stared up into a ceiling of faded shirts and graying undergarments hanging from a web of clotheslines. A haunting tenor voice sang a few bars in Italian. Hollis picked his way past piles of trunks, baskets, and cardboard boxes. And barrels! There were so many barrels down here, he wondered if the hold doubled as barrel storage. He was careful not to step through the middle of any conversations—the last thing he wanted was to disturb anyone and draw attention to himself. Off to one side, he was relieved to see the framework of a partition, separated from the main area by a wall of sheets, with the silhouettes of bunks on the other side. Perhaps most of the steerage passengers slept in there and came out here to socialize. Then he noticed the SICK BAY sign tacked to one of the crossbeams and turned away.

Directly in front of him was a crudely drawn portrait of an infant in a crib. It was nailed to a thick support beam that stretched all the way up to the ceiling. More drawings, along with a few letters, were pinned up around the portrait, their edges overlapping like tree bark. Hollis stepped back and took in the full sight: pictures of people and animals, scraps of paper with names and hearts and addresses. Just above his head, someone had fastened a wooden cross, upon which a realistic carving of a beetle was crucified.

A girl's voice brought his attention back down to the floor of the hold.

"Lookee here, Chester."

The girl stood as tall as Hollis. Her hair was a knotty mess of red tangles that flopped out of a handkerchief tied beneath her chin. Her left eye was an angry slit ringed with a fresh bruise. The boy she called Chester was heavily built but not quite fat, with tight black curls on his head and pencil-sketch hints of hair on his upper lip. She jabbed him playfully with her elbow.

"I think we got ourselves a mighty fine society boy."

Avoiding their eyes, Hollis tried to push between them. A thick, powerful hand on his shoulder held him back. Chester slammed him up against the crates. Hollis's breath exited his throat in a sudden rush. All at once, the girl was in his face. Her open eye was bright green and brimming with liquid, as if she'd been stockpiling tears.

"Not so fast," she said, examining him up close, nostrils flared. "What brings you down here?"

"Maybe his shoes need shinin', Maggie," suggested Chester.

"Nah," Maggie said. "Society boys don't wear shoes, they wear golden slippers—ain't that right?"

She glared expectantly, waiting for Hollis to confirm this.

"I wouldn't know." He tried to swallow and made an audible, embarrassing gulp. "So, um, where you all headed?"

Maggie wiggled a finger inside an improbable tube of ringlets that stuck out next to her ear. Chester said, "Who cares? Anywhere's better than New York."

Despite Chester's iron grip on his shoulder, Hollis found this interesting. "But isn't that where the work is?"

Maggie laughed. "Yeah," she said, "if you wanna drown in some sap pit or choke in a propeller factory. I figure if I'm gonna starve, I'm gonna go starve somewhere I can breathe."

Hollis knew that people had booked passage on the *Wendell Dakota* for all sorts of reasons—plenty of first-class passengers just wanted the maiden-voyage bragging rights.

Second class was generally split between vacationing families and business travelers. Third class was full of single men and women seeking various fortunes around the world—the kind of traveler Marius would be if he hadn't signed on with the company. But Maggie and Chester's reverse immigration was new to him. He listened to the riot of voices surrounding him—Russians, Germans, Hungarians, Swedes—was everybody down here headed back to the Old World?

"So . . . you're leaving the country? For good?"

Chester snorted. "Seems a genius has wandered into our humble midst." He nodded at the satchel. "What's in the bag, genius?"

"I bet it's his church clothes," Maggie said.

"Or chocolates," Chester said hopefully.

"Give it here," Maggie said, grabbing at the strap. Hollis swatted her wrist. At the same time, silver metal flashed in her hand. *Switchblade*, Hollis thought. She pointed to her half-closed, swollen eye.

"Little keepsake from my last visit to your neck of the ship," she said, eyes flicking upward as if she could see through the dozens of floors and ceilings between steerage and first class. She held the blade to the side of Hollis's face. He tilted his head away so it wouldn't slice his cheek.

"Now, hand over the bag."

"I can't do that," he said, trying to speak without nicking his skin. The thin edge of the blade so close to his face made his body tingle.

"No kidding? Why's that?"

"Because it doesn't belong to you, Margaret Keenan," explained a familiar, matter-of-fact voice. The tension in Hollis's body gave way to sweet disbelief as Delia's face appeared behind the would-be muggers.

Without taking her good eye off Hollis or her blade off his cheek, Maggie said, "You're just in time to help me explain the finer points of the steerage tax."

Delia laid her hand gently against Chester's arm, and he dropped it from Hollis's shoulder. Maggie mumbled a curse.

Hollis shot Delia an astonished glance. "You *know* them?"

She ignored the question and tried the same gentle pressure on Maggie's arm. "This one doesn't get taxed. He's my friend, okay?"

This one? Hollis thought.

"Not good enough," Maggie said, but her knife hand wavered. Hollis held his breath.

"Yes," Delia said, moving shoulder-to-shoulder with Hollis and staring her down. "It is."

Maggie seethed. Hollis thought she might cut him out of spite. But after a moment, she flicked the blade closed and said, "We won't forget this."

Delia reached into her own satchel and pulled out a loaf of bread wrapped in paper stamped with the Dakota insignia.

Maggie shook her head. "Keep your charity. We're getting along okay."

Chester muttered something and accepted the loaf. Maggie looked like she was about to hit him, then she turned and stalked away. Chester gave Delia a rueful smile—*here we go again*—and followed Maggie, tearing off a hunk of bread and stuffing it into his mouth.

Hollis watched the untamed frizz of Maggie's hair disappear behind a long line of passengers jostling and pushing for position around two immense, steaming vats. A queasy feeling rose from his stomach to the back of his throat as two men in filthy smocks spooned shapeless lumps from the vats into bowls clutched in eager hands. Hollis watched a father fill a bowl for his pale son and tried to imagine his own family waiting in an endless line just to eat boiled potatoes and stringy beef. The nagging sense of shame he'd felt inside the old couple's tent blossomed again. He reminded himself that nobody was forcing these people to be here—they had paid for a steerage-class ticket of their own free will, knowing full well what that entitled them to. Somehow, that made him feel worse. He turned to Delia.

"If you hadn't come along when you did, I think those urchins would've gutted me."

"Just forget it," Delia said with a quiet fierceness that took Hollis by surprise.

"Sorry I didn't quite make it to the message drop. If you want to lead the way, Rob's probably waiting for us."

"We're already here." She rapped a knuckle against the paper-covered beam.

Hollis ran his eyes across the assemblage of odd scraps. He'd imagined a neat postal window. "Listen, Delia, it wasn't my fault your friends tried to kill me, okay? How in the blue skies do you know them, anyway?"

Delia shut her eyes and stood very still except for a slight quiver in her shoulder, as if she'd coiled all her energy inside and was struggling to keep it from exploding outward. For a moment, Hollis felt just as alone and scared as he had when the blade was against his cheek. Maybe Delia agreed with Maggie; maybe she thought of him as just another simpering rich kid with no idea of how the world really worked. Either way, he supposed there were more urgent matters.

"Forget it. We're being hijacked."

Delia opened her eyes, and the strange tension between them vanished so suddenly, Hollis wondered if he had simply imagined it.

"Figured as much," she said. "I crept all around the lift chambers and didn't see Chief Owens. Lots of unfamiliar folks hanging around, though. I did find *this*, in that same little office where we saw Mr. Castor."

She produced a baton of rolled-up paper that smelled like a musty attic. Together, they unfurled a detailed sky-chart smudged with frantic pencil markings: arrows, loops, and triangles that someone had clearly been drawing, erasing, and redrawing for years. Blue lines—known air currents—curved and swirled like fingerprints. In the center, a thick X had been traced over so many times that crumbs had settled in the grooves.

"The East Coast," Hollis said, pointing to the legend in the upper left corner. "Airstreams and weather patterns from Maine to Florida."

"It was in the safe, so I grabbed it."

"You know how to crack a safe, and you never showed me?"

"It's boring. Does this map mean anything to you?"

He studied the mess of lines and shapes. "Well, we're already headed south." He placed a finger on the X. "Maybe this is where Castor's taking us." He shook his head. "But that doesn't make sense—it's the middle of the sky. It's nowhere."

He waited for Delia to offer her opinion, but she was gaping at him in stunned silence. Then she came to life. "Castor's behind this? As in Jefferson Castor, your stepfather?"

"Soon to be former stepfather, I think. But yes. Him. Rob's dad."

"My God." Her hand worried at the buckle of her satchel. "I'm so sorry, HD."

"Why? It's not like he's my real father. He's just the guy who's married to my mother." He let a sudden wave of despair wash over him. "And I don't even know where *she* is, after all that sneaking around I did." He tapped a fingernail on the map. "But you found this. You're way better than me at this stuff." *And at everything*, he thought.

"Here, this was in the safe, too," Delia said, handing him a typewritten list of names.

"Juniper," he read from the page. "Wellspring. Reynolds. Germain. It's a list of first-class passengers, followed by . . ." Next to each typed name was a handwritten number, some as large as eight figures. "Dollar amounts. Which makes sense." He told Delia about the conversation he'd overheard outside the bridge. "He's ransoming the richest passengers. People were practically fighting each other to book staterooms on the first flight of the great uncrashable airship. They're all here. He could get millions from Edmund Juniper's relatives alone."

"He doesn't even have to go to the trouble of kidnapping them," Delia said. "Once he's got the ship, where are they gonna go?"

"He just had to get my mother out of the picture first." Hollis didn't much like the way this sounded when he said it out loud.

"Don't look at it that way," Delia said quickly. "He needs her alive. The company will want to ransom her, too."

"Jefferson Castor's not stupid, he's not going to—"

Suddenly Rob appeared, out of breath, glancing nervously over his shoulder. Hollis stuffed the list into his pocket and let go of his end of the map. It curled back into a baton in Delia's hand.

"What'd I miss?" Rob panted. "Different world down here, huh?" He eyed the slop buckets and swallowed hard.

Hollis pointed to a greasy blemish that stained Rob's face around his upper lip and chin. "What happened to you?"

"It's spirit gum from the fake beard. I couldn't get it all off."

"You wore a beard?" Delia asked.

"Yes, I wore a beard," Rob said. "It's a basic part of what we call 'tradecraft' in the spying profession. Anyway." He looked hopefully at Hollis. "You were saying something about my father?"

Hollis opened his mouth, but no words came out. It hadn't occurred to him until this moment that he'd have to break the news to his stepbrother, and that once he did, things would never be the same between them. *Well*, he thought, *there's no way around it*. He took a deep breath and gathered his last crumpled reserve of courage.

"Yeah," he said. "I found him."

"**I**S THE OLD MAN OKAY?" Rob demanded.

"Well," Hollis said, "I didn't exactly get to talk to him. It was kind of . . ." He couldn't bring himself to say anything else. Rob scratched the back of his head, sliding the brim of his cap down on his forehead. He turned to Delia.

"What's his problem?"

Delia shrugged.

"Spit it out, Dakota," Rob said.

Hollis felt like he was going to be sick. "We're friends, right, Rob?"

"*What* are you on about?"

"Just answer me."

"Fine. Yes, we're the two best friends who ever roamed the skies."

"And we can tell each other things, right?"

Rob picked at the gummy residue along his jawline. "I'm gonna go ahead and say yes to this."

"Right. Good answer. Okay. So here's the thing. We're being hijacked. I made it to the bridge, I saw it happening."

Rob put his hands on Hollis's shoulders. His eyes were wide. "I *knew* it! This is crazy. This is really crazy. It fits with what I saw, though. Some of the crew movements didn't make any sense. They're acting more like they're herding passengers, instead of helping them with things. I mean, they're hanging around like guards, instead of popping up when they're needed and then moving on to something else when it's finished."

"Our award-winning customer service."

"So they got *both* our parents. That explains why I couldn't find my father."

Hollis let the lively murmur of a hundred nearby arguments and jokes wash over him. Delia coughed and turned away politely.

"That's the thing I was getting at," Hollis said. "They didn't get your old man because he's sort of the one doing the getting. You see what I mean? *He's* the *they*. That porter we met in the lift chamber, he's part of it. He works for your dad, I guess, and there's a lot more like him. You saw them everywhere—you said so yourself."

Hollis had to look away from his stepbrother's face, which was pinched in disbelief. His eyes drifted down to rest on the four tiny stitching holes in Rob's top shirt button as he related the events on the bridge and the chase across the deck. When he stopped talking and the dull roar of the steerage hold rose up again, Hollis made himself look his stepbrother in the eyes.

Rob seemed to be calm. His face had slackened into a faraway look, as if he'd been listening to Hollis describe one of his dreams—a look that said he was sort of interested, but mostly just waiting patiently for the story to be over. Hollis glanced at Delia and gave her a tiny *what's next?* shrug.

"Hmm," Rob said. "Well then, I guess there's only one thing to do."

"Sabotage," Delia and Hollis suggested in unison.

"I was thinking of something more like this," Rob said, and planted his fist across Hollis's chin. The punch sent Hollis spinning sideways. He saw the extension of his step-brother's skinny arm as his neck whipped around. The noise of the steerage crowd slowed to a smear of sound until his knees hit the wooden slats of the floor. Someone yelled "*fight*," and people began to gather in a circle around them.

Hollis staggered to his feet and wiped the back of his hand against his mouth. It came away stained with a mix of blood and spit. A ringing was somehow in his ears and his eyes at the same time.

Rob punched me, he thought.

It didn't seem any more or less real than all the other strange things that had happened on the *Wendell Dakota*. Delia grabbed Rob from behind in a bear hug. Arms and legs flailed wildly toward Hollis as Delia struggled to hold on. Hollis worked his jaw, which clicked painfully.

"Hey!" Delia said. "Ease it down now, Castor."

The words echoed inside Hollis's throbbing head. He saw flashes of the map Delia had found.

"*Low-born lying scum!*" Rob wriggled free of Delia's grasp, pushing her away. "I'll knock you outta the sky!"

Hollis stepped forward and stopped a few inches from his stepbrother's face. His heart was pounding. "Try it."

Delia squeezed between them, brandishing a strange pistol. Two metal rods ran down the length of the weapon and extended beyond the wooden barrel. She pulled the trigger and the short antennae were suddenly connected by a jagged, sparking burst of electricity that reminded Hollis of the transmitter. When Delia released the trigger, the burst disappeared.

"Take a swing," she said sternly, "either one of you, and get zapped."

Hollis and Rob each took a single step back. The crowd, disappointed that the fight had been stopped, milled about uncertainly. Rob's face twisted into a hateful sneer that Hollis had never seen before.

"I'm sorry," Hollis said, "but it's the truth. Why would I lie about something like this?"

"Because crazy runs in your family," Rob said. He brushed off his sleeves and flicked the top of each hand—a habit passed down from his father.

"You *are* my family, Rob."

"I'm not even your friend, Dakota." With that, Rob turned his back and stalked away. Delia mumbled a curse as

Hollis's last name swept through the lingering spectators in a cascade of whispers.

"*Dakota?*"

"*That's the Dakota kid!*"

Hollis felt the curious gaze of the crowd turn menacing, a change as instant and unwelcome as the gust of wind that had carried the christening dirt back onto the rail. He watched Rob stomp up the stairs to the tent city and wondered when he'd see him again, and if that single punch had wiped out years of skipped classes and shared adventures. But what else was he supposed to do except tell the truth? Why should he feel bad for things he had no control over? It wasn't his fault that Jefferson Castor had decided to hijack the *Wendell Dakota*, just like it wasn't his fault that steerage-class passengers had to travel in the crowded hold. So why did he suddenly feel like he was being forced to take responsibility for both? What could he have done differently?

"Delia," he said, "is it true that I used to be decent?"

"Compared with what?"

"The way I am now, I guess."

She paused. "I don't know how to answer that."

Most of the time he appreciated Delia's candor. Right now he just wanted to hear her assurance that he was an okay person, becoming better, not worse. Which was the opposite of how he felt. The fact that he was worrying about himself right now probably meant that he was morally deficient in some way, he thought glumly.

"He popped you good, huh?" It was Maggie, pushing her

way to the front of the crowd. She pointed to his mouth. "Got yourself a gusher there."

Chester, thick arms folded across his chest, appeared next to her and surveyed the scene while he chewed the last of the bread.

Hollis used the inside of his collar to wipe the blood from his upper lip. Hesitantly, he reached toward Delia's electricity gun. "What do you call that thing?"

She shoved it back into her satchel. "Cosgrove Immobilizer. Patent pending, of course. Probably won't kill you, but it'll give you quite the knock-out jolt."

"*Probably?*"

"I wasn't really gonna use it on you and Rob." She held up her right hand. "Apprentice Beetle Keeper's Honor."

"Pretty nifty gadget," Maggie said, sticking a frizzy tangle behind her ear.

"She's an absolute genius," Hollis said. He wanted this knife-wielding maniac to understand that he was better friends with Delia than she could ever hope to be.

"Yeah, we made quite the pair, me and her," Maggie said.

"So you're from Hell's Kitchen," Hollis said, triumphantly deploying his one tidbit about Delia's childhood.

"Yep. Delia's just like me," Maggie said, "only smarter. Smarter'n all the girls at St. Theresa's combined. Smarter'n you, too."

"Honestly, Keenan," Delia said, "that's enough."

"St. Theresa's . . ." The name was naggingly familiar. It

took Hollis a moment to recall where he'd seen it. "'Know your saints,' right?"

Delia's face fell as he reached inside the transmitter bag, feeling for the picture cards. Hollis supposed she'd completely forgotten about them. Her grip tightened on the immobilizer as his fingers closed around one of the cards, but the desperate, calculating look on her face—like she couldn't decide who to zap first, him or Maggie—made him leave the card in the bag. He showed Delia his empty hand and moved on.

"I have a question about the transmitter you made for me." Hollis shot a quick glance at Maggie. "Can it be reversed?"

"What are you getting at, HD?"

"If I can get us to central communication, can we tap the wires? I mean, can we sort of turn the transmitter inside out and use it to listen?"

Delia chewed the inside of her cheek, thinking hard. "I'm not gonna say we can . . . but I'm not gonna say we *can't*, either."

"Because if Jefferson Castor has control of the bridge and the lift chamber, I figure he's also got the main prop tower and everything else. He's probably even infiltrated the furnace rooms. And he's not sending messenger pigeons to give his orders. So maybe—"

"If we find a way to listen to his telephone jabber, he might let slip where he stashed your mother and Chief Owens and whoever else he's grabbed."

"Right. And where he's taking us."

Hollis pictured the construction schematic for the

Wendell Dakota tacked up on the wall of his mother's office, next to the portrait of President Lincoln in his retirement cottage, flashing the smile that had turned famously cock-eyed when the man reached his nineties. Thin black lines representing telephone wires snaked from the prop tower to the bridge to the lift chambers to a hundred other locations. The details were too intricate to remember, except for one: almost exactly amidships, the lines were bundled inside a central shaft, which had to dead-end somewhere beyond the wall at the other end of the hold.

"Hey, Maggie," Hollis said, pointing toward the far side of steerage, "is there a way out through there? Like a tunnel, or a hallway, or a space between the walls where you go to . . ." He wondered what kids did for fun down here. "Drink gin?"

Chester perked up, as if Hollis's words had reminded him of some important task he had to complete. He mumbled good-bye and hurried away. Maggie aimed a dirty look at his back and then turned to Delia. "I talk to the society boy, you let me borrow your moblizer."

"Immobilizer," Delia said. "If you help us, it's yours. I have a spare."

"You got a deal, Cosgrove." Maggie grinned at Hollis. "Follow me."

ROB CASTOR took the stairs two at a time, stirring up little clouds of sawdust. His mind skipped back through the day, only this time when his stepbrother barged into Delia's room at some stupid predawn hour, Rob imagined shoving him away and diving back into *Brice Blank and the Carnival Barker's Mask*. That simple act might have saved them both a lot of grief. He longed for the mind-erasing secretions of the Chinese paladin fly, harvested by the daring archaeologist Atticus Hunter in Rob's own funny-book series (working title: *Hunter*), which currently existed in a sketch pad hidden in his underwear drawer. A little drop of paladin juice on the tongue for Hollis and another for Rob, and *ZAP*—they'd be friends again like nothing had happened. If only it were that easy to start over.

At the top of the stairs, he stopped to shake out his

throbbing hand, ignoring some old man's braying about soup. He picked his way through the tent city and along the catwalk, hopping onto the teeming gangway and retracing the steps that had brought him down into the hold. His body was still jumpy with adrenaline from the aborted fight. He felt like he could float his way out of steerage. A sudden tug at his sleeve almost made him lash out. It was a little girl.

"Excuse me."

He picked up his pace without meeting her eyes. The passage up to the third-class bunk rooms was just ahead.

"Excuse me!"

"I'm kind of in a hurry here."

"You dropped this."

He stopped. A neatly dressed girl of six or eight or ten (he wasn't good with ages) handed him a small packet of Herrimann's pistachios, which he'd bought from a snack cart by the Mount Olympus fountain in the largest first-class ballroom.

"Thanks," he said, tearing them open. "You want one?"

"What are they?"

"Ancient bird eggs."

She giggled. "Eww."

He held one out for her inspection. "Take it."

She placed it in her upturned palm and peered into the gap in the shell.

"Let me know what you think," he called back over his shoulder. As he headed into the corridor beyond the hold, lined on either side by trunks and blankets, his anger flared back up and he imagined Hollis's face as nothing but a pulpy lump. The notion of his father—Dakota Aeronautics' chief operating officer!—hijacking the airship was ridiculous. Actually, he was glad Chinese paladin fly secretions didn't exist, because he didn't want to start over. He wanted Hollis to remember that punch for the rest of his life. His only regret was losing his temper and screaming like a maniac in front of Delia. Popping Hollis a good one and then walking away silently, that would have been—what was that word?—*debonair.*

Rob had never come right out and asked, but he was pretty sure that Hollis blamed Rob's father for his own father's death, as ridiculous as that was. Sometimes Hollis's feelings were so obvious they might as well have been on display in the window of the Bloomingdale's aboard the *Secret Wish.* Other times, everything was bottled up and stoppered tight. Like Brice Blank, Rob considered himself a detector of hidden truths, and in his professional opinion, Hollis was casting blame like a beetle net. Wendell Dakota had had the rotten luck to lean against a decrepit section of railing at the edge of the old D.C. Sky-dock. If anything, it was Wendell's own fault for refusing to get some underling to oversee the renovations. What kind of company president personally inspected some second-rate dock? His own father had taught him that a boss doesn't do everything himself—he masters the art of delegating responsibility.

What Hollis couldn't get over was that Wendell Dakota's death was an accident, no more or less tragic than Rob's mother's death in a hospital bed seventeen minutes after he had entered the world. This was something he often hurled at Hollis in the imaginary arguments he conducted in his head: *At least you got to know both your parents. I only ever had one.* He forced himself to relax his jaw, which popped at the hinges when he clenched his teeth.

The piles of steerage-class belongings ended when he turned the corner and entered third class. Someone had painted drippy hotel signs on the doors of the cramped bunk rooms. Past THE WALDORF-ASTORIA, THE PLAZA, and THE RITZ, he came to an impromptu tavern that had sprung up in a sparse common room. The mingling smoke of a dozen cheap cigars made his eyes water. Someone inside began to sing in a strong but slurred voice.

As much as he could go for a hot lemonade to help pull himself together, Rob kept moving. He took measured breaths, trying to control another dizzying swell of anger. His hand reached inside the transmitter bag. Putting miles of corridors and staircases between himself and Hollis Dakota didn't mean anything with instant communication at his fingertips. The machine ruined the purity of a clean break. *Throw it down a garbage chute*, he thought recklessly. *Smash it.* He needed that clean break, at least until he figured out what was really going on.

He imagined trying to explain to Delia Cosgrove why, exactly, he'd felt the need to destroy her invention. Then he shifted the bag so it hung behind him where he couldn't see it. He was on his own now; he just had to find his father. Surely there was an explanation for the crew's behavior. He'd been too hasty in his excitement to uncover some grand conspiracy. Maybe the crew went on strike at the last minute and left his father no choice but to replace them with transients and strike-breakers. That would explain their disheveled appearance. And the weather alert seemed to be true: the storm was so big out over the ocean, they were even catching the tail end of it along the coast.

The only thing he couldn't figure out was why Hollis would make up some crazy kidnapping story about his mother. Maybe he'd just dreamt the entire thing. Rob decided not to care. He was done thinking about Hollis.

At the end of the hallway, he stepped onto an abrupt swatch of sea foam carpeting that led to second class. The stairs were guarded by two men and blocked off with a braided rope. Behind them, a series of framed illustrations depicted the joyful life of a shipyard worker, muscles glistening as he hammered rivets, nailed boards, and hoisted a foamy mug after a satisfying day on the job.

Rob approached with bold steps. No more sneaking around.

"Gentlemen," he said, tipping his cap.

"No passage here, kid," said the guard on the left, whose sleepy-looking face drooped like a hound's.

"I'd be much obliged if one of you would take me to see Mr. Jefferson Castor."

The other guard, a teenager a few years older than Rob, produced a rag from his back pocket and blew his nose with a great, wet honking noise.

"I said clear the air," said the older man.

The younger man studied his rag in amazement. "Look at this, Will!"

Will ignored his partner and gestured back down the hall. "Come on, kid, don't make it hard on yourself. Just get outta here."

"My name is Robert Castor. I'm Jefferson Castor's son."

Will studied Rob's face.

"No," said the young one, imitating his partner's squint, "you ain't. 'Cause we're all of us keepin' a sharp eye out for Robert Castor. We got *orders*. So I think we would know if he up and walked right to us, wouldn't we, Will?"

"I don't know," Will admitted.

"Then just tell me where my father is," Rob said, "and I'll find him myself. Don't let me interrupt your analysis of that handkerchief."

"Here's what I'm thinking, Will. What if he's *not* Mr. Castor's son, and—hey!"

Rob ducked beneath the rope and charged up the center of the staircase. Will plodded behind him, but the younger guard was quick. Rob felt a tingling whoosh of air from a swiping hand that missed by an inch. Around the corner, he plowed into a startled tangle of doughy flesh, stiff uniform fabric, and flailing limbs. He squirmed and wriggled, but it was no use: he'd run straight into the middle of three more guards. After much yelling and confusion, they righted themselves. Two strong pairs of arms pinned him against the wall. Three pairs of eyes bored into him. He had no idea if these men were waiting for some kind of explanation or just catching their breath before beating him senseless. It was also possible that they were too dull-witted to do anything but hold him until someone else came and took charge of the situation.

"Really should've stayed in bed," Rob said to himself.

"What's that?" asked a panting bald man whose breath smelled of onions and tobacco.

"You wouldn't understand."

The man chuckled. "Whatever you say, kid."

MAGGIE LED HOLLIS and Delia into a neighborhood of clotheslines and quilts. They scurried to keep up as she darted between battered trunks and baskets, the worldly possessions of entire families packed into squares no bigger than Hollis's bedroom. In this labyrinth, Hollis felt safer. People were too preoccupied with mending clothes or preparing meals to give him a second look. Hollis marveled at the fresh set of sights and sounds. It was as if an enclave had sprung up within the city of steerage, itself merely a small part of the greater metropolitan area of the *Wendell Dakota*.

"How did you become friends with that one?" Hollis asked Delia quietly, keeping an eye on the messy knot where Maggie's kerchief joined a clump of hair.

"I've known her for a long time."

Hollis thought for a moment. "That doesn't really count as an answer."

They turned sideways to follow Maggie down an aisle of crates packed with skinny chickens. Their smell reminded Hollis of the petting zoo on the leisure deck of the *Secret Wish*, where a llama had slurped oats from his hand and left his palm slimy and warm.

"There's a lot you don't know about me, HD. Just like there are things I don't know about you. It's not that big a deal."

"You can ask me anything." He paused. "Go ahead." Met with silence, he thought about bringing up St. Theresa's, then changed the subject. "Hey, look. Pigs."

The aisle widened, and suddenly they were flanked by animals in big, sloppy pens. He'd never been around so many pigs—or even a single pig that he could recall—and he was surprised at the low, guttural noises they made. Ahead, Maggie stopped and turned.

"Not everybody was born with their heads in the clouds."

"I was born in Richmond," Hollis said.

"Me and Delia watched each other's backs. You know what that's like?"

Delia sighed. "C'mon, Maggie, lay off."

But Maggie had that fiery gleam in her good eye that Hollis recognized from their first meeting. She stretched her arms out wide, and Hollis had a sudden memory of his father standing in the shipyard.

"So now that you've seen how it is," Maggie said, "you don't seem like you got much to say about it. Delia was wrong about you—you *are* just like all the rest."

Delia winced. "Godsakes! Shut up."

Maggie kept talking, but Hollis didn't hear a word. *Delia was wrong about you*. . . . It dawned on him that it had been Delia's idea to meet in steerage. "You set me up!" He pointed at her, finger trembling slightly in disbelief. "You planned this whole thing. You *knew* they were gonna ambush me down here."

"I'm sorry, HD. She took it a bit too far—I only wanted you to see what it was like. I should have planned it better, but everything happened so fast."

"A bit too *far?*" Hollis was yelling now—he couldn't help it. "She almost cut my throat, Delia. My mother is still missing, and now, thanks to you, we're running around down here"—his eyes flicked to one of the pens—"with the *pigs.*"

Shink went Maggie's switchblade.

"Keep your voice down, or I'll stick you like one," Maggie said, pointing the knife casually toward the middle of his chest as if she were handing him a pencil.

"Put that away!" Delia said.

Maggie laughed and lowered the knife. "Relax, Cosgrove. I'm not gonna slice up your swanky friend. He don't rate at all with me, one way or the other."

"All I'm saying," Hollis said to Delia, "is that you could've picked a better time to take me on a tour. We're kind of in the middle of something important here, you know?"

Maggie gave Delia a look that was easy for Hollis to read: *I told you so.*

Delia said, "Let's just keep going."

Maggie turned without another word and led them past the final row of pens and into a long, half-open shelter that ran along the edge of the hold. One side was propped up by vertical slats and boards, hastily nailed together. They passed through brief sections of darkness where the wall was complete on both sides, then a quick slice of steerage life returned, followed by another plunge into darkness. This happened again and again, as if someone were flicking a switch.

"This place was supposed to be divided up into sleeping quarters," explained Delia as they followed Maggie through the half-finished tunnel. "But early on, they decided the carpenters would be put to better use elsewhere. Then I guess they just forgot to finish."

"Who's *they*?" Hollis asked, dreading the answer.

"Your dad, mostly."

What did Delia expect him to say? That his dad wasn't perfect? He knew that.

"Hey," Delia said gently, "I said I was sorry, and I meant it, okay?"

"Fine." Hollis felt itchy. "I'm sorry, too. Let's just get to the wires."

They walked through a few long seconds of darkness, and when the wall opened up again, Hollis had a direct line of sight into the candlelit interior of the sick bay. A woman was setting a table of overturned crates for a small boy whose shirt drooped from his skinny body like a wizard's robe. At the center of the table rested a steaming bowl of lumpy stuff from the vats. An older girl stepped in front of the blanket flap, which had been clothespinned back. She met Hollis's eyes for a moment, but didn't seem to register his presence. With a practiced motion, she raised a wadded-up rag to her lips and muffled the wet sandpaper sounds of a coughing spell. Through the triangle of space defined by the girl's bent, spindly arm, Hollis watched the woman deposit a spoonful of stew into the boy's mouth. Then he kept moving, and the wall closed up.

THE SECOND NOTE from Hezekiah Castor arrived two weeks after the first. This time, the message was a crude drawing of a burning sky-canoe. In the middle of the canoe, spiky flames engulfed a charred stick figure waving his arms and screaming in agony. Beneath the ship were the letters *H.C.*

Samuel sat dumbly at his desk, gaping at the drawing. He had a brief, horrible vision of the Dakota compound in flames, his men rushing from their barracks in shirtsleeves to fling buckets of water at the inferno as it engulfed the——

"Mr. Dakota, sir!"

Samuel placed the bottle and the note into a drawer and slid it closed. "Come in!"

One of his assistants cracked open the door. The tip of a long nose poked inside. "General Grant's asking for you, sir."

Samuel sighed. "Thank you."

The nose withdrew.

Samuel strode across the low-cut grass of the testing ground toward a small white tent. General Ulysses S. Grant had arrived this morning to field-test the new flying weapons against Stonewall Jackson, the Confederate general whose army was camped a few miles away at the edge of the Shenandoah Valley. Through the half-open barn door of the main hangar, Samuel could see his chief builder performing final inspections on the eighteen sky-canoes they'd managed to churn out in frantic anticipation of Grant's arrival. Each canoe was fully steerable, thanks to Pembroke's billowy sailcloth oars that locked in place on either side like oversized lawn-tennis rackets.

Samuel had spent much of the past week aloft, paddling through patches of dead air to find the gusty space where he could lock the oars and let the sails harness the wind. At first he'd been hesitant to ride the stronger currents, but after a few more test flights, he began to crave the sudden stomach-flipping glide when the ship dropped from stillness into a powerful airstream. He began to imagine that he could actually *see* the currents winding through the empty skies, like shimmering paths to new worlds. Samuel Dakota lost himself in these happy moments. He even managed to forget that the true purpose of his joyful experiment was to make Lincoln's Northern war machine all but unstoppable. General Grant's arrival was an abrupt reminder, like waking from a delicious strawberry-rhubarb dream to find himself once again camped out in the mud.

He stood at attention just outside the flap of the tent, waiting for his invitation from the general, who was sitting with his two aides at a small table strewn with maps and a bottle of bourbon. When one of the aides cleared his throat and said, "General, Mr. Dakota for you," Grant looked up and waved his hand dismissively at Samuel's upright military posture.

"At ease, beetle man. I don't much care for formality." Grant paused to sip from his glass. "Make yourself at home."

Samuel stepped inside. Grant flicked his wrist idly in the direction of the tent flap.

"Give us a moment, gentlemen."

The two aides left without a word. Samuel sat down at the table.

Grant cleared his throat and spit in the grass next to his chair. "I understand you have the magic moonshine distilleries here, Dakota."

"That's right, sir. If you like, I can have a sample brought over for you." He noted the dark hollows around Grant's eyes, as if they'd been shaded with charcoal. The general was clearly exhausted, or drunk, or both. Even his beard looked droopy and tired.

"I drink bourbon," Grant said, and for a long time, neither man said anything. Eventually, Grant drained his glass and refilled it, and with a startled grunt filled an empty glass and slid it across the table to Samuel.

"Where are my manners? There you go."

"Thank you, sir." Samuel took a tentative sip, wishing desperately to be alone in the sky.

"What do you think of all this . . ." Grant made a circle with his forefinger over the topmost map, a mess of squiggles and jagged lines pockmarked with blue and gray dots. "All this . . . war?"

"Well." Samuel considered for a moment. "I suppose I want it to end as soon as possible." General Grant raised an eyebrow. "With a victory for the forces of emancipation and reunification, of course," he added hastily.

"As do I, Dakota. As do I. But have you given any thought to what an ending *means*?"

"I'm sorry, sir—I'm not sure I understand the question."

"What will you do after the war?"

"Well, hopefully Dakota Aeronautics will expand . . ." Samuel thought off the top of his head. "Maybe into, I don't know, commercial transportation." It was a good idea. The war had already displaced millions of people. The postwar travel industry could be a gold mine. Proud of himself for thinking of a new business plan on the spot, Samuel smiled. Grant drained his glass once again and let it slam down upon the table. His next words came out thick and muffled.

"And then there's the question of my own *what's next*, which I'm having to ponder much sooner than I expected, thanks to you and kindly old Mr. Gatling over here." He jerked his thumb at what seemed to be a blanket tossed over a large telescope.

"I'm sorry," Samuel said. "Mr. *Gatling*?"

"Yep," Grant said sharply. "Brought down Gatling and

fifty of his brothers to arm your flying machines. You did build fifty, yes?"

"Er . . . we got very close."

Without leaving his chair, Grant whisked away the blanket.

The telescope was a gun with a barrel the size of a small artillery piece mounted on an axis between two wheels. It looked like a miniature cannon. Samuel had heard of Mr. Gatling's fearsome spinning crank gun, but had never seen one up close. He imagined a terrified Confederate soldier crouched in a ditch, staring up in disbelief as rapid-fire death rained down from a fleet of flying canoes. For a paralyzing second, Samuel felt the imaginary soldier's fear as if it were his own.

What have I done?

The answer, he knew, was that he had changed the world, and there would be no going back and canceling what he had created. He had made good on his promise to President Lincoln and created a weapon to destroy the Confederacy. He should have been deeply satisfied. But now, sitting next to the huge gun in the pungent haze of General Grant's bourbon breath, his achievement seemed cruel and sad.

Grant read the look on his face.

"What did you think we were planning to do once we were up in your air boats, Dakota? Pelt the rebels with pebbles?"

The general fell into a sort of halfhearted laughing fit. Samuel stared at his glass and suddenly felt very ill.

"The attack begins tomorrow morning at 0500 hours," Grant said. "That should give you enough time to choose your flagship and perform final inspections. And may I suggest quoting some mighty-sounding hogwash in your speech to the pilots before the launch?" He nodded in the direction of his aides, who were waiting outside the tent. "They can find you some Tennyson or something."

"*Speech.*" Samuel sounded out the word as if he were learning it for the first time. "To the pilots?" He looked stupidly at Grant, then all at once he understood. He shook his head, finding his voice. "With all due respect, General Grant—"

"Save it, Dakota; my mind's made up. They tell me you spend most of your time in the sky. Who better to lead the attack?"

Samuel swallowed the lump forming in his throat. He thought quickly. "Someone with command experience. An officer. I'm just a civilian."

"You haven't been discharged from your duty as a soldier."

Samuel was incredulous. "My duty? I'm . . . I was just a private. I slept in the mud."

"Congratulations," Grant said with a grim smile. "You've just been promoted."

"To what?"

Grant ran a finger along the ragged corner of a map and

thought for a moment. Then he stood up and assumed a formal pose with his chest puffed out. Samuel noticed for the first time that the general was wearing a long sword attached to his belt.

"Gentlemen!" he called to his aides, who hurried back inside the tent. "I'm pleased to introduce the commander of the Union Air Cavalry, Sky Captain Samuel Dakota."

"**THIS SHOULD DO YOU** just fine," Maggie said as she slid a piece of loose wood away from a rough-hewn hole in the wall.

"Thanks," Delia said, rummaging in her bag and handing over the Cosgrove Immobilizer, which Maggie hefted expertly, sighting down the barrel with her good eye. *This girl has fired guns before*, Hollis thought. Maggie nodded goodbye at Delia and turned to make her way back down the half tunnel.

"Been a pleasure, Maggie," Hollis called after her.

"Piss up a rope," she called back before disappearing around the corner.

"Here." Delia handed Hollis a handkerchief. "You still got . . ."

Hollis wiped flakes of dry, crusty blood away from his

lips. He pictured the back of Rob Castor's head climbing up onto the catwalk, getting smaller and smaller, disappearing from his life forever. He felt like he was driving people away simply because he was born a Dakota.

"You know what happened at the launch?" Hollis asked as he wiped away the last of the blood. "I did the christening, with the dirt and everything."

Delia shook her head. "I was already belowdecks."

"Yeah, well, I screwed up."

Delia laughed. "Doesn't matter. It's just a dumb ceremony."

"But what if it *does* matter?" Hollis asked. "What if I caused all this?" As crazy as it sounded when he said it out loud, it felt good to tell someone. Maybe that was the true nature of a curse: secrecy gave it power.

"There's nothing you can do about it now," Delia said, "except try to put it right, which is what we're doing anyway. But listen, about setting you up like that . . ." She hesitated.

Hollis's eyes went to a dark knot in the board over Delia's shoulder. "I get why you wanted me to see it down here. I do. It's not lost on me, okay?" He wasn't ready for a face-to-face conversation about something he would need a long time to sort out. "But I can't do anything about it at the moment."

"Please look at me. I'm trying to apologize."

"I accept your apology. I just don't want to talk about this right now."

"You're going to run things someday, HD."

She was using her logical problem-solving voice. Its matter-of-fact tone made Hollis want to scream.

"Delia," he said as calmly as possible, finally meeting her eyes, "if Jefferson Castor goes through with this, if we let him *take the ship*, there will be nothing left for me to run. No steerage-class accommodations for me to improve. Surely the smartest girl at St. Theresa's Industrial School can grasp that."

Her stone-faced gaze was fixed on Hollis.

"I'm sorry." He shook his head. "I didn't mean to say that. What *is* an industrial school, anyway?"

"We should get going."

"Is that where you learned electronics?" She didn't answer. "So what, then? What happened to you that you can't talk about?" He squeezed his eyes shut. "I didn't mean that, either. I don't know what's wrong with me right now."

Delia spoke as if she were gradually easing her thoughts into words and didn't want to get them wrong. "If you were anybody else . . . I mean, if you were still *you*, still *Hollis*, but just not Hollis *Dakota* . . . well. Dakota Aeronautics is you, and you're Dakota Aeronautics, and there's no way around it. It's all tied up together. Like I said, you're going to run this place one day. You'll be my *boss*."

"Why don't you just come out and say that you don't trust me?"

"Why don't you take me to Sunday dinner at Il Bambino's? Why haven't you ever had me over for tea in your stateroom?

Because there are parts of your life that can't involve me. I accept that. And I'm just asking you to understand that it works both ways."

It occurred to Hollis that he already had what he needed: the name of her old school. When this was all over, he could make inquiries and find out everything he wanted to know. He was sure that Delia had already realized this. Maybe this was her way of asking him not to do it.

"You know," he said, "I could bring you something from Il Bambino's if you want to try it. I don't recommend the rabbit."

Delia rolled her eyes. "Come on, Hollis." She grabbed his arm and began pulling him into the dark passageway beyond the hole in the wall.

"Okay, okay, just promise me one thing," Hollis said, thinking of Rob's parting words and nearly losing his grip on whatever emotional blockade was holding back a flood of tears. "Promise me we'll stay friends, whatever happens."

She let go of his arm briefly, but only so she could take his hand and give it a squeeze. He swallowed hard and felt the stinging ache from his throat to his nasal cavity that meant the dam was as good as broken. He distracted himself with a quick mental list of things he would rather do than cry in front of Delia, like eat a bowl of minced glass or hammer his front teeth out. Then tears leaked out anyway. There was nothing he could do about it. He let her lead him through the passage.

Once they rounded a bend and the hole in the wall

finally disappeared behind them, Hollis lost track of his own feet. Delia didn't try to say anything to make him feel better, and for that he was grateful. When he'd recovered enough to speak, he kept his voice to a whisper.

"You got a lantern in that bag?"

"I got the second Cosgrove Immobilizer, the sky map, some linseed oil, a few pencils, Rob's smelling salts, and a little bit of salted pork jerky. And some other stuff, probably."

Hollis's mouth watered at the thought of spicy, smoked meat. "I wouldn't say no to a piece of that jerky."

A thumping noise up ahead made him hush. Together they waited, silent and still, listening to muffled voices in the dark.

Eventually they crept forward on tiptoe, feeling their way along the unsanded wall with their fingertips, barely skimming the surface of the wood to avoid getting handfuls of splinters. The passageway turned sharply and ended at the bottom of a crude staircase. Dim light floated down from the top, along with the voices. Hollis nudged Delia and held up two fingers that were barely visible in the gloom.

Delia listened for a moment, then shook her head and held up three fingers: three men at the top of the stairs. She reached into her bag and pulled out the second immobilizer and the bag of salted pork. Then she rummaged quietly at the very bottom of the bag where the odds and ends lived, producing a novelty three-dollar bill, a metal ring over-crowded with keys, and a bag of marbles. Hollis motioned for the marbles and very gently took them from her hand. He wasn't exactly sure what he was going to do next— maybe fling them up at the men to create a distraction? Then Delia leaned so close that her mouth brushed against his ear. With a whisper as soft as a shallow breath, she told him to set them along the bottom steps and get out of the way. Hollis got to work. Delia brandished the immobilizer and melted into the shadows alongside the staircase. Marbles in place, Hollis cupped his hands around the sides of his mouth and made a loud, ghostly *WOOOOHOOOOOOOOOOOOOOOOOOOO*. It sounded exactly like an invitation to a ridiculous trap. He winced.

Someone muttered, "Damn steerage rats," before heavy feet clomped down the stairs. Hollis pressed back against the wall opposite Delia and waited, heart pounding. The first man fell sideways as marbles skittered everywhere, sounding like a thousand rather than the handful Hollis had placed. The second man pitched forward, tripped by his companion. Before either man could right himself, Delia sprang from the shadows and gave them both a jolt of jagged lightning. They lay crumpled in a heap at the bottom of the steps while Hollis and Delia, breathing hard, glanced nervously at each other.

Where was the third man? The marbles had scattered to new places and stopped. The passage was silent once again. Hollis and Delia climbed over their unconscious victims and hurried up the stairs, which brightened as they ascended. At the top, a flickering lantern hung on the wall next to a door marked CENT COMM. The air was thick with the smell of lamp oil and sawdust.

"See?" Hollis pointed to the sign. "I knew exactly where we were going."

He pushed open the door, and the fine hairs on the back of his neck started to prickle. He turned in time to see a squat, bullet-headed man lock a meaty forearm around Delia's neck and lift her up off her feet.

"Oopsy-daisy," the big man said.

Delia let out a strangled yelp as he tightened his chokehold.

16

THE ELEVATOR to the command post at the top of the main prop tower was a rattling metal box. There was barely enough room for Rob and his three escorts, and they stood silently, pressed against each other like toy soldiers in a tin. The limited air was humid with whiskey breath and sweat.

"If you're lying—" warned one of the men.

"I'm not lying, you dunce," Rob said for the hundredth time. His captors were reluctant to bother Jefferson Castor with the ravings of a crazy—though remarkably well dressed—third-class kid. But they seemed at least a tiny bit scared that he might be telling the truth, which was enough for them to escort him to his father, who was supervising something in the prop tower. What, his captors wouldn't say. They were also frustratingly mum on the subject of who they were and why they were on the ship, despite being half drunk and annoyingly forthcoming about Alabama women and a host of other subjects.

The elevator bumped to an abrupt halt. A guard with a pockmarked face pulled a lever. The door slid open to reveal a metal grate. He pulled another lever, the grate clattered up, and the men pushed Rob out into the command post. The air wasn't exactly clean, but the metallic tang of combustion was preferable to the gamy stink of the guards. In the hollow of the tower beneath his feet, the great motor churned, spinning the main propeller with the kind of turbine-driven force that disintegrated unlucky birds on impact and dragged the enormous airship through the sky. Rob was no math genius, but he figured this propeller to be roughly a gazillion times the size of the chocolate replica he'd been solely blamed for stealing (despite the abundance of melted evidence on Hollis's face and clothing). Here in the command post, cutting-edge soundproofing dampened the operational noise. Only the dense baritone *whoosh* of the rotation vibrated through the steel-reinforced walls.

In front of him, the room was sectioned off like a chessboard with a walkway down the middle. Blond squares of polished floorboards alternated with dark, fenced-off holes that provided access to the engine room below. Steam escaped from the holes and drifted lazily along the floor like poured molasses. Rob watched as six technicians were ordered down into one by a spry old man with a rifle. The technician in front opened a gate in the fence with a trembling hand and began climbing down a metal ladder. The man watched with fierce concentration until all six had vanished, then he walked over to Rob and his escort.

"Who's the kid?" he asked from the left side of his mouth while the right side clamped down on an unlit cigar.

"He's goin' on about bein' Mr. Castor's son."

"Well, Mr. Castor's lookin' for his son."

"This ain't him, is it?"

The old man shrugged. "*You* wanna bother Castor about it, be my guest."

As the men talked it over, Rob stepped aside to give himself a clear line of sight. At the far end of the command post, a long oval window appeared to be painted a single shade of drab institutional gray. Beneath the window, a row of dials set into thick pipes poking up from the engine room displayed the ship's airspeed, the primary concern of any prop tower crew. To the right and left of the speed gauges, crewmen spoke into telephones while others routed calls, trading cords between two switchboards with practiced ease.

A sharp *crack*, barely audible above the rumbling, brought all activity to an abrupt halt. As the guards turned to look toward the window, Rob thought of how Brice Blank was always getting a "sense of foreboding" before massive life-changing events started to pile up around the middle of every issue. In his own drawings, he made sure that Atticus Hunter was blindsided by the twists in the story. Rob had always considered that to be the more realistic approach. How much foreboding could one person possibly handle? And what was that "sense" supposed to feel like, exactly?

But now Rob felt it acutely: the dread of something inevitable and out of his control that was going to send him reeling. Each freight-train blade swinging past the command post was suddenly loud and distracting.

SHWOOMP. SHWOOMP. SHWOOMP.

The second *crack* brought everything speeding back into focus. The guards herded Rob up the walkway as they ran to investigate, their footsteps displacing steam in puffs of clarity. The men at the machines turned back to their work as if nothing had happened. Rob began to feel ill. He wondered what Hollis and Delia were doing.

Closer to the oval window, what had looked like a solid sheet of gray became a roiling storm cloud with several shades of darkness blossoming within. From this vantage point, high above the main deck, Rob should have been able to see the bow of the ship. But the whole sky was the sightless void of the cloud.

"Everything okay, sir?"

Rob turned toward the voice and felt a simultaneous flood of relief and terror. The "sir" was his father. He was holstering a pistol.

"It is now," his father said. Then his eyes found Rob, and he froze like he had on the catwalk of the lift chamber. The body of a large man was sprawled facedown at his feet. One arm extended straight out toward Rob. On the man's hairy-knuckled finger was a gold ring in the shape of a puffed-up, gaseous beetle.

Chief Owens.

Rob's mouth was too dry to speak. He swallowed gummy saliva-paste and managed a whispered "*Dad?*"

His father thought for a moment. "How'd you like to see the bridge?"

KICKING AND FLAILING, Delia forced her attacker to press his back against the wall to leverage his chokehold, and he narrowly sidestepped a neck-breaking tumble down the stairs. The uneven wooden slats of the floor creaked in protest, and Hollis had a horrible split-second vision of the center shaft popping out of the ship like a cork, spilling the three of them into the empty sky. A backhanded fist glanced across his forehead; that swinging anvil of a hand was keeping Hollis at bay, and his loafers offered little traction. Changing tactics, he darted forward, staying low, and reached into the bag pulled tight across Delia's chest. When his fingers closed around the immobilizer, he yanked it free. Delia's body drooped as she gasped for air. Hollis pulled the trigger and slammed the jagged lightning-burst into the man's exposed forearm, right next to a tattoo of the name *Beatrice* scribbled inside a heart.

The big man shuddered as his body closed the electrical circuit. When Hollis pulled the weapon away, the man's eyes rolled back in his head and he slid limply down the wall to the floor.

"'Night, Beatrice," Hollis said, so that when Delia told the story of how he'd saved her life, it would have a jazzy ending. The immobilizer felt tiny and feather-light in his triumphant grip. Then he wondered with a kind of dull horror if the man was dead. The weapon seemed to gain weight as his adrenaline retreated.

"Delia?"

She wasn't moving. He knelt and rolled her over until she was faceup. Her breathing was shallow. Hollis rummaged through her bag, past Castor's map of the sky and the packet of pork jerky, until he found the bottle of smelling salts. He heard Rob's voice in his head: *Strong stuff. Trust me.*

"Shut up," Hollis muttered, twisting off the tiny cap and holding it under Delia's nose. The sharp smell of ammonia filled the air. She began to cough and sputter. Hollis helped her sit up.

She opened her eyes and stared dumbly at Hollis before recognition seeped into her face. She glared at Hollis's hand, which was still clutching the immobilizer.

"Next time," Delia said, snatching it away from him, "remember that if two people's bodies are touching, they're both going to conduct the current."

"Right," Hollis said, pretending he'd known that all along. "Sorry."

"You really should start going to school. But thanks. That arm smelled like boiled ham." Delia let herself be pulled to her feet, where she wobbled and steadied herself against the wall. She nodded at the cent comm door. "I'm okay. I'm ready."

Hollis eyed the man slumped against the wall. "Is he . . . I mean, did I just . . ."

Delia shook her head. "He'll wake up soon. Same as the two downstairs."

"Oh, good," Hollis said, at the same time realizing how absurd that sounded. "Not good. You know what I mean."

Together they stepped into a room about the size of Hollis's bedroom closet, with endless dark space above their heads instead of a ceiling. And instead of shirts and trousers, telephone lines dangled and branched off into neat holes drilled into the paneling. Next to each hole were pencil markings indicating the terminus of each line: GALLEY 3, AUTOMAT, PROM DECK STBD, and so on.

"What's the difference between these directions and those signs?" Hollis asked, indicating more formal squares tacked up next to sets of telephone lines bundled into groups and secured with thick twists of wire.

But she was already deep within the Republic of Delia. With a quick touch, her magnifying glass deployed from her headband.

"Transmitter," Delia said, gesturing toward Hollis's satchel. Hollis handed it over and watched, transfixed, as she used her bracelet's charm to unscrew a bracket and disconnect the two wires that joined the receiver to the telegraph sounder.

"Knife," Delia said, holding out her hand. Hollis dug though the bag and came up with the salted pork, but no knife. He popped a piece of jerky into his mouth and slipped back out into the hall. Their attacker was slumped against the wall, eyes closed, a string of drool connecting his half-open mouth to his left shoulder. Around the man's waist was a leather tool belt. Hollis unsnapped each little compartment until he found the handle of a long switchblade, more minia-ture sword than knife.

"Some blade this guy's got," he said, handing it to Delia. She clicked it open and set to work, carefully slicing away a strip of the black rubber casing that covered one of the telephone wires. She had chosen one from the bundle labeled PROP TOWER that branched off into a hole marked FURNACE 3. Hollis figured it out: areas vital to the ship's operation required the bundles—the thick arteries on the blueprint. Places of lesser importance got one or two lines— the veins and capillaries. It made sense. While the bridge had to function as the nerve center, there was little need for Nico's Café to maintain a ready line of communication with the squash courts or the lift chambers. When lines absolutely had to be connected, the switchboard operators performed the handoff.

"Okay," she said. "Cross your toes."

Using fabric from her dress to shield her hands, Delia

touched the thin, exposed strands from the spark-gap transmitter to the unprotected telephone wire. Hollis felt his body tense up, anticipating some kind of explosion. Instead, the sounder began to squawk gibberish.

"What *is* that?" Hollis asked, leaning close to listen to what sounded like a broadcast of irritated water fowl.

"Dunno," Delia said. "Lemme patch into another one."

"Go for the bridge."

Delia transferred the wires to another dangling line. This time the sounder emitted a human voice. Distant and fuzzy, Hollis thought, but definitely human. Now if only they could learn something useful before the three unconscious hijackers woke up. They held their breath and listened. The static faded, and a melody emerged.

"What's the one thing you can't find in the sky? It's worry! It's worry!"

Hollis grabbed Delia's arm. That was Wendell Dakota's voice coming from the sounder, singing Elmer Berman's hit tune, "Airship to Paradise." Hollis reached out to touch the wire as if it were his father, alive and in the flesh. Delia pulled his hand away.

"What's never darkening an eagle's mind? It's trouble! It's trouble!"

He's here, thought Hollis, pressing his ear almost flush against the transmitter, eager to absorb the vibrations. *He's on the ship.* Everything that had happened since the launch faded away, became the hazy background for this new development. It seemed completely plausible. His world had realigned. It had been thrown wildly off course but had somehow righted itself.

"*So-oh-oh pack those bags and stamp those tickets——*"

"Cute, Marius." A woman's voice that Hollis didn't recognize cut in, silencing the song. "Very cute. It's a good impersonation. I'm just sorry it was wasted on all those pointless telephone calls. Lucy Dakota might be a lot of things, but easily frightened isn't one of them."

Wendell Dakota's voice changed abruptly into that of the young crewman.

"Can you feel it? They can. They know their mother is near."

"Have you been drinking?" The woman sighed. "Of course you have. Stay at your post and make some coffee. Jefferson and I are in the middle of something up here, and we don't have time to——"

Click. The connection went quiet, along with Hollis's mind. He was unable to think about anything at all. His shock was a blank, out-of-time space that enveloped him completely. It was almost blissful, until it resolved into a state of panic. "What was *that*?"

"Hollis." He felt Delia's arms around him.

"What *was* that? *What* was *that*?" Saying these three words over and over again was all he could do.

"Shhh," she said. "It's me. It's Delia."

"What. Was. That."

"It's okay, Hollis. It's okay."

Eventually he became aware that they had been going

back and forth like this for some time. Delia watched as he returned to himself, practically holding him upright until he could stand on his own.

"That wasn't my father," he said.

"No."

"It was Marius."

"That's right."

Hollis saw his mother's stricken face, just before the launch, and a lump formed in his throat. "The stoker."

"What stoker?"

"Remember when I told you about that telephone call my mother got on the bridge, right before the launch? It's happened before. She said so, right before they took her, she asked one of the kidnappers if it was him . . . and all this time it's been Marius, pretending to be my father." His eyes met Delia's. "Why?"

She thought for a moment. "It's the long game, HD. You don't just wake up and decide to hijack the airship carrying the richest passengers in the world. You have to approach it like a scientist would, figuring out all the different parts. For years you'd have to plan it, in order to control the variables. And your mother's a pretty big variable. Maybe Castor's been trying different things to keep her off balance."

"But Marius was saying something else about my mother, too." Hollis tried to extract a thin strand of hope from what he'd just heard. "We're near. We're close to her. Something like that."

"He said *they*, Hollis. *They know their mother is near.*"

"But—okay, then who was he talking about?"

"I don't know. I think we need to examine this from all the angles." Delia was treating him gently, as if an argument in his fragile state would send him right back over the edge. "Who does the other voice belong to?"

Hollis thought back to his frantic dash away from the hijackers and his escape up to the promenade deck. "There was only one woman on the bridge when I was there. She looked like . . . I don't know, a schoolteacher or something. She had a table full of books. And maps."

"Maps like this?" Delia pulled the rolled-up paper from her bag.

"I don't know, I didn't get a good look. I was kind of in a hurry."

She slapped the page. "X marks the spot, just like in *Brice Blank and the Sandworm's Gold.*"

"You can't be serious."

Her face flushed, something he'd never seen before. "Rob let me borrow it."

"So what does X mark the spot of?"

"The sandworm's gold."

"How about in the map we've got?"

"What if 'they know their mother is near' is some kind of code? Maybe it's a rendezvous with other ships."

Hollis had a disturbing vision of Castor's men at the helm of the *Secret Wish* and the *Windy City.* He shook his head, chasing it away.

"It doesn't matter."

Delia was taken aback. "Of course it does."

"Not if we make sure he never gets there."

Hollis had swerved dizzily from zapping a man unconscious to blank astonishment at his father's voice and had reached what his mother would call *sharpness*, the moment of clarity that settled in after weathering a headache. He was being borne along by the rage he felt at Jefferson Castor, at Marius, at everyone who had been so senselessly cruel.

He would silence them all.

He looked up into the darkness of the shaft and pointed to where the telephone lines vanished up the wall.

"What would you say to climbing up there and cutting the lines?"

Delia attached the fearsome switchblade to her knapsack and eyed the lowest peg sticking out of the wall. A few feet above that, another peg bent at an awkward angle. "Which lines?"

"All of them."

"I would say that knocking out the ship's communications is an extremely dangerous thing to do. And stupid. I would say: Hollis Dakota, that's a stupid idea."

"But would you do it?"

"Yes."

"Okay. Really?"

She set to work detaching the two little wires from the line and twisting them back into place within the hollow dictionary. When she was done, he stuffed it into his satchel.

"On the port side of the sun deck, there's a slop room

for parkas and boots," he said. "If you can get up there, it should be a good enough place to hide out and wait for me."

"Where are you going?"

"That line you tapped from the bridge—what was at the other end?"

"The library."

"Then I guess it's time to check out some books." Hollis waited for a reaction. Delia raised an eyebrow.

"You shouldn't go by yourself."

"I'm bringing friends."

Delia hoisted herself up onto the first peg. Hollis moved swiftly and silently out of the little room and down the stairs, ignoring Delia's last whispered question.

"*What friends?*"

THE BRIDGE of the *Wendell Dakota* was a hive of peculiar activity. Rob watched a crewman scrub at a dark stain that had soaked into the wooden floor. Cursing and sweating, the man splashed his rag into a bucket of suds and attacked the stain with vigor. Rob didn't ask what had spilled.

Sky Captain Quincy was gone. Most of the Dakota officers had been replaced with a mismatched array of people commanded by Rob's father. He figured they must have snuck aboard as passengers and stolen uniforms, meaning that somewhere on the ship were the underwear-clad members of the real crew. At least, he hoped they were locked away onboard and not littering the ground below. He didn't ask about that, either. The two genuine crewmen still on the bridge—navigators with specialized skills—were monitoring gauges with guns shoved between their shoulder blades.

His father was barking into three different telephones with a voice that Rob had never heard before: shrill, demanding, hysterical. It was as if an alien were occupying his father's body, like in *Brice Blank and the Riddle of the Moon*. He shuddered at the idea of his father's arm becoming a crystal tentacle. Left alone for the moment, Rob tried to make sense of the new personnel.

There was a large group that seemed out of place on an airship. His escorts to the prop tower were a prime example. Rob had noted their inability to shut up about the South rising again. He wondered where his father had found so many of these characters—maybe they were some sort of militia? Why would they be led by Jefferson Castor, who had left Virginia early in his life and never looked back?

The second type was harder to pin down. They seemed quietly menacing rather than boisterous. Their pistols and rifles and knives were spotless. None of them looked like they were having half as much fun as the South-will-rise coalition, though some were just as liquored-up, sipping from flasks. Rob dubbed these characters the mercenaries. As his father's business dragged on and Rob had more time to observe, he decided they filled the role of officers.

The third group of hijackers was by far the smallest and most puzzling. They congregated around a table piled high with maps and books that rivaled the tomes on Delia's shelf. Studious and aloof, they seemed to have wandered in from a university lecture hall. With their sallow complexions and hunched postures, they would never be mistaken for the muscle of this operation; at first Rob even thought they might be hostages. And yet as soon as he'd reached the bridge, the first thing Rob's father had done was exchange words with the woman who presided over the odd little group. A silver chain attached to her reading glasses draped around the back of her neck. Rob nicknamed her the librarian. She had a heated discussion with his father about one of the maps on the table. When she stepped away for a telephone call, Rob caught a glimpse of a bulky paperweight in the shape of a beetle. It could easily be from the gift shop in the Newark Sky-dock, and yet there was something homemade about it, an off-kilter hitch in its design.

Thoughts of gift shops and company trinkets ushered in a sudden memory of their most recent family trip, to the private sky-dock in the Statue of Liberty's crown. Hollis had acted like a sullen five-year-old, answering Rob's father with one-word grunts and silent shrugs. That afternoon Rob had wanted to give his stepbrother the Betzengraf special: an open-handed slap on the back of the head. To think that all this time, Hollis had been *right*. But right about what, exactly?

Under different circumstances, he would have given anything to be here on the bridge, with its magnificent view and otherworldly stabilization gauge, which was like something from a delicate planet of glass. Instead, he wished he could turn back time to the launch so he could fake a terrible illness on the Newark Sky-dock and be taken down to a hospital. His father would have had to go with him, and none of this would be happening. Hollis would still deserve that slap.

"So find someone who knows how to fix it!" his father exclaimed before dumping all three telephones into the hands of an attendant. Rob and his father were both pale and dusted with freckles, but right now Jefferson looked positively ghostly. Rob watched him struggle to relax the tense, pinched muscles in his face.

"I'm sorry you had to see all this," he said gently.

Rob's mind raced through several of the biting retorts he'd prepared while his father had been barking into telephones. And yet all he could manage was the most basic of questions.

"What are you doing, Dad?"

Outside the window, clouds seemed to whirl and spin. It was as if the propeller were whipping the air into a froth. Rob had always imagined the bridge as a place of brilliant sunshine glinting off polished steel machines. To see it for the first time cast in such an eerie pall seemed wrong. Behind him, the man scrubbing the stain pounded the floor in frustration.

"It's not what you think," his father said.

"I don't know what I think it is," Rob said, which was true. His mind was like a kaleidoscope: just as he latched on to a single thought, the image shifted and the thought became something else.

"Jefferson!" The librarian was trying to get his father's attention. Rob noticed that she was the only person on the bridge who didn't address his father as "sir."

Rob's father motioned to a mercenary jotting something on a clipboard.

"Go see what she wants. Tell her I'm trying to have a conversation with my son."

"Yessir."

Rob didn't know what was expected of him. There was no *Brice Blank and the Parent Who Turned Out to Be an Airship Hijacker*. His father seemed like he was waiting for him to say something.

"Why?"

Jefferson Castor wasn't used to explaining his decisions, so it was interesting for Rob to watch his father gather himself up for a big talk. His lips appeared bloodless, almost blue. Rob wondered if they had always been like that and he'd never noticed.

"You mean more to me than every person on this airship combined. I've never lied to you about anything, and I'm not going to start now. But these are hard truths, Rob, and I want you to promise me you'll try as best you can to really understand the things I'm going to tell you."

"I promise," Rob said. The words came out squeakier than he'd hoped. His heart was pounding.

"The most important thing you have to understand is that I'm not some common criminal. The Dakotas owe me." An argument broke out between the navigators and their captors. His father ignored it. "They owe us both. And I've waited a lifetime to make them pay up."

"But you're chief operating officer. Can't you just give yourself a raise?"

His father sighed. "The Castors and the Dakotas go back a long way, Rob. Their debt to us is about far more than just money."

"So why are all these other people here?"

"They're here because airships don't hijack themselves."

Rob found it hard to believe that his father had so many secret friends willing to risk their lives for him. "I mean what are they getting out of this, if it's not about money? Pride in a job well done?"

A sudden thunderclap rattled the bridge like one of the California earthquakes Miss Betzengraf had told them about. Rob's father pulled him close. He was soaked in sweat.

"Listen to me very carefully. In order to get what you want in this world, you have to be willing to buy loyalty. And that doesn't come cheap. There are passengers aboard this ship with more money than they know what to do with. Their families on the ground will buy their release, and they'll all troop merrily back to their summer cottages and coastal estates without even having to sell a single diamond from their ballroom chandeliers to finance their safe return. Their wonderful lives will be completely unchanged, except they'll have a fascinating new story for this season's banquets and parties. They can compare notes over cocktails. And we'll be able to pay our hardworking employees, with plenty of capital left over. Everybody wins."

Rob noticed that his father had started using *we*, as if they'd planned the hijacking together. "Except for Chief Owens."

His father was silent.

"And Hollis."

"Have you seen your stepbrother?"

"Not since I punched him for making up lies about my dad."

"Pay attention, Rob. I am not in the business of hurting anyone. I am in the business of planning and carrying out operations for a large aeronautics firm. Think of this as just another task for me, and part of my job is to see everyone through safely. And to do that, I need you to be a man and keep your priorities straight, because I require your help. It's always been just us two, and I want to keep it that way after this stage is over with."

The alien was gone. Rob felt a surge of love. At the same time, his mind screamed at him: *Chief Owens!* He tried to ignore the persistent image of the outstretched hand with the beetle-shaped ring. Maybe Chief Owens had pointed a gun at his father. Maybe the whole thing was self-defense.

"What do you mean, *this stage*? What comes after this?"

His father's eyes went to the librarian and her comrades. "Castor Aeronautics."

"What are you talking about? Who are those people?"

"I'm talking about finally setting things right."

A grim-faced hijacker manning the switchboard turned

in his chair to face Rob and his father. "I think you need to see this, sir."

Rob's father swore under his breath. "You have five seconds to convince me you've got a serious problem that requires my personal attention."

The hijacker pounded a telephone receiver on the desk in front of him, then put it to his ear. He shook his head.

"There's nothing, sir."

"What do you mean, nothing?" Jefferson Castor reached for the telephone in disbelief.

"Nobody's home."

"Try another one."

"It's the same with all of 'em, sir. Looks like some damn fool cut the lines."

CHESTER HAD LICE.

At least, that's what Hollis surmised. He'd spotted the frizzy red mess of Maggie's hair from the half-light of the unfinished tunnel at the edge of the hold. She was leaning against a stack of crates, sharing a cigarette with Chester, who was seated in front of her so that she could slide her hand along the top of his head. When Hollis had crept through the crowd to the other side of the crates, he realized she was shaving off his curls. The dry scrape of the razor against Chester's scalp made Hollis feel slightly ill.

"Question is," Maggie was saying, "what're we gonna do with Delia's little zapper?"

"I say we sneak up amidships," Chester suggested. "Find us an easy mark stumbling out of a tavern."

"On their way *out* they ain't got no money," Maggie said. "Hold still. Don't you know how much a head cut bleeds?"

Hollis took a deep breath and stepped up to them, not at all sure of what he was going to say.

"Hello," he began. He accompanied his greeting with a timid little wave, which he immediately regretted. The flare of confidence he'd experienced in the cent comm room had evaporated. "Airship to Paradise" was playing in his head on a never-ending loop. He'd been so sure of his ability to recruit Maggie and Chester, it hadn't even occurred to him that they had no reason to trust him, especially without Delia by his side. Chester stared at him, slack-jawed and speechless. The razor glinted in Maggie's hand. Hollis figured he should cut to the chase.

"The ship's been hijacked."

Chester picked at his teeth with a splinter of wood. Maggie blew a huge puff of smoke before crushing out the cigarette beneath her shoe. Then, to his relief, she set the razor down on a box. A hearty laugh resounded from somewhere behind him, and as it caught on, the dull murmur of the hold seemed to swell hysterically for a moment. Hollis felt like it must be aimed at him and pictured a hundred fingers pointed at the back of his head. Warmth crept into his cheeks and forehead.

Hollis continued in a rush, "The leader of the hijackers is my stepfather, Jefferson Castor. He's holding passengers for ransom. He also kidnapped my mother, and I'm on my way to pay a visit to somebody who knows where she is. But I think it'll be the type of visit that requires a certain kind of . . . persuasion."

He paused, making a point of glancing down at Chester, who was imposing even when seated. No reaction, except for a smirk that curled the edges of Maggie's mouth. He tried a new tactic.

"Castor's changed course. We're heading south, instead of across the Atlantic."

Maggie chuckled. "Already got that weather report."

He thought quickly. "We can stop at a first-class infirmary. I can get you some ointment for your . . ." He waved his hand vaguely in Chester's direction.

"My what?" asked Chester.

"Your, um, lice. Your head lice."

This time Maggie glared at him while Chester burst out laughing.

"He don't have lice," she said coldly. "He just likes my haircuts."

Hollis forced himself to stand his ground.

"Fine. Look, I know you have every reason to hate me, but—"

The *Wendell Dakota* interrupted him by lurching starboard. Maggie's makeshift haircut station collapsed. The razor spun away, and Hollis fully expected it to wind up buried in his flesh. His loafers skidded awkwardly. Trunks and boxes crashed to the floor of the hold. Chester's shoulder sent Hollis spinning into Maggie's arms. Together they tripped over a laundry basket and went down in a tangled heap. As they struggled to free themselves—Maggie shrieking, "*Get off me*," in Hollis's ear—the bow of the ship began to creep skyward. All around them, helpless passengers lost their grip on the uneven floorboards and tumbled backward to join the growing mess of linens and food and dishes crushed against the newly sloped wall. Pained wailing harmonized eerily with high-pitched screams. A knit scarf snaked out of nowhere to cover Hollis's nose and mouth. All over the hold, people convinced this was their last chance made sure to squeeze in a final *I love you*. Chester lunged to wedge his fingers into a gap between the boards. Even with Hollis and Maggie clinging to him, he managed to keep steady. A woman nearby was gasping her way through a rushed Hail Mary. Possessions rained down from the tent city. A sharp pain in Hollis's rib cage made him wonder again about the whereabouts of that razor. *I love you*, he thought. He didn't have anyone to say it to right then, and yet his brain was forcing it on him.

But these weren't anyone's last moments. The ship leveled off, leaving passengers free to right themselves. Stirred-up dust thickened the air.

Delia must have finished cutting the lines.

Without careful instructions from the bridge, the beetle keepers were suddenly flying blind. And if Big Benny Owens's team had been replaced by Mr. Castor's amateurs, the voyage of the *Wendell Dakota* was about to get a lot more turbulent.

Hollis untangled his legs and scrambled to his feet. All

around him, the chaos of the hold had taken on a frantic edge as parents searched for their children. Dozens of men and women covered in sludge from the food vats wandered like ghosts, while others pawed at the steaming mess with blankets. Maggie ignored Hollis's outstretched hand and pushed herself up. She joined Chester in helping an old woman gather her spilled possessions, placing them inside a wicker basket. Hollis looked around, wondering what to do, desperate to help someone with something. Here they were in the midst of a crisis, and he was just standing around like the selfish rich boy they all thought he was. He went down on one knee and began picking up scattered playing cards. When he couldn't find their box, he placed the cards neatly inside an empty tobacco tin, then arranged the tin on a small crate next to an ashtray, as if he were straightening up an end table.

Then he wondered what the hell he was doing.

Maggie stared at him curiously, giving him the disturbing impression that she was reading his thoughts. "Do these hijackers of yours know how to fly this thing?"

"It's not that." He wondered if Maggie still had that switchblade on her. "Delia and I cut the telephone lines."

"Which ones?" Maggie asked.

"All of them."

Chester had somehow managed to keep his toothpick, and he pulled the tiny wooden spike from his mouth to point it at Hollis. "So what you're saying is . . ." He turned to Maggie. "What's he saying?"

"That he's a few dozen clams short of a bake." She narrowed her eyes at Hollis.

"It was the first step in a plan," he said. "A real plan. I swear. This ship has my father's name on it, and I'm going to take it back with or without you, but I'd be honored if you'd help me."

Suddenly the steerage hold shook violently a second time and listed to port, sending Hollis sprawling across a frazzled young mother's blanket. A baby shrieked. After a few seconds, the ship righted itself. Hollis leaped to his feet.

"Okay," Maggie said.

"So you're with me?"

"For now," she said. "And it don't mean we're a team, or that I like you, or that I won't accidentally kill you and not lose sleep over it. It just means I don't wanna die today." She tucked the Cosgrove Immobilizer into her belt. Hollis and Maggie turned to Chester, who was watching them skeptically.

"We'll be traveling through several kitchens," Hollis said.

Chester cracked his knuckles.

AFTER THE DARKNESS of the cent comm shaft, the gloomy vista deck seemed spacious and bright to Delia. The long, windowless compartment (crew members called it the vista deck as a joke), sandwiched between the third-class bunks and second-class staterooms, was used to store goods that American companies were exporting to Europe. It was a peaceful place: livestock traveled in steerage.

Delia mopped her brow with a complimentary Dakota handkerchief. Slicing the wires had been hard work. Climbing those rickety pegs had been scary enough to fuel a lifetime of claustrophobic nightmares. Despite all that, she had done it. Every single line had been severed. She often thought of airships as living creatures—many beetle keepers did—and now she felt a twinge of guilt. She had shut down the nervous system of the *Wendell Dakota*, cutting off its brain from its limbs.

Delia stuffed the soggy handkerchief into her bag and stepped away from the half-size door that led back into the shaft. She squeezed between casks of whiskey-sap piled from floor to ceiling. In small countries like Belgium, whose airship industry consisted solely of sky-canoe tourism, genuine Dakota whiskey-sap was a luxury item.

A few feet in front of her, the row of casks dead-ended at a wall of crates marked LIGHTBULBS. Delia pictured each bulb, lovingly swaddled in a nest of straw, and wished she could crawl inside, pull the lid over her head, and take a long nap. Maybe when she woke up, this would all be over. She ran her hand along the knotted wood, resisting the urge to pry it open.

Keep moving, Delia.

Her year at St. Theresa's Industrial School for Girls had taught her how to confront unpleasant things. It was easy to keep your head down and say your prayers—much more difficult to outsmart a system designed to mold you into an agreeable young woman, to wring the streets of Hell's Kitchen out of you like dirty dishwater. The rules at St. Theresa's were easy to remember: don't talk back to the sisters; recite your assigned Bible passages with enthusiasm; embrace the arts of cooking, cleaning, and respecting a future husband; know your saints. When you ran out of rules to obey or tasks to complete, there was always more atoning to be done for the sin that had landed you in St. Theresa's: getting pregnant or picking pockets or falling in with the wrong Bowery crowd. Or helping Margaret Keenan's uncle build homemade explosives.

When her apprenticeship at Dakota Aeronautics began, Delia had been certain that some higher-up would get around to digging into her past and give Chief Owens no choice but to send her back down to earth. Recently, however, she'd finally started to relax: such a massive company could churn along forever, indifferent to the history of one apprentice beetle keeper. But now she would have to make up a story to satisfy Hollis's curiosity. She'd said it herself: if his last name had been anything but Dakota, she would have simply told him the truth—that Maggie's uncle was a kind man, generous with his scientific knowledge, who had given her the tools to make a better life for herself. And who would build anything for the right price, no questions asked.

A noise like a tin can hitting the floor—*clinkclankTHUD*—made Delia's heart leap. Thanks to the arrangement of goods, there was only one way to go: down another aisle, toward the noise. If she retreated, she'd be trapped against the wall, faced with a blind descent down the cent comm shaft. She took a left and stopped—this section of the vista deck was in shambles. All of the neat, orderly rows that separated the storage space into dry goods, machine parts, perishables, and clothing had been destroyed. Her first thought was that an army of raccoons had run roughshod over everything, gnawing open sacks of wheat and barley, tearing into slabs of salted beef, slurping up candies until the air was cloudy with powdered sugar.

From the piles, a voice muttered, "Aww, sassafras." It sounded like a boy. Ahead and to the right, flimsy boxes marked MASHED POTATO FLAKES had been left mostly untouched, so that they formed a little nook. Delia held the hijacker's fearsome knife out in front of her and slid her feet quietly until she was able to peek around the corner.

The boy was about ten. His overcoat had seen better days, but the crewman's cap nested in his hair was spotless. He was perched on a stool, pawing through a box. Thin potato flakes covered the floor like snow on a toy train set. Delia revised her theory: the vista deck had definitely been picked clean by looters, but they had walked on two legs rather than four.

"You have to add water to those," Delia said. The boy froze with his hand in the box. His eyes darted to her, and he relaxed when he saw that he'd been caught by a girl. He tensed up again when he realized that girl was brandishing an eight-inch blade. Slowly, he removed his hand from the box and sat on his stool. Behind him, Delia noticed a rifle leaning against a garishly striped box labeled PEPPERMINT STICKS.

"I ain't got no water," the boy said cautiously.

"Too bad," Delia said, wondering what she would do if the boy reached for his gun. "Where'd you get the hat?"

The boy reached up as if to remind himself that he was wearing one. "My pa."

"Your pa work for Mr. Castor?"

The boy shifted on his stool. "He's a lieutenant in the New Army of Northern Virginia," he said proudly.

"So what's he doing on an airship?"

The boy looked at her skeptically. "I don't think I'm supposed to talk about it."

"It'll be our little secret." She stepped forward into the nook.

He eyed the blade. "I ain't never seen no girl with no big knife before."

Delia saw herself as the boy saw her, a girl with dirty hands, a smudged dress, and a sweat-smeared face, looking pinched and desperate with her heavy blade. She almost gave in to the urge to touch her headband and display her homemade magnifying glass. *I made this—I'm not what you think!* It had worked with that startled personnel clerk in the Fourteenth Street Dakota Aeronautics office—he'd introduced her to Big Benny Owens, and now, two years later, here she was.

Instead, Delia tightened her grip on the knife and leveled her steeliest gaze at the boy. There were times when growing up with Maggie paid off.

"The New Army of Northern Virginia is known for its bravery and self-sacrifice in defending the Confederate homeland," the boy said quickly. He was clearly parroting someone, or a recruiting leaflet. "Which is why we been asked to join this glorious battle against the servants of Lincoln."

"Uh-huh. What else?"

"Ain't nothing else. We get paid and then we go home to fight the second War of Northern Aggression."

"When's that supposed to happen?"

"Could be next week. Could be next year. We'll be ready."

Delia's mind was connecting threads. In order to maintain control over an airship the size of the *Wendell Dakota*, Castor would have to command a considerable force. It made sense that he would use a ready-made militia for muscle—offer a sweet enough chunk of the ransom, and he'd have a temporary army at his disposal. If he could play to their sympathies, all the better for him. He probably got this crew at a discount rate.

"How big is the New Army of Northern Virginia?"

"Eight squads, I reckon. Something like that."

"So if you had to guess a number . . ."

The boy's knee began to bounce up and down. "Numbers ain't my thing."

"If everybody who came aboard with you and your pa to help Mr. Castor was all standing in one big room, and you counted all the heads, how many heads do you think there would be?"

"Us and them other folks too?"

"Them other folks, they're another militia?"

The boy scowled. "Yanks. My pa hates 'em. He says as soon as we get off the ship, he ain't never so much as lookin' at one again, 'less it's down the barrel of his gun."

Delia lowered her knife. The boy was getting

fidgety—saying the word *gun* seemed to remind him that he had one within reach. She smiled. "Yanks really are the worst. I'm from Savannah, myself. Too bad your pa has to work with them."

"Buncha Yanks and a buncha heathens, too."

"I can't stand heathens. Did your pa happen to mention the *kind* of heathens that are aboard?"

The boy's entire face wrinkled in disgust. "Beetle worshippers."

For the first time since she'd found the map and the passenger list, Delia's heart began to race with the excitement of discovery. The problem was, there were more than a dozen active beetle cults, each with its own agenda and rituals. The broadsheet Rob had discovered on her bookshelf only hinted at the cult-related materials—books, pamphlets, the odd totem—she had been collecting under Chief Owens's supervision. Rob's voice echoed inside her head: *Delia, tell us the truth—are you in a cult?* She wasn't, of course, although one of them had tried to recruit a few Dakota Aeronautics employees; she still had the business card given to her by an earnest young man with thick glasses and a cheap suit.

Delia slipped the knife back into the bag—*See? We're just having a friendly chat*—and made her question as offhand as possible. "Do these beetle worshippers happen to have a name? Any strange tattoos or jewelry you can remember? Funny words they like to say over and over again?"

"You don't sound like you're from Savannah."

A dull book called *Beetle Deification: A Survey* catalogued the groups, and Delia tried to remember the names she'd skimmed in her reading. "Sons of Solomon? Order of the First Beetle? Insect Liberation Front?"

"I ain't sayin' another word."

Delia sensed that she was reaching the limits of this boy's secondhand knowledge, anyway. "Remember what I said about our talk."

"What was it again?"

"Our little secret. You didn't see anybody in here."

"I didn't see anybody in here," he repeated dutifully. As she backed away, his eyes flicked almost imperceptibly to check the location of his rifle. Without another word, she took off sprinting, past wheels of Wisconsin cheese and bottles of California wine. She didn't waste a second looking over her shoulder; the son of a militiaman was probably a crack shot. She hurdled a pyramid of animal cracker boxes and zigzagged past bundles of patchwork quilts.

The possibility of gunfire seemed to add an urgent dimension to everything the boy had said. Her mind raced. The beetle cults were breeding grounds for conspiracy theorists, disgraced scientists, and aimless loners in search of a home. What could a group of crackpots possibly have to offer a man like Jefferson Castor? They didn't do anything except preach outlandish "facts" about the holy origins of the beetles and perpetuate wild rumors about Hollis's grandfather. She doubted if most people at Dakota Aeronautics had ever given them a second thought. Yet Jefferson Castor, the man least likely to tolerate their brand of insanity, had taken them aboard the ship. Why?

Behind her, the boy hadn't fired a shot. Maybe he couldn't bring himself to draw a bead on a fleeing girl. She almost convinced herself it was okay to go back and ask him a few more questions. Without knowing specifics about the "heathens," she had little to go on, but at least now she could look beyond a ransom scheme—Castor seemed to have more on his mind than just getting rich.

The ship lurched violently. Delia kept her footing by bracing herself against a pile of olive-drab coats. Straight ahead, directly opposite the place where she'd emerged from the shaft, was a door. She quickened her pace, but the door didn't get any closer. It was a nightmare hallway.

No: she was running uphill. The ship was tilting. Behind her, the boy's shouts were drowned out by splintering wood and breaking glass. She thought of the boy's spilled mashed potato flakes—now the least of his problems—as an avalanche of quilts tumbled toward her. The ones that had torn free of their packaging floated past her head like jellyfish.

Delia thrust her hand forward and lunged for the door. It swung open and she climbed inside. She grabbed hold of a wooden railing with both hands, curling herself around it like a shipwreck survivor clinging to a piece of driftwood. *I did this*, she thought. *I made this happen.* What if she and Hollis managed to put a stop to Castor's plans, but sacrificed the ship in the process? What if they never saw Rob again?

It was a curious situation. Earlier, she had invented a new way to communicate. Then she had put the ship in grave danger by taking away that very same ability. She wasn't sure if that was an example of irony or simply a coincidence. The difference was fuzzy. The nuts and bolts of language bored her.

She was supposed to be a scientist.

Panting, clutching the rail, Delia admonished herself as the ship began to level off. She knew better than to make stupid, impulsive decisions. The scientific method was there for a reason. When the ship was steady enough, she forced herself to let go of the railing. There was work to be done. They would only know if the ends justified the means when they actually reached the end.

Reaching for her bracelet, her fingers went to the charm; besides those few old-fashioned picture cards, it was her only keepsake from St. Theresa's. The face of St. Albert, patron saint of scientists, was imprinted into the cheap metal, but had become nearly unrecognizable since she'd been using it as a screwdriver. Delia thought about the location of the vista deck and the way she'd been moving. The ship hadn't just listed to one side; the bow had shot upward. Even without a direct line to the bridge and the prop tower, beetle keepers should be able to keep the airship from breaching like a whale—especially with the new automated compartment system.

Stupid! She had seen the unfamiliar faces. The chambers were full of amateurs. Her place was down there, helping them. So what if they were Castor's people? Allegiances wouldn't matter much if the *Wendell Dakota* flipped over. She hoped that Hollis would figure out she wasn't coming and go on without her.

At the top of the stairs, she was greeted by sounds of laughter and good cheer. She stepped into a second-class hallway decorated in a pretty floral pattern. Passengers overflowed from a bistro, clinking glasses and smoking cigars. The tables inside had overturned, so they'd simply elected to stand. They didn't seem worried about the change of direction, the turbulence, or the armed crewmen patrolling the ship.

"Is that all you got?" shouted a plump, red-faced man in a tweed jacket with patches at the elbows, shaking his fist at the ceiling. "It'll take more than that to send the *Wendell Dakota* down to earth!"

He was met with howls of approval. Lingering here was a waste of time, but Delia could only watch, horrified, as a young man escorted his wife to the party.

"You're being alarmist, Sylvia. I assure you, it's perfectly normal for an airship to experience periodic bumps, especially since we've skirted the edge of that Atlantic storm."

"There was nothing normal about that!" Sylvia removed his arm from her shoulders. "Something's terribly wrong, and I'm going to find out what it is."

"Why, my dear? What are you going to do? Let's have a drink, and try to remember you're on an airship that's scientifically uncrashable."

WENDELL DAKOTA had never been much of a singer. He was more of a tone-deaf whistler. In Marius's impersonation, the ghostly voice of Wendell Dakota had sounded, for the very first time, on-key.

Hollis wondered why something like this would occur to him. Did other people's brains spring these shameful little traps? He closed his eyes and tried to recapture the fleeting confidence he'd possessed in the cent comm shaft. It was no use. At least that burst of inspiration had been for Delia's benefit, so it hadn't been entirely wasted.

"I'll tell you one thing about first class," Chester said, wiping his mouth with the back of his hand. "You people got some good cheese."

Hollis took a bite of his own ragged, misshapen sandwich, hastily assembled on their journey to the private reading room in which they now found themselves. There were eight such rooms that could be entered from a single hallway, on the other side of which was the library. Each room was decorated to represent one of Wendell Dakota's superlative qualities. The theme of this particular room was "foresight," signified by the imposing brass telescope that seemed to look straight into the wall, providing a view of nothing.

"Funny place for a spyglass," Maggie said, placing her good eye against the scope.

"The lens actually goes all the way through the hull," Hollis explained. "You're looking out into the sky off the port side."

Flecks of crusty baguette fell to the floor. He'd only eaten a third of his snack, while Maggie and Chester were already done. He was a prim chewer, he realized, and then forbade himself to be self-conscious about his *chewing* when they were minutes from confronting Marius. While he waited for Maggie to tell him what he already knew—*it's stormy out there*—he wondered why the decorator had taken a literal approach and painted so many eyes on the wall. It made him uncomfortable.

Chester arranged his bulk in one of the shiny leather chairs.

Maggie pulled away from the telescope, gesturing for Hollis to have a look. Even knowing what to expect, his heart sank: the *Wendell Dakota* was floating inside a fog as thick as Delmonico's stew, meaning Jefferson Castor had lost all visibility. He hoped Captain Quincy and Chief Owens were still alive. With Jefferson in charge and the telephone lines severed, Hollis knew the ship could emerge from the storm above the clouds, overloaded with beetles, trapped in an out-of-control sprint for the heavens.

"Okay," Hollis said. "Status report. What I'm seeing here is that visibility's at zero and it's a good bet we're too high in the sky."

Chester was cleaning his fingernails with his toothpick. "You can tell all that from one little peek into a cloud?" he asked, mildly interested.

"I've lived aboard every airship in the fleet. I can tell when we're rising above our cruising altitude. The air feels wrong, even inside all these walls. And the thing about low visibility is that rookie beetle keepers always pour on the juice. Nobody wants to crash, so everybody's first instinct is to load the compartments with beetles and let them feast."

Hollis paused, listening to every little creak and groan of the ship, trying to anticipate the next shake-up. He imagined the bow nosing down while the stern flipped up like the sudden snap of a diver in midair. He pictured a great gash in the hull and wondered what went through people's minds when they were plummeting toward the earth.

In the weeks following his father's accident, Hollis had obsessed over pictures of the D.C. Sky-dock, tracing a finger from the broken railing down to the ground, imagining what his father could have been thinking at each moment. He'd heard the old stories about life flashing before your eyes, but he had trouble imagining what that was like. Did time become so elastic that you relived every moment and felt every feeling over again? Or was it a single blinding flash, a total overload of memory and emotion? Most of all, he wondered what his father's very last thought had been. His wife's face? His son's voice? Or was it just some random brain activity, a tasty breakfast he'd enjoyed one morning in 1906?

"So we're still uncrashable, yeah?" Maggie asked, startling him. "I gotta admit, you're makin' me nervous." She glanced around. "Maybe it's just all these eyes, lookin' at me."

Hollis considered how best to explain this. "The ship has sixteen lift chambers, which is a record number, so even if we lose a bunch of them in a freak accident, we won't drop. It's uncrashable because these new spider machines react to a million different things, like wind and airspeed. They make dealing with the beetles a science, so it's not possible to fly too high or too low."

"So then what's the problem?"

Her genuine curiosity made Hollis feel like they really were working together and that she probably wasn't going to stab him.

"Why are you looking at me like that?" she asked.

"I'm grateful for your help. I thought you hated me."

"It doesn't matter if I *like* you or not."

"I kinda like him," Chester admitted.

Maggie glared at him. Then she turned to Hollis. "You were talking about the machines."

"Right. Well, they can be turned off. Or broken. Or just messed up by people who don't know what they're doing. If the machines aren't pulling us down a little bit and keeping us steady, it's a good bet the hijackers are just working the chambers themselves. And it's the machines that make the ship uncrashable—it's not the ship itself."

"Then what the hell are we waiting for? Let's go see what your friend knows."

"Marius isn't my friend." Saying this out loud made Hollis think of what Delia had said about his name. "He never was. He's just a guy who works here."

Chester stuffed a few more slices of cheese into his mouth.

"Did you have those in your pocket this whole time?" Hollis asked. Chester stood up from his chair, ignoring the question, and slipped on a pair of brass knuckles.

Hollis opened the door and peered out into the hall. There were a few passengers milling about, but the path to the library door was clear. Most people had taken to their staterooms following the shake-up, and those who hadn't were holed up in bars and restaurants. Hollis led them across and pushed open the door-sized mural of Don Quixote tilting at a windmill.

The library was sectioned off by topic—they had entered into Military History. The floor was covered in books that had been thrown from the shelves. On the wall was a massive painting of a Revolutionary War battle. There was General Washington astride a horse at the forefront of the colonists' lines, his hair as white as the stylized puffs of cannon fire that burst around him. How strange to see a battle fought entirely on the ground. Hollis wondered what it would be like to face down a row of muskets.

Chester took the lead, peering around the corner, then motioning for them to follow him past the grinning, bespectacled face of Teddy Roosevelt presiding over Biographies. When Chester's hand went up, Hollis froze. Maggie pulled the immobilizer from her belt.

There was a wet, mindless gibbering coming from just beyond the next set of shelves. Hollis saw his braver self put a hand on Chester's shoulder: *Stay here. I'll take a look.* But instead he just waited for the bigger kid to check it out.

Chester looked, then slapped the non-brass-knuckled hand over his mouth. He stumbled back, wide-eyed. Maggie cursed and leaped to his side, immobilizer at the ready. A second behind her, Hollis wrenched a copy of *Middlemarch* up from the floor and held it over his head, prepared to strike.

It took all of his willpower to keep his half-digested sandwich down.

Marius was suspended in the air. His shoulder nudged a chandelier as he bobbed gently up and down. He was shirtless and barefoot, wearing only his uniform pants, and his lean upper body was covered in a riot of lurid tattoos ending just below each wrist. In the center of his chest was a distorted picture of the Dakota beetle—its legs and feelers bent and twisted into impossible shapes.

Hollis dropped the book. He'd seen that same corrupted beetle on the business card he'd found in Delia's satchel. Even more disturbing was Marius's lumpy, distended belly, which undulated as if something was squirming beneath his skin.

"Is this the guy?" whispered Maggie.

But Hollis was speechless. Marius, on the other hand, was blubbering and smiling to himself, eyes twitching every time he nudged the light on the chandelier.

"Marius," Hollis said finally.

The floating man looked at Hollis curiously, then began to retch. His body jerked in the air, arms and legs tossed about like a doll's. A dribble of amber slime emerged from his mouth. Chester jumped back.

Marius began making a hoarse gagging noise. His torso seemed to rise, his entire body in great distress, then he sank a few inches as he expelled a beetle from his mouth. The insect floated over the shelf toward Poetry.

"Hollis," he rasped, "can you feel it?"

"Um, I don't think so."

Hollis noted the empty bottle of moonshine and the containers of sap that littered the rug beneath Marius. Behind him, a holstered pistol was slung across a chair. "Have you been . . ." The words were hard to find. "*Eating* beetles?"

Marius coughed. "I feel what they feel. I know their mother—*our* mother—isn't far."

Chester began slowly working his way along the shelf to

the back of the room, keeping as much distance as possible between himself and the floating man. Maggie stood her ground at Hollis's side.

Marius clearly didn't have much time. His skin was covered in a sheen of sweat. His eyes were straining upward in their sockets.

"I need to know about *my* mother, Marius. Where is she?"

"Don't know about your mother," he rasped. "Only father."

Hollis shifted his interrogation. "What do you know about my father?"

Marius made a convulsive noise that sounded like a gurgling faucet. Then he fought for control of himself. "So sorry. Always liked you, Hollis."

Hollis wasn't afraid anymore. His mind had tinted everything red. He stepped forward and almost lost the sandwich again; the smell was unbearable.

"What are you sorry for?"

"I . . . pushed him." Marius began to droop, his head lolling on his neck.

"*Don't you die yet.*" Hollis gave *Middlemarch* a vicious kick. The book slammed into the wall. "Not until you tell me why you did it."

At the other end of the room, Chester picked up the gun. "Maggie!" Hollis snapped, pointing. "Stop him."

Marius lifted his head, ever so slightly. "Castor," he muttered.

"Castor. Jefferson Castor told you to do it."

"Mmm."

"He hired you to kill my father."

Maggie sprang to life and followed Chester's path to the chair. Marius began to quiver, then shake violently. His flailing arms snapped their bones. Maggie sank to the ground, burying her face in her hands.

Chester raised the pistol and aimed it at the back of Marius's head.

"Not yet!" Hollis screamed. Chester's hand began to shake.

Marius's entire body was thrust upward into the ceiling, broken limbs splayed, as the beetles inside him feasted. His mouth was twisted into an agonized grimace. His nose leaked fluid. Chester lowered the gun without firing and collapsed into the chair.

"Please," Hollis begged the floating corpse, "not yet."

THE PISTOL ROB HELD was heavy and cold, as if it had been kept in an icebox rather than locked in a cabinet beneath a bumpy map of Greenland. Rob looked at it in his upturned palm and tried to imagine pointing it at a person and pulling the trigger. To contrast with Brice Blank's pacifism, Rob had gleefully made Atticus Hunter very handy with guns, and quick to use them. Now he felt like a fraud and vowed to revise every issue, scrubbing out the weapons with his gummy eraser. The no-going-back consequences of such a thing, the inability to unshoot someone, made his knees feel rubbery.

"I gotta say, Dad, thanks but no thanks," Rob told his father after contemplating the heft of the pistol for a full minute. Being presented with a loaded gun by the man who didn't let him keep a slingshot in the stateroom was somehow the most unbelievable horror in the day's parade of them.

"That is a semiautomatic Colt M1911," his father explained quickly. "It's a single-action pistol. You've got seven shots before you need to reload. This is the safety—" His father pulled out his own identical gun and clicked a lever on the upper part of the grip. "Make sure it's off if you need to use it and on when the gun is in your pocket. I don't have time to teach you how to fieldstrip it. You probably won't need to do that."

The alien hadn't vacated Rob's father's body. It had simply burrowed deeper into his brain. Rob had never heard his father mention guns before, and now he was rattling off directions like an army instructor.

The pool of blood oozing from Chief Owens's big lifeless body had been black, not the vibrant candy red Rob had always imagined. He looked his father in the eyes.

"I don't know if I can take this."

"I'm not asking. Now listen to me." All around them, his father's crew paced grimly. An atmosphere of tense preparation had descended upon the bridge. "These men who cut the lines, I can promise you, they're not going to stop with a single act of sabotage. So this is what you're going to do. You know how to get to the life-ships?"

The life-ships were emergency sky-canoes; larger versions of Samuel Dakota's original. Each one was equipped with the proper number of beetles for a safe descent, along with a portable mixing kit that injected moonshine whiskey into the beetles' normal diet of sap to produce buoyancy at a moment's notice. On the *Wendell Dakota*, there were eighty-four of these ships docked in hollows inside the hull. Larger collapsibles for third-class and steerage passengers were stowed belowdecks.

"I'm not leaving you here," Rob said.

"Yes, you are. Take the gun and go. I'll send two of my men with you."

"Have you seen the weather out there?"

"Do you know what staying in here will mean for you? Do you think the men coming to break down the door will stop to think about who is in their sights? They will be firing at anything that moves. And make no mistake, if you can't pull that trigger, you don't belong here right now."

Rob closed his eyes. *Hijacking.* It sounded like a thing that happened to other people, unfortunate souls who weren't Rob Castor. If he stayed with his father, did that make him a hijacker, too? Once he accepted the gun, his innocent-bystander status was probably revoked.

His father grabbed his shoulders. "Focus, Rob. I need you to be strong. What would what's-his-name, Brice Blank, what would he do?"

Rob opened his eyes, surprised his father even knew the name of the funny-book hero. "Brice Blank hates guns, Dad. He'd probably turn himself in because of his faith in the legal process."

His father frowned. "Oh." He pulled Rob close and buried his face in Rob's suit jacket. Rob heard sniffing.

"Dad, are you *smelling* me?"

"I'm so sorry," his father said.

"If I'm gonna go, I need to understand why you're doing this. Because if I don't get to see you for a while, if something happens . . . I have to know."

Slowly, his father raised his head. Rob's shoulder felt warm and wet from his father's tears. He had never seen the man cry before.

"Jefferson!" the librarian yelled across the bridge. "A word, please."

His father ignored her.

"Sir!" A mercenary with bullet belts worn across his chest came running up. "The prisoner wants to see you. Says it's urgent."

His father closed his eyes. For a moment, he was very still. Then he pressed his palm against his forehead and slid it down his face as if it were a towel.

"Come with me." He led Rob across the bridge, ignoring crewmen at two different chart stations pleading "mission-critical" issues. Halfway down the port side of the bridge, a gap in the viewing windows was filled by a raised platform encircled by railings. It reminded Rob of a pedestal for a politician on a whistle-stop tour, in which an airship dripping with campaign banners would descend upon small towns all over the country and hover just above the ground while the politician gave a speech.

"It's time for you to know that the invention of flight was dependent upon a Castor just as much as a Dakota."

"A Castor?" Rob asked as they ascended the steps. Every child knew the story of how Samuel Dakota had changed the world with his special blend of whiskey and sap. He didn't see how one of his own ancestors could possibly have played a part in such a well-known tale.

They crossed the platform and paused while Jefferson unlocked a door marked CAPTAIN'S QUARTERS. There were several keys attached to a loop of his belt, and while his father struggled to find the right one, Rob switched the gun to his other hand so he could wipe his sweaty palm on his jacket. He told himself that as long as he didn't put the weapon in his bag, he hadn't officially accepted it. Willing the key to be missing, he shifted anxiously from heel to toe and back again. Rob didn't want to meet his father's prisoner. He didn't want his father to *have* a prisoner.

"It's just me!" his father called out as he knocked twice, then unlocked the door.

The sole occupant of the sparsely furnished room was Lucy Dakota. She was sitting in a chair between an empty shelf and a bare desk. Rope bound her wrists and ankles to the arms and legs of the chair. Flustered, Rob slipped the gun into his pocket. He hoped she hadn't seen it in his hand.

"The ship is too high," she said immediately, ignoring Rob, addressing his father. "Don't tell me it's not. And we're still ascending. Why aren't the chambers lowering our altitude? Where are we? Where's Hollis? What's going on out there?" She craned her neck as best she could, as if a single glance out the door would explain everything.

"It's not your concern," his father said.

"Everything about this airship and this company is my concern. There's a reason my name isn't Lucy Castor."

Rob had heard them use these exact words in arguments about the price of candles for the second-class spa and the brand of peanuts for the third-class bars.

"Just be quiet for one minute, Lucy, please."

"Is Chief Owens still in charge of the chambers? Eliminating him would be a disaster. I hope you know better than that."

"This is my ship. And soon it will be my company. These concerns are mine alone."

"Jefferson. Listen to yourself."

"No. You listen to me. It's a simple matter of justice."

Lucy looked at Rob for the first time. "Well," she said, arching her eyebrow at him, "this ought to be good."

THE HISTORY OF FLIGHT IN AMERICA

PART

FIVE

SHENANDOAH SURPRISE!
Aerial Navy Routs "Stonewall" Jackson

The Washington Evening Star
August 12, 1862

Steel-Frame Air Boat Deflects Enemy Fire;
Secretary Stanton Orders 500

The Philadelphia Inquirer
August 29, 1862

The Army of Northern Virginia Retreats;
General Lee Vows Counterattack

Charleston Mercury
September 15, 1862

Portrait of a High-Flying American Hero:
Samuel Dakota

Harper's Weekly

October 2, 1862

Richmond in Flames! Dakota Bombers
Scorch Confederate Capital

New-York Tribune

October 27, 1862

ON A CRISP AFTERNOON in November of 1862, Samuel Dakota left the Appomattox Courthouse in Virginia and walked down the stone steps to his personal sky-canoe. He had just witnessed the complete and unconditional surrender of the Confederate forces. As predicted, Samuel Dakota's airships had ended the war in months rather than years. The Congressional Medal of Honor had been draped over his neck by Lincoln himself, and the picture of the ceremony made the front page of all the major northern papers. He had renewed his contract with the United States government for half a million dollars.

So much sky left to conquer, he thought as he gazed up at the clouds drifting lazily above the courthouse. He closed his eyes and saw fluffy outlines against the backs of his eyelids. They looked a bit like twin sky-canoes, with smoky wisps connecting the stern of one to the bow of the other. Gradually they expanded into bursts of radiant color. Inspired and deeply moved, Samuel realized that he was a visionary, and like most blessed men, the next phase of his life was to be a lonely one. He snapped his eyes open, jumped into his canoe, and rummaged beneath the seat for his sketchbook.

Every man's journey to the heavens is lonely, he told himself— *I'm just lucky enough to be able to get there on my own terms.* Suddenly his hand brushed against something glassy and smooth, and his heart sank as he pulled out a bottle with the letter *C* scratched into the bottom. He glanced around the bustling town square and up the steps of the imposing courthouse at the jovial men in dress uniforms. There was no sign of his tormentor, but Samuel had long suspected the man had help. Perhaps even a friend at Dakota Aeronautics.

Inside the bottle was the expected note.

HEY MISTER DIKOTA,
KILLIN MEN IS EASY FROM UP IN
THE SKY, AINT IT? WHEN YOU DONT
HAVE TO SEE THERE FACES?

H.C.

Samuel stuffed the note back into the bottle. It was as if Hezekiah Castor could read his thoughts. Attacking from the sky hadn't even felt *real*, raining bullets and bombs down upon the little gray ants and their tiny model cities far below.

But his life was about to enter a new and glorious phase, and if Hezekiah Castor was going to be a constant thorn in his side, the man would have to be dealt with. As much as it irked Samuel to have to revisit that shabby little corner of his past, it was time to put an end to this. Who knew when Castor might graduate from threats to sabotage?

Samuel Dakota spread the whiskey-sap along the sides of his ship, removed a few choice beetles from their golden box (a gift from General Grant), and set them in place. Much to the surprise of the Union dignitaries who had been promised an escort back to Washington by Sky Captain Dakota himself, everyone's favorite war hero rose into the sky above the town square and caught a light westerly breeze. President Lincoln and his cabinet shielded their eyes against the glare of the noonday sun as Samuel's sky-canoe disappeared beyond a distant ridge.

An hour later, he touched down in a clearing in the dense woods a few miles from the Dakota manufacturing complex. His heart was pounding as he checked to make sure his pistol was loaded and holstered securely at his side. At the far end of the clearing was a decrepit, lopsided cabin with a roof that sloped down low enough to graze the tops of two old rocking chairs.

Next to the cabin was the broken-down, rusty still where Hezekiah Castor had made his moonshine. Inside that moonshine was the combination of fermented grains that, when mixed with sap from certain Virginia maple trees, became the fuel that inflated the beetles and released their gases. He remembered the day in his other life as a Union Army soldier (had it really been less than a year ago?) when his regiment had crossed this very clearing and encountered the skinny, unkempt man with sunburned arms and a floppy straw hat. Surprisingly, it had taken four men—including Samuel—to wrestle him down and hog-tie him. Then they had taken their time drinking from his still, filling bottles for the road. All the while, Hezekiah Castor watched helplessly, squirming and sputtering in the dirt. And as a parting shot, Samuel had grabbed an ax that had been leaning against the side of the cabin and smashed the still to pieces, obliterating tin cups and copper pots that had been marked with the letter *C*.

He'd never really felt bad about it. Moonshine thievery was a minor offense compared with the atrocities committed against civilians by both sides. And anyway, they had left the man alive.

As Samuel approached the house, he saw that the still remained a bent and twisted piece of ugly wreckage. He was about ten feet from the porch when the door swung open and banged against one of the rocking chairs. Hezekiah Castor stepped out into the shade of the overhanging roof. He put his hands on his hips. Samuel stopped. He couldn't see Castor's eyes, which were hidden beneath the brim of his straw hat. But he could see the man's small mouth working on a plug of tobacco, which he spit into the grass alongside the house.

"Thought I'da seen you sooner," Castor said, his voice measured and calm, with an unexpected hint of friendly hospitality. "Been some time since I spied you behind your big ol' fence." He chuckled. "Imagine that. Never thought I'd be seein' your face again, and there you were, struttin' and hollerin' at your workers. Nearly jumped outta my skin."

"How did you find out my name?"

"Your man at the gate was mighty helpful, long as I promised to quit botherin' him. Reckon you got my notes, then."

"I've been busy."

"Oh, I heard, Samuel," Castor said. Then he tilted his head back to glance at the sky. "I seen."

"What do you want?" Samuel asked, bracing himself for an angry, rambling speech during which Hezekiah Castor, creator of the magic moonshine, claimed to be entitled to a chunk of Dakota Aeronautics' profit. The formula was a military secret, of course, but the company had grown so quickly that even Samuel had trouble remembering who was supposed to know certain things and who was not. And he had been giving so many interviews lately, all of them a blur.

"Well, now, lemme see," Castor said, crossing his arms. "How 'bout you start by replacing what you done broke?" He nodded at the wreckage of the still. Samuel was taken aback. Castor was upset about a few tin drums and some piping?

"Your *still*," Samuel said, buying time while he figured out the man's angle.

Castor spit a thin jet of brown liquid between his front teeth. "Darn right, my still. You know how scarce tin's been round here? And if you can believe it, I ain't exactly prosperin', neither."

"That's it, then?" Samuel was incredulous. "You want to be, um . . . *compensated* for the damage to your property."

"That's about the long and the short of it, yes sir."

"What about the notes?" Samuel said, his nervous fingers resting on his holster. He still didn't quite believe that Castor had gone to the trouble of sneaking him threats in bottles because he was upset about the piece of junk in his yard. Was it possible that Castor didn't even *know* his moonshine was the original ingredient in beetle fuel? That all this time he had simply wanted Samuel to replace what he had broken?

"Like your last one," Samuel pressed, "about how killing men from the sky is easier. What did you mean by that?"

"Well, ain't it?"

"I suppose it is. Yes."

Castor just shrugged. "Don't matter no more, nohow."

Samuel's dress uniform began to itch. "Listen, Castor, I'm . . . sorry about your, all your, uh . . ." He started to apologize for the hog-tying, but thought better of it. "I'm sorry I stole your moonshine. Quite the interesting formula you've got there."

Castor stepped off his porch and squinted at Samuel. "Now what do you mean by that?"

"Tasty stuff," Samuel said quickly. "Very smooth." He reached into his pocket and felt the pleasant heft of his money clip. Just a few dollars, and he was free. "I pay you now," he said slowly, so there wouldn't be any misunderstanding, "and you leave me alone. No more notes in bottles, no more sneaking around Dakota Aeronautics and bothering my men. And this is the last time we ever speak."

Castor laughed, which became a wet cough that culminated in another brown gob of spit in the grass. "You sure are a strange bird." He put up his hands in a gesture of mock surrender. "You kick me some good Union currency, we're square. Don't have to fret about me spoilin' your sky party no more."

Samuel produced the money clip and was about to peel off a few crisp bills when a sudden flash of movement in the doorway of the cabin—*ambush!*—made him drop the money and fumble for his pistol. Hezekiah whirled around as a pale boy with reddish-blond hair, clad in dirty overalls, stepped out onto the porch. Samuel, who had managed to bring his pistol up in the direction of the ambush, felt hot shame creep through his body.

I am pointing my gun at a child.

His heart was pounding. But it was as if his thoughts existed in another universe from his actions, and he couldn't make himself lower the gun right away. The boy looked at him curiously, then made a pistol shape out of his thumb and finger and pointed it at Samuel.

"You're a thief, mister," the boy yelled, jerking his hand back to mimic the recoil of a gun being fired. "Pcheeww!"

"Jefferson Castor!" Hezekiah yelled. "You git back in the house!" He turned back to Samuel with an apologetic shrug, and his eyes widened when he saw the gun—the real gun—aimed at his boy.

What happened next would replay over and over in Samuel's mind every night before he fell asleep, and then again in terrible dreams where the tree branches crept across the clearing, their impossibly long shadow-fingers pointing at him in silent accusation like little Jefferson Castor's gun hand.

Hezekiah Castor lunged for the gun, putting his body between the barrel and his boy.

It just went off.

Samuel made the excuse even as he pulled the trigger; maybe even a split second before he did. He had been jumpy all day, and his finger slipped.

It was self-defense.

A reflex.

An accident.

It just went off.

The next few minutes were a series of still images in his mind: Hezekiah Castor lying on the ground next to the wad of cash, his arm bent unnaturally back behind his head. Little Jefferson Castor frozen, midstride, between the porch and his father's body.

And finally, the merciful blue emptiness of the sky as Samuel Dakota made his escape.

DELIA LOWERED HERSELF into the primary lift chamber. At each rung, St. Albert's wry face seemed to appear, inches from her own. She wondered if Albertus Magnus would have sympathized with the beetle cults. He'd been an open-minded man: bishop and alchemist, saint and scientist. A doctor of the church who also discovered arsenic. Beetle keeping had taught her to see the wisdom in these contradictions. Lifting an airship into the sky required both rational thought and faith. The best machines amounted to a pile of scrap if the beetles suddenly refused to consume whiskey-sap halfway through the flight.

If St. Albert were alive today, she decided, he would have written a work of great scholarship about the cults. Something better than *Beetle Deification: A Survey*, from which she could recall only the sketchy facts she'd retained before the book's bone-dry text drove her away. Now she wished she'd paid more attention.

She hopped down onto the catwalk and ducked behind an abandoned lunch cart. Earlier, the place had been full of strangers. That had been disconcerting enough, but now something else was nagging at her.

The noise.

The primary lift chamber was home to the largest of the *Wendell Dakota*'s sixteen brand-new Sorter/Picker/Dispenser machines. Yesterday, Hollis and Rob had been able to hear the rhythmic shuffle from all the way up on the catwalk; spiders didn't exactly run whisper-quiet. But now, the distant sounds were human rather than mechanical: the sharp echo of orders being given, revised, given again.

Refill on eleven, two liters.

Four won't close. They're coming back up here.

Siphon forty-one into twenty-nine!

Delia pressed her forehead against the side of the cart. These were the sounds of amateurs trying to manually operate the compartments that fed whiskey-sap to the beetles. Now she was sure that Chief Owens was a captive, or worse. There was no way he would allow his crew to shut off the spiders and work for the hijackers.

She had to get down to the chamber floor. Maybe she could take out a few guards with the immobilizer and try to restart the spider. Even if she succeeded, it was still only one of sixteen. But what else could she do? She turned her wrist and glanced at St. Albert's face on her bracelet. Then she stood up.

"Are there any more of those exquisite jelly rolls back there?"

Delia found herself face-to-face with a woman who had been about to peek behind the cart. She was delicate and thin, with long eyelashes and a pale, high-cheekboned face. Her hair curled beneath the brim of her felt hat. She looked like the kind of young society lady who strutted about beneath a twirling parasol, except her skirt and blouse were covered in clotted whiskey-sap. A hint of black ink peeked above her neckline along her shoulders. Delia remembered that the Sons of Solomon liked to ink toy trains on their bodies, while the Order of the First Beetle preferred a corrupted version of the Dakota logo. And the Liberation Front's insignia was a raised fist, but she didn't know if the members tattooed it on themselves. If only there was a way to ask about the woman's ink without arousing suspicion. Her questions would have to be much less direct.

"Jelly rolls!" Delia said. "I was just looking for them myself."

The woman laughed. "Perhaps we can share one. Did you just come off shift?"

Delia thought quickly. "Sure did," she said. "In chamber two."

The woman began sifting through the shelves of the cart.

"Nothing. Too bad. I'm on break, and I'm starving."

Delia marveled at the woman's calm. She'd assumed everyone down here would be frantic.

"I'm Delia," she said, extending her hand.

"Nice to meet you, Sister Delia. My name is Ada." The woman clasped Delia's fingers in some kind of intricate pattern.

"How's everything going in your chamber?"

"Oh, fine," Ada said. "The beetles do all the work. They know where they're going." She smiled dreamily. "We are so near, Sister Delia."

Delia's heart pounded. Ada's words recalled Marius's: *They know their mother is near.*

"I was sort of worried when the telephones went dead, since we turned all the spiders off."

Ada seemed taken aback. "The tools of enslavement?"

"I know we had to shut them down. It's just a little scary to be flying blind."

"Blind!" Ada was incredulous. "Their womb-seeking instincts will guide us."

Now Delia had it. The Order of the First Beetle believed that Samuel Dakota had discovered a powerful mother beetle. According to the Order, flight was only a small part of what these creatures were capable of, and they were going to prove it by recovering Samuel's long-lost ship, where the mother was supposedly stashed away, oozing with undiscovered potential. That was all she could remember.

"Sister Delia, are you all right?"

Delia tried to smile sweetly, but she was hopelessly distracted. Jefferson Castor had placed the fate of the greatest airship ever built into the hands of a Confederate militia and a beetle-worshipping cult. She wondered if the only true motive for the hijacking of the *Wendell Dakota* was complete and utter insanity.

She willed the muscles of her face into a vacant smile. "Of course, forgive me. Sister Ada, may I ask you something?"

"Yes, Sister Delia."

"Do you ever worry that we've come so far, but we—they—still won't be able to find the ship?"

"You poor child," Ada said, pulling Delia in for an embrace. "We all wrestle with doubt from time to time."

Delia wriggled out of Ada's grip as politely as she could. "I'm full of nerves today, that's all."

"Remember our words, Sister."

"I do."

"Say them with me."

Delia mumbled along while Ada said, "As the mother delivered her beetles unto us, so we deliver our beetles to the mother."

Delia thought of the X on the map in her bag. These people actually believed they were taking the beetles home. "Thank you, Sister Ada. Very inspiring."

"Come, take a shift alongside me. Extra hands are always welcome in chamber one. It will remind you that our work is not in vain."

"That's . . . actually a good idea."

From catwalk to ladder to ledge, sidling past steel casks of whiskey-sap, they descended. Halfway down, in the center of the chamber, was a glass bubble dotted with reflections from the lamps that hung from the walls. This was the spider's head, where keepers helped guide its movements. The bubble was empty. Lower still, with Ada chattering on, Delia studied the dormant limbs. Eight thick legs angled upward from the base of the control bubble, each an assemblage of pipe and wire, tightly wound. Jointed pistonlike to each main limb, a trident of three lesser segments pointed toward the floor. Splitting again and narrowing, these twenty-four arms became forty-eight stumpy aluminum hands, out of which burst two hundred and forty hoses. At the bottom, Delia and Ada shuffled through dendrites of legs-become-fingers, hundreds of nozzles dangling above the compartments they'd once fed.

The machine's stillness depressed her. Everywhere she looked, Order acolytes were pouring whiskey-sap down the hatches in the hull. They were chanting in Latin; Delia recognized the language from mass at St. Theresa's. Militia hijackers poked warily about the forest of limbs, while others patrolled with rifles over their shoulders. Above her head, a convex sliver of glass distorted their movements.

"I'll just go make myself useful," Delia said absently, trying to avoid the eyes of the militiamen. All around her, the chanting of the false keepers became fervent.

"Blessings!" Ada held out her hands with palms down, parallel to the floor, and wiggled her fingers. Then she was gone. Delia moved swiftly. Underneath the bubble was a ladder that would take her to the meeting point of the main limbs. There she'd find a trapdoor. Maybe she could go unseen long enough to get the spider started again.

"I think this one is really trying to commune with me," said a man as Delia flitted past. He had paused in his work to examine a beetle up close. "Look at its little feelers!"

Delia had been trying not to think about it—the idea of behaving like a cult member made her ill—but there were times when she felt a majestic vibration rippling through the beetle population. Sometimes she could get a single beetle to respond, like a pet, to whispered coaxing. Other times they were simply mindless insects.

Nearby a woman giggled excitedly.

"It doesn't taste that bad!" she exclaimed.

Delia gagged and forced herself to keep moving. She might be willing to entertain a wild notion or two about the beetles, but she drew the line at actually *eating* them.

Movement off to her right: a small group of militia coming closer. The ladder to the bubble was about thirty feet away. If she made a run for it, they would see her. She was tempted to pull the immobilizer from her bag, but she knew she couldn't zap them all. Going against everything she believed in as an apprentice beetle keeper, she walked casually to the nearest compartment, pulling it open. The dark space beneath was swarming with beetles. Delia grabbed hold of a feeding tube and turned the handle. She chanted nonsensically. Without looking up, she sensed the patrol no more than a few steps away. Instead of passing her by, they stopped. She felt eyes upon her and reluctantly looked up to meet them.

The armed porter from yesterday's trip to chamber two was studying her face.

"I know you," he said.

She smiled dumbly, shrugged, and resumed her chant.

"You're not one of them. Who are you?"

The militia men weren't budging. She dropped the Order act. "I just work here."

"Do you?" His hands rested casually on the ivory grips of his pistols. "Then it's time you met the boss, cupcake."

"**I SEEN THOSE TATTOOS** before," Maggie said. "Painted on a wall."

Chester agreed. "All the way over by the pier, crawling up a lamppost. And on a sammich board down at the Four Aces."

"My father thought they were kind of funny," Hollis said. "The beetle religions. The cults, I mean."

"Yeah, real funny," Maggie said. "Until you find yourself coughing up beetles and floating."

They were sprawled along three rococo divans, a fraction of the expensive furniture that lined the walls of Edmund Juniper's personal storage space. At one end of the long room, the splintered door was propped awkwardly in its frame. Chester's shoulder had succeeded where Maggie's lock picking had failed. The two guards who had been stationed outside were slumped against the wall, unconscious, hands trussed with scaly rope from a box labeled SNAKE-CHARMING SUPPLIES.

All three of them were shell-shocked and spent. But Marius had not confessed to the murder of Chester's father, or Maggie's. For them, fear was the end—they could begin putting the gruesome spectacle behind them. For Hollis, it had opened a wound, a blossoming, painful thing. The wound trumped the mystery of the tattoos and the woman on the bridge. It trumped the hijacking. It even trumped his mother's whereabouts. Those things were background noise. The last two days had suddenly become old news.

He closed his eyes and watched the railing give way. Saw his father pitch over the side. A person, after a few seconds of freefall, was a person no longer. Just a broken shape. He'd had this vision before, only now there was a figure left standing on the dock. It wasn't Marius. Marius was nobody, and he was dead. It was Jefferson Castor, and he was very much alive.

But not for long.

Hollis sprang from the divan, riding a fresh jolt of adrenaline, or hatred. He felt clear-eyed, as if the room were lit by the sun rather than a row of bare bulbs. Maggie's face looked vivid, the plum-colored bruise seeming almost delicious. Chester's scalp had a juicy little nick from the razor at the very top of his head. Looped around the arm of a divan where Chester had left it was Marius's leather gun belt. Hollis forced himself to sit back down. Attached to the belt was the holster. His knee bounced. Inside the holster was the gun. They had come here to hide, to regroup, but he didn't care. He wanted the gun in his hand, pointed at Jefferson Castor's head, close enough to see the look on his face.

Chester had managed to open one of the trunks pushed up against his divan. He rooted around inside. Hollis rose from his seat and buckled the holster belt around his waist.

"There he is," Maggie said, watching Hollis pace the length of the room and turn. "Wild Earp."

It was a cowboy gun, a six-shooter, and the belt sagged along his hip. Marius had probably won it in a poker game in Deadwood or Carson City. At least, that's the story he would have told Hollis. The fact that Marius's corpse was now glued to the ceiling of the library, drooling whiskey-sap, cast doubt on his past tales of adventure. He had been nothing but a killer for hire, a coward who shoved an innocent man off a sky-dock for money, or whatever Castor had offered him.

Hollis reached into his satchel. Would it be satisfying to send a message? *Your dad's a murderer. Thought you should know.*

His fingers brushed against the business card, and he took it out of the bag. The beetle design really was a perfect match with Marius's tattoo. Bent feelers, twisted pincers. He remembered the way Delia had caressed the living beetle in her dorm room. The little creature had been under her spell.

He folded the card in half, creasing it with a thumbnail.

"Hey, Maggie, what kind of place is St. Theresa's?"

"Delia never told you about it."

"No."

"Guess she's got her reasons."

"It won't be hard for me to find out. You might as well just tell me."

"Ask Delia."

"I can't."

Hollis tucked the folded card back into the bag. If only Delia were carrying the second transmitter instead of Rob. He could find out if she'd reached the slop room, tell her he wasn't going to meet her there. *Oh, and by the way, are you in some kind of beetle cult?* Maybe this was a more accurate glimpse into the future: crossed wires, missed connections, a flurry of breathless messages.

He sat down and removed the gun from its holster. The metal felt hot in his hand. It seemed like a simple enough mechanism: you pulled the hammer back until it clicked, then you pulled the trigger.

"You wanna keep that thing pointed somewhere else?"

Maggie was sitting up now, poised like she was ready to dive to the floor.

"Sorry," Hollis said, laying the gun next to him on the divan.

"How about putting it away?"

"It is away."

"Holster it before you blow your head off."

He put his hands up in a surrender pose. "I'm not even touching it, okay?"

"Hey!" Chester shouted triumphantly. He had popped

open a second trunk and was holding a carton of cigarettes, displaying them proudly to Maggie and Hollis. "Chesterfields!"

On any other day, Hollis would have been horrified to learn that Juniper's possessions had been even lightly jostled in transit. Now he just reached out a hand.

"I'll take one of those."

Chester pulled out three and dumped the rest back into the trunk. He stuck the cigarettes in his mouth and patted his pockets until he located a book of matches. He lit all three and handed them out, then went back to rummaging.

Hollis's mouth filled with smoke, and he coughed it out in a single explosive cloud without pulling it into his lungs. He hated the taste, but he was trying to think of himself as a killer. And killers, from what he could gather, tended to smoke. Maggie took a satisfied puff. Chester explored an armoire full of motoring jackets.

Hollis looked at the gun, then at Maggie, who was reclining with her eyes closed.

"Have you ever killed anybody?"

She opened one eye. "You serious?"

He took another pull on the cigarette and scorched his throat. He began to hack and sputter.

"First time?" she asked.

He shook his head. Then he dropped the cigarette to the floor and stubbed it out with the toe of a loafer.

"Do you want to know about just me, or me and Chester both?"

"Both, I guess." His mouth was dry. He wished that

Chester had found a canister of spring water instead of a carton of cigarettes.

"Hey, Chester," she called to him. "How many people you killed?"

"I lost track."

"Me too." She shrugged, but her mouth twitched with the hint of a smile.

"Okay, I get it. Sorry I asked."

"Here's a piece of advice from one killer to another."

"Uh-huh."

"Don't point that thing at somebody unless you're sure you can pull the trigger."

"How will I know if I'm sure until I point it at him?"

Chester pulled a hacksaw and a chisel from a trunk labeled EGYPT. "Killers don't ask questions like that," he said. Then he thought for a moment and upended the entire trunk, spilling its contents onto the floor: shovels, pickaxes, and little pieces of sandstone. Leftovers from Edmund's five-month obsession with archaeology.

"What kinds of questions do they ask, then?"

"Yeah," Maggie said, sitting up, looking curiously at her friend. "What kind of questions do killers ask themselves, Chester?"

He got down on his knees and put out his cigarette on a cracked stone plate. Then he began sifting through the pile. "I didn't say that right," he said. "What I mean is, if you have to ask yourself if you'll be able to shoot your old man's murderer, then you ain't got what it takes for killing. Because it don't get much cleaner than that, when you're talking about reasons and . . ." He paused, thinking hard.

"Justice," Maggie said.

Chester examined a spiral-shaped blade caked with dust and pointed it at Maggie. "Justice."

Hollis was light-headed. The room was full of smoke. He was angry at himself for letting his rage simmer while they sat among the trappings of Edmund Juniper's life. He had wasted a rare moment of sharpness. Now he thought he'd be better off just giving the gun back to Chester.

His divan began to vibrate in a stuttery rhythm.

"What the hell is that?" Maggie asked.

It took Hollis a moment to realize that his transmitter was active. He pulled the dictionary from the satchel and opened it up.

Maggie peered at the machine inside the hollow. "What the hell is *that*?"

"I think it's Rob," he said.

LD IN CAPTNS QRTRS

"LD," he said. "Lucy Dakota. In captain's quarters. Why would he tell me that?" He looked from Maggie to Chester.

"Because it's a trap," Maggie suggested. "How do we get there?"

"You have to go through the bridge," Hollis said.

"There you go."

He looked at Chester, who was happily sorting the mess of tools into two piles. "Sharp and dull," he explained.

Hollis stood up and holstered the gun. "I think we can find another way."

Maggie crushed her cigarette into the floral-patterned fabric of the divan. "Wild Earp to the rescue."

THE BOOK WAS CALLED *Prince of the Cosmos*. It had arrived on Rob's seventh birthday wrapped in Dakota Aeronautics gift-shop tissue paper, a present from his father. Long after he'd forgotten the story (something about a boy and his pet star), Rob remembered the pictures of the constellations. Now, as he gazed out the viewing windows at the front of the bridge, he picked out Hydra. The storm had passed, leaving a clear, starry night in its wake. That was the good news.

The bad news was that the *Wendell Dakota* had begun to tremble. Rob had been on thirty-one airships and never felt anything quite like it. He was used to the constant hum of distant machinery, the churn of the propellers, the rattle of malfunctioning gadgetry. He had witnessed engine fires, turbine failure, and faulty smokestacks. And there was always turbulence. But this was something new: a tickle in his feet that crept into his calf muscles and was making his stomach feel queasy. As soon as the stabilization gauge had confirmed the tremor, ball-bearings quivering in the argon, his father had rushed to the librarian's side to pore over a map. They seemed to be excited. His father even put his hand on her shoulder.

Alone behind the gauge, Rob had transmitted Lucy Dakota's location to Hollis. This he had done without his father's knowledge, after deciding that his father had lost his mind. Rob didn't know what a head doctor's medical diagnosis would be, but his father's obsession with vengeance had clearly infected his brain, and Rob was the only one who could help. There were people aboard the ship who would not hesitate to kill Jefferson Castor, and others who were fanatically dedicated to helping his cause. Rob's plan fell squarely in the middle—he was going to save his father's life and get the airship back down to earth in one piece.

The plan had been inspired by the story of Hezekiah Castor's murder. Before his father had even reached the end of the family history lesson, Rob's mind had begun unspooling plot threads with a fervor he recognized from the nights he'd gulped several coffees to stay up late working on *Hunter*. Stray ideas stuck fast to one another, forming unwieldy clumps of scenes and endings.

Samuel Dakota had started it. Anybody could see that. He'd built the company on the backs of lies and death. Rightfully, it *should* be called Castor Aeronautics. Yes, Rob's father had acted criminally, but then again, the man had seen his own father shot down before his eyes. Rob didn't know much about trial law, but he figured a jury would have to take that tragedy into account. The tricky part was getting his father to give up peacefully, and that was why Rob broke transmitter silence: he needed Hollis's help.

The lynchpin of his plan was Lucy Dakota. For everything to fall into place, Rob and Hollis would have to sneak into the captain's quarters and persuade Lucy to change the name of the company. She'd also have to make Rob's father president of Castor Aeronautics, right there on the bridge, in front of Jefferson's men. Perhaps she could also proclaim his father captain of the *Wendell Dakota* for good measure. It would all be for show, of course—but if his father thought he had what he wanted, then perhaps his brain sickness would ease up just enough for him to understand that he had to take the ship back down.

Jefferson Castor would be arrested at the sky-dock—Rob had no illusions about that—but at least he would be alive. They would *all* be alive. And Rob could enlist the best lawyers and the best head doctors—

"Attention! If I could have everyone's attention, please."

His father was resting his hands on the ship's wheel in the center of the bridge. Rob moved away from the stabilization gauge to join the members of his father's crew gathered around the wheel in a loose semicircle.

"When sorrows come," his father announced gravely, "they come not single spies but in battalions."

Rob tried not to laugh. He wondered if his father had ordered someone to write him a speech. And shouldn't it be "they come not *as* single spies"? At least he'd forgotten all about banishing his son to the life-ship.

"But I say to all men"—his father raised his eyes to the table where the librarian and her assistants were ignoring him—"and women aboard this ship that if our sorrows come in battalions, our triumphs on this night shall come in legions!"

He raised his fist to a smattering of tepid applause. Rob clapped five times, loud and sharp. Behind him, someone gave a fierce rebel yell, and Rob turned to see militiamen spread out along the perimeter. He realized his mistake: Hollis and Delia would probably be shot on sight by some trigger-happy drunk. He had acted too hastily, summoning his stepbrother here. They needed a safer meeting spot, somewhere Rob could outline his plan. The conversation would also involve apologizing to Hollis for punching him—Rob didn't have any illusions about that, either.

"So," his father said, clearing his throat, "I'm told we're almost there. In just a few minutes, the world of aeronautics as we know it will cease to exist."

Rob reached inside his bag. He wondered if it was possible to tap out a message without looking. His fingers wriggled beneath the cover of the hollow dictionary.

"You are witnessing the end of one era. . . ."

His father held up a sign with the Dakota insignia printed

on it. He raised it above his head and rotated slowly so that everyone could see. Behind him, a freestanding chalkboard full of equations collapsed onto its face with a hard slap. Two mugs and a stack of papers slid off a filing cabinet. The half-raised shades along the viewing windows began to knock against the glass. Rob's vision skittered.

"And the dawning of another!"

His father flipped the sign to display a sleek letter C enclosing a ramshackle machine—Hezekiah's whiskey still, Rob realized after a moment. Several hijackers hustled back to their posts, securing unbolted chairs and stray maps. Beyond his father's Castor Aeronautics logo—still held aloft—Rob spotted fresh activity at the other end of the bridge. Up on the platform, the door to the captain's quarters was open. Lucy Dakota had emerged, unbound, and was making her way down the stairs. His father, aware of movement behind him, lowered his sign and turned. The librarian was leading a chant in a language Rob vaguely recognized as Latin. The tremors reverberated inside his body, toes to forehead. Lucy Dakota was outlined in jittery ghosts.

Before Rob fully understood what he was doing, he was striding toward the platform. Hollis was in the doorway of the captain's quarters, then at the rail, looking out across the bridge. His face and shoulders and arms were coated in dust and splinters. His shirt was lacerated. His hand was full of silver. Flanking him were two equally dirty strangers, a stocky lump of a boy and a frizzy-haired ferret of a girl. The lump held a pickax over his shoulder, the ferret a pointy shovel. Hollis raised his silver hand. *Gun.* It was pointed over Rob's head, toward the wheel.

Hollis is going to shoot my father.

He screamed his stepbrother's name and reached into his pocket. Hollis slid his gun along an invisible axis so that it was pointing at Rob, who brought his own pistol up so that Hollis's face was bisected by the sharky little sight at the tip of the barrel. For a terrible, weightless moment they were frozen like this.

The last page in *Prince of the Cosmos* had no words. It was just the boy waving good-bye to his star, which had taken its rightful place in Ursa Major. Rob had drawn a Dakota airship into the picture, a crayon outline hanging awkwardly in the night sky. Once he'd shown it to Hollis. Why had this come to him now? He had the prickly sensation that the *Wendell Dakota* was alive, that it knew something he did not and was trying to tell him something.

There was a sound like cannon fire. Had he just been shot? His feet left the ground. The cannon became a steady roaring in his ears. There was a shriek, loud and terrible. Hollis and the lump and the ferret were in the air above the platform. And then the platform ate itself, along with the railing and the door. He wondered if Lucy Dakota had ever reached his father. He wondered if he was dying or already dead.

At least it didn't hurt. It didn't feel like anything at all.

ON THE EVENING of December 31, 1899, three generations of Dakotas were together for the first and only time.

Wendell Dakota was in the accounting office of the Virginia manufacturing compound, checking the weekly report from the whiskey-sap department. He was mumbling to himself and tapping a pencil against the desk with his right hand, while his left curled around the belly of his infant son, Hollis, as he bounced the boy on his knee. He'd offered to watch the baby for the night so that his wife could accompany her friends to a formal New Year's ball in Richmond. Big fancy parties made him anxious and uncomfortable. He only attended them to prove that he wasn't a crazy recluse like his father, Samuel, who spent his days in total isolation, locked away inside his massive personal hangar in the center of the compound.

Samuel Dakota had never met his grandson and hadn't seen his son in years. Wendell knew the old man was still alive only because of the endless clanking and pounding from inside the hangar. His father had always been withdrawn and obsessive—quite different from the man profiled in *Harper's* magazine at the end of the Civil War, an article Wendell had read countless times as a boy, trying to reconcile the brooding father he knew with the dashing, cavalier war hero he *wished* he knew. Once Wendell had grown up to marry Lucy and prove himself a capable leader of Dakota Aeronautics, Samuel Dakota seemed to decide that his duties as a human being were finished and abruptly retired to his hangar.

Then the rumors started. Dakota Aeronautics was keeping Samuel's body in a top-secret ice chamber to be unfrozen in a hundred years. Samuel had leprosy. Samuel had created a weapon so dangerous it could never be used. Samuel had succeeded in breeding mutant beetles with all sorts of strange powers: speech, artistic talents, poker, and—Wendell's favorite—invisibility. At first, he had almost lost his mind trying to stop the spread of these rumors off the compound. Then, after his wife yanked yet another silver hair from his head, he decided to stop trying. Let people talk; he had bigger things to worry about. He forced himself not to care.

Wendell made sure that trays of food were slid daily through a small hole in the door, and his father slid them back when he was finished eating. That was the extent of their relationship, which explained why Wendell almost dropped his own son in shock when the door to the accounting office opened and Samuel Dakota walked in, pulled up a chair, and sat down as if it were the most natural thing in the world.

The first thing Wendell noticed was the smell. Anyone who worked closely with beetles was accustomed to the rancid odor of the gas they released after slurping up whiskey-sap. But the stench coming from his father was the tangy onion reek of someone who hadn't washed or changed his clothes in a very long time. Samuel's dirty-blond hair was much more dirty than blond, and it had twisted into a greasy clump surrounded by frizzy coils. His cheeks, mouth, chin, and neck were hidden by a thick beard, ornamented here and there with little bits of food. He wore the tattered remnants of an expensive suit, and a broken stopwatch dangled from his breast pocket.

"I'm leaving," Samuel rasped. "Wanted to say good-bye." He peeked up over the desk. "Who's the little one?"

Wendell Dakota was speechless. His father sat back in his chair. For a while they just looked at each other until Wendell managed to ask, "Where are you going, Dad?"

"I made a mistake. A bad mistake. Long time ago. Last day of the war."

"What mistake? What are you talking about?"

"Killed an innocent man."

"Well, it was a *war*, Dad. I know it wasn't pleasant, but you had to do things for the good of the Union. And you know what? That doesn't excuse—"

Wendell cut himself off. He didn't mean to sound so angry, but he couldn't help it: his father had disappeared from his life because of his guilt about the war? That was what this was all about? He continued, trying to calm down.

"Why couldn't you have told me this years ago, instead of just . . . hiding? I could've found you some help. Plenty of war veterans have nightmares and things of that nature."

Samuel shook his head. His beard shed a sandstorm of cracker crumbs. "Living on earth is the nightmare."

"Listen." Wendell had regained some of his composure. "Let's just relax. Let's first get you into a bath. I mean, what in the blue skies have you been doing in there?"

Samuel reached up to scratch his neck, and Wendell recoiled in disgust. The old man's fingernails were at least three inches long and had turned a sickly mustard color. Some of them had even begun to curl at the ends.

"I'm going to heaven," Samuel explained. "I found a way to sneak past the gates. Won't get in unless I fly there myself."

On Wendell's lap, Hollis squirmed and cried out. Wendell realized that he was clutching his son like he'd clutch the wheel of an airship in a storm. He tried to relax.

"Okay," he said calmly. "Don't do anything rash. Let's talk about this."

Samuel jumped out of his chair. "Nothing to talk about. Just saying good-bye."

"Wait!"

But Samuel turned and rushed out of the office. Wendell couldn't exactly chase him down with his newborn son in his arms. And anyway, he wasn't sure it was necessary. The old man had clearly lost it, and come tomorrow, Wendell would break into the hangar with a team of nuthouse professionals. Maybe, with the proper guidance, they could salvage their relationship and Hollis could get to know his grandfather.

Wendell Dakota told himself this, but the truth was the encounter had deeply unsettled him. He stared at the accounting ledgers; the numbers swam together. Maybe he *should* go after him right now. What was all that talk about heaven?

He sat pondering the empty chair where his father had been sitting, half convinced he had hallucinated the whole visit. After a while, Hollis began to cry, and Wendell stood up to rock him gently. He went to the window of the office and looked out across the empty testing fields of the compound. Everyone was elsewhere, celebrating the end of another year that had promised—and delivered—so much progress to mankind. He wondered what the world would be like for Hollis.

Long after Wendell's son fell asleep in his arms, he continued to stare out into the deepening Virginia night, his eyes coming to rest on the gloomy hangar that loomed over the field: Samuel Dakota's self-made prison. He sighed—and almost dropped his son once again as a terrible *CRASH* shook the office. The baby's eyes snapped open, and he resumed his shrill cry. Wendell's first thought was: *Bomb!* But then he saw something dark growing out of the roof of his father's hangar. He strained his eyes, staring in awe as the enormous shadow-thing clawed its way up into the sky. As it floated away in silhouette against the clouds, it *became* a cloud, camouflaging itself like a chameleon. But that was impossible. He blinked, and the shadow revealed itself to be an airship shaped like a long funnel. The claws he had seen were pieces of the roof splintering back as the ship crashed through. He strained his eyes to track its flight, but the night sky swallowed it up. He stood at the window for hours, seeing the shimmer of the vanished ship again and again in what always proved to be stars, until he was sure of one thing.

Samuel Dakota, the father of human flight, was never coming down.

THE SMELL DRAGGED Hollis up out of darkness. The smoke ignited a cough that racked his body. His rib cage felt poorly assembled, bone grating against bone at odd angles. He coughed again, retching violently. All at once, he was painfully, regrettably awake and alert. He was stretched out on his side, covered in dust. He lifted a broken piece of wood off his leg and examined it. Buffed and shiny. A floorboard from the promenade.

The promenade?

Hollis pushed himself to his feet and fought a brief rush of nausea. He was on the bridge. Or what was left of it. All around him, the nerve center of the ship was reduced to splinters, broken glass, and frayed wires. Borders had been dissolved, walls shifted and crushed, so that it was difficult to tell where the bridge ended and the corridors began. He had been thrown clear of the platform and suspected he was somewhere near the back of the room, which had the bombed-out feel of a condemned building, its guts exposed and helpless.

The air was filled with poisonous smoke and drifting ash—and beetles as big as his fist. He watched in slow, dreamlike fascination as a monstrous insect floated past his head. Its pincers were the length of his thumbs, its belly round and inflated to the size of a baseball. Dozens more flitted in and out of the smoke like black balloons. The smell was worse than the lift chamber; it was as if he were buried inside a pile of spoiled vegetables.

He recoiled in horror as a mutant half-beetle appeared in front of his face, its belly and rear segment completely gone. Then the rest of it blinked forth out of thin air and the beetle became whole. Hollis rubbed his itchy eyes.

What was that?

Hollis pulled his torn shirt up to cover his nose and mouth. He was aware of other people moving through the smoke; human-shaped impressions appearing, silhouettes receding. He couldn't make himself call out. The very idea of opening his mouth made him retch again.

There was a persistent high-pitched ringing. The volume felt connected to his stomach, and louder meant sicker. Covering his ears just made it worse: it was coming from inside his head.

Something big brushed against his back. He spun away, imagining a human-sized beetle, pincers squeezing his chest, jaws enveloping his face. There was a sharp pain in his heel, and he remembered, just before he lost his footing, about the ridiculous loafers. He tumbled blindly to the edge of a jagged hole in the floor. A credenza appeared to have been jammed down into it at an angle by some giant hand. Its glass doors were shattered except for one, which still sheltered a pair of sky-boots.

Right in front of his face, huge beetles were rising up out of the hole in grapelike bunches, flickering in and out of existence, floating up into the sky.

The sky?

The siren in his head forced him to close his eyes. The last thing he saw before the world went dark was an eye patch. It was lying on the floor next to him. He had seen it before. Somewhere.

MAGGIE'S HANDKERCHIEF covered her nose and mouth. She was slapping Hollis in the face and calling his name. Once he was able to hear her voice and feel her hand on his cheek, he sat up. Some of the smoke had cleared. The wreckage wasn't as bad near the viewing windows, but the floor was strewn with rubble. The stabilization gauge had disintegrated, leaving a web of thin metal crutches to support nothing but air.

Maggie helped him to his feet. The siren was piercing. She seemed to understand that real conversation would have to wait. Instead, she pointed to the switchboard, which was intact and serving as a rallying point. His mother was addressing a group of hijackers. For a moment, Hollis's relief beat back the noise in his head to a distant, muted wail. He pointed himself in the general direction of the switchboard and tried to walk. The siren returned. Pain rooted him to the floor. He swayed, and Maggie tightened her grip on his arm.

"Easy there." Her voice was trapped at the bottom of a well. "Don't worry about her. Some of those men are on our side now. Or maybe there ain't no sides anymore."

Hollis watched carefully. Behind his mother, Chester was holding a blueprint of the ship. She pointed to a spot on the floor plan, and three hijackers ran off. She was giving orders, and they were obeying.

"She's good," Maggie said. "Course, without Castor, these guys would probably follow a cow off a cliff, but still." She began to wave. "Hey! Lady! Found your kid over here!"

Maggie's face began to join her voice, slipping into a distant fog. Hollis thought he might have said something about needing to lie down. His mother was okay. Castor was gone. He could take a little rest.

"UP YOU GO, HOLLIS."

His mother's voice. He was kneeling down near the edge of the hole. He blinked the world into place. His mother was stooped, propping his body up, trying to help him to his feet. She smelled like burnt hair. Had he passed out? How long had his mother been holding him like this?

"Hollis?" Her voice was a muffled roar. She planted a

gentle kiss on his forehead. "No? Not yet, then. Okay. We'll get you some help."

He could see over her shoulder. There was Chester, talking to some passengers on the bridge. People he recognized. A woman in a frilly nightdress, a man in a trenchcoat. He was supposed to know their names.

He met his mother's eyes, imploring her to understand. *I'm sorry I let them take you away.* Was he actually forming words? *I'm sorry I ran.* He thought he might be making a strange noise, harmonizing with the wailing in his head.

". . . and you'll see that he stays right here?"

Hollis felt himself being handed off to Maggie. His mother said something else, something about a doctor, then she thanked Maggie and was gone.

"I ain't holdin' you if you're gonna be dead weight."

Hollis nodded weakly. This time his scratchy voice came out. "I can sit up."

Maggie let him down easy, until he had arranged himself cross-legged on the floor with his chin propped on his fists. Together they peered into the hole. She gave a low whistle.

"You and me and Chester were lucky. That thing didn't even come in through the bridge but it still tore it up bad."

"We *hit* something?"

"Something big. The rest of the ship can't be too pretty."

But Hollis was barely listening; he'd spied Rob's transmitter bag dangling from a broken floorboard.

"I gotta get down there," he said, fighting a wave of nausea as he lifted his head.

Maggie followed his eyes. "Nah—let him find his own way. That's how it's gotta be at a time like this."

Hollis shook his head.

"Then I'm coming too."

"Listen—" He cleared his throat. "Maggie. Listen to me." His voice was returning. "Life-ships. Ask my mother where to go. Take Chester and get in one."

She snorted. "They're for them. For the passengers."

"As of right now, you're first class, you ride with anybody. Tell my mother I said that."

"Tell her yourself."

"Maggie," Hollis said, surprised at the strength of his voice, "please go."

She regarded him with her good eye and straightened the kerchief on her head. Her eyes scanned the bridge, and after a moment, she nodded. "Deal. But you take this"— Maggie tucked the Cosgrove Immobilizer into his satchel— "so you don't have to go killin' anybody."

"Get out of here." Each word sank Hollis further into exhaustion. "I'll see you on the ground."

She grabbed him by the chin. "Don't forget about us."

Then she was gone, skirting around a barricade of fallen cabinets. Hollis slung his stepbrother's bag over his shoulder and dropped into the hole, hanging on to the ruined floor by his fingertips. With great effort, he worked his way along the edge until he was hanging above a king-size bed. Then he let go.

HE WAS SITTING UP in bed next to a toppled dresser. The state-room was a museum of things that no longer mattered: fine china, custom-tailored suits, priceless antiques. The noise in his head was a faraway drone.

He remembered that he'd been pointing a gun at Rob. They'd been pointing guns at each other.

A gang of beetles floated past. It was easier to think of them as living things when they were so big. There were parts of them he had never noticed before. Fine cilia, once microscopic, now as long as his hair. When they were gone, he climbed out of the bed. His shoulder felt heavy; he was carrying two satchels.

The gun in its holster was slouching beneath his right hipbone.

In the sitting room, Rob was bent over the sofa, holding a stocking to a nasty gash on a young woman's forehead. On the floor by his feet, another stocking was soaked in blood.

"Rob." His voice had returned to a dry whisper.

With quick-draw speed that seemed to surprise him as much as Hollis, Rob spun around, gun drawn, pointing at Hollis's chest. His face was sporting a bruise under one eye and a jagged scrape along the jaw.

Hollis was too weak and slow to do anything but display his empty hands.

"Please," was all he could say.

Rob didn't move.

The surge of fear and adrenaline turned up the noise in his head. Hollis's knees buckled, but he stayed up. Slowly, he reached across his body and removed Rob's satchel from his shoulder. He held it out as an offering.

"You forgot this. I won't tell Delia."

Rob flinched at her name. "You were going to shoot my dad."

"I swear, I wasn't. I couldn't do it." How could he possibly explain himself with a fuzzy head and the barrel of a gun two feet from his heart? "Be careful with that. Put it away."

He swatted a ghostly half-beetle from his face, hand brushing the fuzz sprouting along its pincers. The beetle glittered like crinkled aluminum and faded away. Hollis wondered if he'd gone insane. Crazy did tend to run in his family.

"Just put down the gun, Rob."

"You take yours out of that holster and throw it on the floor."

Hollis took a deep breath. "You first."

"That doesn't make any sense."

"A gigantic Christmas light of a beetle just sailed by, Rob. Then it *disappeared*. And that woman's bleeding. Shooting me's not helping anyone."

In his hand, Rob still held the stocking. He glanced at it, then over at the pistol. "My dad gave this to me." He shook his head and looked blankly at Hollis. "My dad gave me a gun." He laughed. "We really have no idea what's going on in our parents' heads, do we?"

Hollis thought of his father. If only they could have had one more year together, or two, or three. He'd have asked his father why he never replaced the old, rickety spectacles that always slid down his nose. He'd ask all sorts of things about airship design and Samuel Dakota. And he'd write the answers down so he could keep his father's words forever. *Swear.* Hollis thought of his mother, who had married Jefferson Castor, of all people. Why? Simply because he'd been nice to her? Because he'd been so helpful when she suddenly found herself alone? Rob was right, it was impossible to really know.

"Your dad wore those yellow suspenders that one time," Hollis said. "With the birds on them. Just that one time. Then it was back to pinstripes."

The lights flickered. Hollis braced himself for the plunge into darkness, but they came back on. Rob put the gun in his pocket and took the satchel from Hollis's outstretched hand.

Hollis's vision swam. He was dizzy with relief. Behind Rob, the woman was saying something about girls. Over and over again: "my girls."

Hollis tried to calm her down while Rob wiped her forehead.

"She needs water," Rob was saying. "We have to find some water."

The bathroom wall was gone. Inside, a porcelain tub had been reduced to what looked like a pile of broken plates. Then he forgot why he had come in here in the first place. The man was lying facedown, wearing his dressing gown and clutching a toothbrush. His eyes were open.

Dr. Wellspring, Hollis thought. Then he found himself very close to an eye, a mustache, a spot of blood in the corner of a mouth.

THE LITTLE GIRL slung over Hollis's shoulder twisted the tail of her toy pig. *Pop goes the weasel.*

She felt heavier than a skinny six-year-old should be. He was in no shape to be carrying anyone, but they didn't have a choice. This particular first-class corridor had been lined with Ming Dynasty showpieces encased in glass; now the carpet was full of shards.

"Junie?"

"My name is Jessie."

"I'm Junie!" said the girl Rob was carrying.

They were in a single-file procession. Mrs. Wellspring, the stocking wrapped around her forehead, shuffled numbly between Hollis and Jessie, Rob and Junie.

"You're going on a little ride, okay? You and your sister and your mother. And you have to be brave."

"I am brave. Are we going to crash?"

"This ship can't crash," her sister said. "Don't you know anything?"

They turned a corner. A pair of Pekingese bounded past their legs, wild-eyed and panting. An overturned mattress leaned against the wall. A man with an attaché case at his feet was straightening his tie in a crooked mirror. The tinny chime of a music box playing "Airship to Paradise" drifted out of an open stateroom door. Hollis peeked in. Empty.

"We're almost there, Mrs. Wellspring," Hollis said, even though she hadn't said anything at all.

In front of the life-ship hatch on the port side of the first-class deck, they bumped into an angry mob. The old man Rob had dubbed Swallowtail Ovaltine was brandishing his cane like a sword, standing before the open hatch. A few men had formed a rough line, just out of his range. The air was tinged with menace—they were getting ready to rush him.

"You men stand down!" Ovaltine said. "God almighty, is there not a gentleman among you?"

"My wife and children are not boarding that ship without me," said a man in a bowler with a boy at his side—the master magician.

"Then you are a coward, sir!" the old man yelled. He swung his cane back and forth. "You're all cowards!"

"Why should we split up our families?" another man shouted back. "I don't see anybody here giving orders."

"It's not supposed to crash!" whined the magician. "You said it can't, Daddy!"

"For God's sake, man, shut that boy up."

"Well, he's right, isn't he? Ten to one, this airship is the safest place to be right now."

"I'd rather be in here than out flying in one of these flimsy air boats."

Everybody was screaming at once. Irate fingers poked the air. In Hollis's arms, Jessie began to cry. He looked at Rob.

He sympathized with the crowd—why *should* families have to split up? Everybody knew the rule—women and children first—but how rigidly was it supposed to be enforced? And who was going to enforce it?

While he was turning it over in his mind, Rob calmly handed Junie to her mother. He pulled out his pistol and fired a shot directly into the wall next to the hatch. The report was deafening. Instantly, the corridor was silent. Fearful eyes were trained on Hollis and Rob.

"General Ovaltine's got it right," Rob said. There was a confused murmuring. "Women and children first. Can anybody here fly a life-ship? All you really have to do is keep it from hitting something."

"I was in the army," volunteered a man wearing three jackets and holding two suitcases.

Hollis wanted to speak up—people were beginning to recognize him—but the pistol shot was echoing in his brain. The edges of his vision were hazy. His forehead felt very warm.

"If you men . . . ," he began. Rob, seeing him falter, took Jessie and lowered her gently to the floor, where she wrapped her arms around her mother's leg. "If you want to make yourselves useful, you're needed at the other hatches. Some of you head starboard—there are more ships over there. Help where you can," he implored. "Please."

Most of the men, thoroughly shamed, dispersed. Hollis leaned against the wall as Rob helped the three Wellsprings through the hatch and into the canvas-topped ship. He noticed Rob was shaking with exertion. The eerie poise that had compelled him to fire his gun had deserted him. Hollis realized that there was nothing to stop those men from simply climbing aboard a different life-ship.

"I know that," Rob said as they moved to the next hatch, and Hollis realized he must have spoken aloud. Rob was running, Hollis was struggling to keep up. "I know that, but what else are we supposed to do?"

CLARISSA JUNIPER refused to leave Edmund's side.

The plush expanse of the Junipers' stateroom carpet was soaked in alcohol. Evidently they had set up miniature drink-mixing stations throughout the vast Presidential Suite, most of which were now in ruins. The couple had also piled the cushions from half a dozen scattered sofas into a cozy nest, which is where Hollis and Rob discovered them.

"I advise you to get to a life-ship," Hollis said wearily. It was difficult to muster any urgency for people who were obviously not going anywhere.

"I appreciate the suggestion, young Master Dakota." Clarissa Juniper poured herself another martini from a shaker and offered one to Rob, who declined.

"I only drink hot lemonade."

She shrugged and topped off her husband's glass.

"Let no one accuse Edmund Juniper of failing to play the man's game to the very end," Edmund said, winking at Hollis and adding olives to a toothpick.

"Man's game?" Hollis asked Rob, heading back to the

stateroom door. The whole incident was making him feel feverish, and he was eager to be moving along.

"Gentleman's game, I think he means," Rob said. "Honor, or courage, or something like that."

As they left the Junipers behind, Hollis could hear Edmund calling after them. "If you happen to pass this way again, we've just run out of olives!"

HOLLIS WAS STARTING to feel better. The ringing had receded to a distant ping. He showed Annabel and Arthur Reynolds how to fasten their belts and was about to discharge life-ship twenty-six when something underneath the seat caught his attention.

It was a woman's bonnet pulled low over a hairy face.

"Get out of there, sir."

"I will not."

"Women and children first," Hollis said. It came out like a sigh. The phrase didn't even sound like English to him, he'd been repeating it so often.

"I will be frank with you—I am very frightened."

"So is everyone else."

"But you see," pleaded the face beneath the seat, "I'm convinced there won't be enough life-ships left over for the men."

"There are seats for every passenger. What kind of air-ship company do you think this is? You just have to wait, that's all."

"Then I'm afraid you'll have to drag me out."

Hollis turned to Rob, who shrugged. "I don't think we should argue with one of the greatest writers in the world."

"Thank you!" said the man, crawling up from his hiding place and removing the bonnet, shaking hands with the women and children who filled the boat. "Julius Germain. Pleased to make your acquaintance."

Hollis turned away. Were all novelists such frightful cowards?

THE SECOND-CLASS TAVERNS WERE FULL.

"Sylvia," a man was slurring, "uncrashable. Un. Crash. A. Bull. Have another drink and get hold of yourself."

Hollis and Rob were creeping toward the epicenter of the damage. The Automat had gone dark; the promenade was strewn with crusts, the floor painted in splatters of cherry filling and applesauce. They moved cautiously through a crispy sea of broken glass.

The men came out of nowhere, dark shapes at the edge of a dust cloud, then Hollis and Rob were among them. Hollis recognized many of the bruised, battered faces as Dakota officers. Stripped of their uniforms during the hijacking, some had assembled ragtag outfits. Others remained in their underclothes.

Hollis's relief flooded his body. He was exhausted, but much stronger. He gave the nearest man, Officer Fitzroy, a hug.

"We need your help," Hollis said.

"Up in first class—" Rob began, but Hollis cut him off. Maggie had asked him not to forget.

"Get to the steerage hold," he said. "Every passenger gets on a ship."

The men vanished so fast, Hollis wondered if they had really been there at all.

ROB WAS PULLING ON HIS ARM.

"Get up."

"I just need to rest for another minute," Hollis said. "I keep thinking about—I mean, she's Delia, so she's probably okay, but still. I wish we'd run into her."

"Me too. But right now we have to find my father."

Hollis couldn't look at his stepbrother. He focused on a rag doll lying next to his foot. "That's not what we're doing."

The collision had turned this part of third class into a maze of twisted nails and knotted beams. Rob examined a clock without hands and tossed it aside. "Well, that's what I'm doing, Hollis. I'm sure you can understand why it might be important to me."

Hollis felt something sharp and hot behind his eyes. He jumped to his feet. "Why, because mine's already gone?"

Rob looked away. "I didn't mean it like that."

"He's gone because your dad had him killed."

Rob put both hands atop his head, like he was opening up his lungs after running a mile. "That's a lie," he said. He dropped his hands and made fists, then put them in his pockets. "You don't have any proof of that. Your dad fell by accident. The medical examiner said so." Hollis could see the outline of the gun in his jacket.

"Marius pushed him. He was working for your dad." Hollis felt strangely deflated, sharing this with his stepbrother. He ought to feel righteous, he thought. Triumphant.

"Listen, Hollis," Rob said. "Your grandfather Samuel killed my grandfather Hezekiah."

Hollis had never heard that name in his life. "Your father's father?"

"One and the same."

Was that supposed to compare with Jefferson Castor having his father killed? That felt like an open wound. Rob's accusation felt like gossip about two strangers in a newspaper article from before he was born. "Are you sure?"

Rob sniffed the air. "You smell that? It's coming from down here." He turned and dropped down behind a massacred sofa.

"Hey, it's not the same thing, you know," Hollis said, following his stepbrother. "Don't just change the subject. Who cares if—ow!" Hollis snagged his shirt on a splinter the size of a penknife and felt the quick heat of a scratch on his upper arm. He joined Rob in a nest of rubble. They both moved very slowly—the third-class furniture had been reduced to kindling.

"That's bad, right?" Rob pulled his shirt up over his nose.

"Smells like . . . I don't know," Hollis said. "Beetles and

something worse." It was as if the pungent beetle gas had been laced with the ammonia the maids used to clean the crystal chandeliers. Then Rob let out a yelp and pointed at their feet.

Hollis and Rob were standing on empty air. The floor *felt* solid and metallic, but it seemed to be made of nothing at all. Hollis knelt and pounded his fist against the void that somehow supported their weight. A hollow echo died away beneath him. When he lifted his hand and unclenched his fist, he found that his pinky was gone.

"Gah!" Frantically, he rubbed at the missing digit, which was coated in a viscous liquid. When he smeared it against his thigh, his pinky reappeared, but the liquid painted an instant see-through path along his pant leg.

Rob knelt, pressed his palm flat against the solid air, and began to wipe back and forth as if he were dusting a table-top. The invisible coating rubbed off, and Rob's hand began to fade like the mutant beetles. Hollis joined him, and soon they had uncovered a patch of rusted metal decorated with a painting of a huge beetle: the insignia of Dakota Aeronautics.

Hollis leaned forward. Something was nagging at him. One of the old family myths his father used to share over an after-dinner brandy.

"That's impossible," Hollis said.

"You're seeing this too, right? The thing we can't see?"

"No, Rob, listen. After Samuel disappeared, there were all these rumors. My dad knew every one of them. They were just stories he used to tell me for fun."

"So what are you saying?"

"I'm saying I think we just found Samuel Dakota."

"Looks like *he* found *us*."

They worked their way across the surface, ducking beneath floorboards, pushing aside debris that had fallen all the way down from first class—unopened lavender soaps, broken martini glasses, fountain pens. Eventually they came to an opening into the interior. Next to it was a thin-fingered hand. Hollis's heart skipped. There was a tiny corrupted beetle tattooed between the first and second knuckles of the ring finger. The body was mostly hidden beneath a fallen trunk plastered with faded stickers from European capitals. Hollis wondered if it was the strange woman from the bridge. He reached to check for a pulse.

The unmistakable sound of a human voice drifted up out of the opening.

"Dad!" Rob said. The voice stopped. Rob swung his legs over the side.

THE FIRST TIME Delia had ever set foot inside the lift chamber of an airship, Benny Owens had personally shown her around.

"Watch your head. It can get a bit cramped down here."

The chamber was small and low-ceilinged—the airship *Hyacinth* was a swift cruiser—and he seemed to forget that Delia (not being a three-hundred-pound man) could move quite easily between the beams. He also seemed to be immune to the horrible smell. She tried not to gag in front of her new boss, but every time she opened her mouth, the stench invaded her throat. She could barely speak and was afraid she might be coming off as meek or dull-witted.

"This is what we call the farm," he explained, thick fingers wrapped around the handle of a door to a cylindrical tank in the center of the chamber. She was waiting for him to open it, eager to see what was inside, when she noticed him glaring off to the right. She followed his gaze—toward what? There were workers manning compartments, measuring out whiskey-sap with flasks and beakers. There was a path at the edge of the chamber, mostly used for extra storage space. Then she saw them: two boys, ducking down behind a massive crate. Hidden from the keepers directly in front of them, but exposed at an angle.

Benny grumbled to himself and stalked off in their direction. Delia wasn't sure what to do, so she followed him.

"Get out from behind there!" he said. The boys jumped up. The taller one with the peaked cap put his hands in the air in mock-surrender. The shorter one kept shifting his weight like his bladder was about to burst.

Benny chewed them out: the lift chamber was a sacred place (he actually said the word *sacred*), and they were profaning it with their tourism. A fleck of spittle landed on the shorter boy's lapel, and Delia could tell he was trying not to look at it. The other boy started laughing. Benny ignored him and glared at the shorter boy.

"Just because your last name's Dakota doesn't give you the right to trample my authority. I'll talk to your mother again if I have to. Now, get out of my sight."

"Who are you?" the taller one asked her.

Delia, flustered, opened her mouth and immediately began coughing.

"What?" Benny said. "Oh. This is Delia, my new apprentice."

"Welcome aboard," the boy said as Benny's hand on her back ushered her away. "I'm Rob, and this is Hollis. I'm sure we'll see you again."

"You won't," Owens said. Then, to Delia, "Don't let them bother you. Damn kids think they run the place. We do real work down here."

"The whole ship doesn't smell like this!" Rob called after her. When Owens turned, displaying his fist, beetle ring flashing, they were already gone.

Delia let her mind crawl through this memory, probing its shadowy edges like a tongue scraping along teeth. There was nothing else but the theater of the past.

She was trapped in a floating tomb.

Thinking about rescue was a pointless indulgence. Even if the Dakotas won the ship from the hijackers, even if life-ships were launched, even if the airship didn't simply fall from the sky, it would take days for anyone to sift through the wreckage to find her. She might as well be stuck in a collapsing building during the San Francisco earthquake.

She had just been caught by the man with the ivory pistols when the ship began to tremble like a terrified kitten. The chanting of the Order had taken on a wanton, gleeful edge. She'd used the distraction to dart away.

Everywhere, compartments were unmanned, left open for beetles to escape. Even Delia caught a hint of the odor. She began kicking them shut. Then there was a hand on her arm; a joyful, vacant expression on a familiar face.

"Sister! Pray with me!"

Ada pulled her down to her knees. Delia shrugged the woman off, spun away. The bucking of the ship made it difficult to stand. She reached out and clung to part of the spider. Gunshots echoed through the chamber. A pair of beetles alighted on a nozzle. They slurped whiskey-sap and floated toward her face. She began whispering to them, changing her voice to the timbre they responded to in her experiments. It didn't matter what she said, so she took Ada's suggestion.

Holy Mary, Mother of God . . .

If St. Albert could see her now. The pair of beetles floated away. What had she been thinking? She didn't know how to ask them for help. They couldn't empathize with her situation. They joined several dozen of their kind and disappeared into the spider's limbs above her head.

Then she'd hugged her piece of the spider and shut her eyes as a noise like an exploding bomb made her cry out. The structure of the chamber came undone around her. The variety of terrible sounds was infinite: screeching metal, cracking beams, breaking glass. Curiously, some came out of her past: the bells of St. Theresa's tolling the hour, Maggie's quick feet on the fire escape, the crackling of the transmitter. Perhaps this was dying: everything all at the same time.

It was dark. She was curled up, knees pressed against her forehead, her body a compact little bundle. The air was putrid, close, and full of choking dust. There were screams, faraway pleas for help. She heard them through miles of broken spider limbs, twisted catwalks, and shattered decks.

She didn't know how badly she'd been hurt. The space was too confined to test her arms and legs. She wondered if the air down here was even breathable. Her body felt like one big bruise. There was no sharp, searing pain. She took that as a good sign.

All she could do was think.

Those fanatics from the Order of the First Beetle had somehow been right all along. What else but Samuel's ship could the *Wendell Dakota* have struck so high in the sky? How wonderful it would be to set foot in that long-lost airship, to sift through the obsessions that had consumed the father of flight.

She was dwelling on this when the voices nearby began to multiply. They seemed to be chirping. Another Order ritual? A gentle breeze stirred the air in her little pocket of rubble. She wasn't alone in here—beetles were drifting through the air pockets of the wreckage as if it were a giant anthill.

She felt the tickle of tiny feet, the barely there shuffle of insects on her arms and neck. Perhaps, like cockroaches, the beetles were an indestructible species, tenacious enough to exist long after the last humans had died out. It was easy to imagine them skittering through rubble like this a million years from now.

It wasn't an Order ritual. The beetles were chirping and

buzzing. They had always been silent before. She whispered to them.

Our Father, who art in heaven . . .

The airship keened, shot through with an eerie deep-sea moan. Tremors shook the chamber; a fresh set of screams rippled around her.

She couldn't keep track of time—minutes, hours, days—so she counted the beetles as they crawled across her skin. She was nothing but a piece of rubble to them.

When the ship began its tilt, she thought she was free. But all it did was rotate her so that she was facedown. She thought about what it would be like to get crushed; snapping spine, shattering vertebrae. Best to get it over with quickly.

Beetle fuzz tickled her lips; they were crawling on her face. She felt the new sound before she heard it—a murky tearing away, high above, descending. Familiar things were growing ever closer. The commotion of a Saturday night in Hell's Kitchen, the dinner stampede in the dining hall at St. Theresa's, Maggie and Delia slapping down trays together. The patter of Hollis and Rob in the dormitory hall, knocking at her door.

Voices chimed in from all over: *I love you.*

There were cracks in the hull. A seam had formed. If cutting the lines had destroyed the brain of the *Wendell Dakota*, the collision had claimed its body. Beetles chirped.

This is what we call the farm.

Back in her dorm room, Hollis was bringing her spare parts for a new electrical project. Rob was reading on her bed. An errant beetle carried a pair of pliers across her ceiling. On the *Hyacinth*, Benny Owens was welcoming a new apprentice. Soon she'd be a full-fledged member of the crew. A girl from Hell's Kitchen, a nobody, an accidental delinquent. Changing the world.

Only the cold knot in her stomach told her it was not real; would never be. The hull panels popped their rivets, millions of metal bolts flung out into the sky to fall like hailstones. It was so loud that she no longer heard anything at all.

Delia saw herself as the girl she had been, watching Maggie's uncle examine a telegraph key. His left pinky had been fused to his palm, so his hand was perpetually claw-shaped. And yet the movements of his good fingers were graceful and precise as they revealed to her the secrets of wires and circuits and fuses. He held the telegraph key in his gnarled hand and invited her to give it a tap.

The silence was a miracle; a gorgeous hush as the ship tore itself in two. She was freer than she'd ever been. There were millions of stars, and she was among them.

"WAIT,**" HOLLIS SAID.** "You don't know how far you're going
to"—Rob vaulted into the darkness—"drop."

Hollis peered after him.

"It's okay!" Rob called a moment later.

Hollis jumped inside and landed in a pile of papers and
books. The air was musty and stale. There was an under-
current of beetle gas. A shaft of light from above illumi-
nated a study strewn with leather-bound volumes. Yellowed
newspapers from the last century were tied in luggage-
sized bundles. Test tubes and flasks poked up through the
mess. A long aquarium, somehow intact, contained three
fat, oversized beetles attached by pipes to a spigot, out of
which dripped the stuff that had coated the ship. A pool of
empty air had formed beneath the aquarium, carving out
invisible rivers between the mountains of books.

"This is bananas," Hollis said. "He was up here in the sky this whole time."

"If this isn't real," Rob said, "then at least we know we're *both* crazy."

Hollis nudged an empty beetle husk with his toe. Had they been molting up here? Shedding one skin for another? He followed Rob through the study, down a passageway decorated with whorls of ink and pencil scribblings; notes and formulas that seemed to curl inward and end where they began. Hollis scanned the homespun ramblings of a man with nothing but time and solitude. The passage was lined with eleven numbered doors, five on each side and one straight ahead. Hollis opened the first one and flung it shut after a quick peek inside. He steadied himself against the wall, breathing hard.

"I think we died," he said. Rob turned to face him. "And this is hell."

Rob eyed the door. Hollis's hand was still gripping the latch. "Let me see in there."

Hollis shook his head.

Gently, Rob curled his hand around Hollis's and pried his fingers from the latch. Then he steadied himself and opened the door. The walls inside the little room were a coral reef of shiny jet-black undulation. The air was dense with hovering beetles. Sitting in a nest of husks in the far corner was a bloated insect the size of a puppy. It was propped upright by an exoskeleton that left its soft underbelly exposed. Pincers as long as Rob's forearm moved at a steady pace, scooping smaller beetles into its wrinkled, fuzzy mouthparts.

Rob slammed the door.

Hollis retched. A long-fermenting odor had been released into the passage.

"Cannibals," Rob said. "Keeping themselves alive."

"They've never done that before," Hollis pointed out. "Samuel must have—no, please don't—"

Too late. Rob opened the next door and two stuck-together beetles tumbled out past his head. He slammed it shut before Hollis could see inside.

Rob stood very still, gathering himself. "Mating," he said quietly.

"I don't think we should open the other ones."

At the end of the hall they were left with no choice. Jefferson Castor was speaking to someone behind the eleventh and final door. Rob put his hand on the doorknob, paused, then turned to face Hollis, blocking his way.

"Leave your pistol out here."

"Don't worry, I'm not gonna use it. I don't think I can."

"Then throw it inside one of these rooms."

"I bet your dad has a gun in there."

"You don't think Samuel does too?"

Hollis did a quick age calculation. He supposed his grandfather could still be alive. Besides, who else was Castor talking to? Hollis imagined walking into a standoff. Three generations of Dakotas and Castors, armed and resentful, together at last. Decrepit old Samuel, who had vanished into the sky when Hollis was a baby. Jefferson Castor in his suit. Hollis and Rob, after what they'd just seen in the corridors of the ship. After what they'd done. Together.

"Okay," he said. "We both do it."

Rob pulled his pistol from his pocket and turned to face the fifth door. "Agreed." Hollis sidled up next to him.

"Same time," Rob said.

He slammed his hand down on the latch and opened the door, leaving just enough room for them to toss their guns through the sliver of space. The room felt as hot as an oven on his fingers. Then Rob shut the door. Hollis unbuckled the holster and hung the sagging leather belt from the latch.

"You dropped this!" they heard Jefferson Castor say. Alarmed, Rob pushed open the eleventh door and Hollis rushed through behind him. The air was thick with fireflies, and the overturned furniture cast eerie shadows. Jefferson Castor was hunched over a broken desk. "I brought it back to you," he said. Hollis and Rob exchanged a glance: Castor was holding a grinning human skull, jamming an empty money clip into its mouth between broken teeth.

"Time to go now, Dad," Rob said gently.

Castor turned and smiled sadly at his son. "Not until he says he's sorry. I think I'm owed at least that much."

Rob looked at the skull and swallowed hard. Hollis marveled at the fact that in reality, skulls were just as scary as you'd think they'd be. He wondered how long Samuel had been rotting up here in his invisible crypt, outlived by his experiments.

"Samuel and I have much to discuss," Jefferson said.

"You're talking to a *skull*, dad."

A violent shiver rocked Samuel's ship. Hollis crashed against the side of a dresser. Fireflies scattered angrily. Jefferson tossed the skull aside and knelt to pull his son in close. Hollis was an arm's length away from the thinning hair at the back of Castor's head. He saw Marius's hands slamming into his father's back, the rail giving way. If he still had his gun, it would be impossible to miss from this distance. Rob would be covered in his father's blood. And what then? Hollis looked away. His eyes settled on the upside-down skull, resting against a broken lamp, ruined mouth flashing silver. He thought of his mother, coordinating the rescue effort from the bridge. She was still up there. He was sure of it. She wouldn't leave until all the life-ships had been filled. Or until the *Wendell Dakota* simply fell apart and sent them all spinning down to earth.

"I want to tell you something." Jefferson gripped Rob's face and looked him in the eyes.

"Stop!" Rob pleaded. "Just come on."

"You're better than I ever was."

Rob wrenched himself free from his father and backed away. In one motion, Hollis pulled the immobilizer from his satchel, sprang forward, pulled the trigger, and slammed the tiny bolt of lightning into Jefferson Castor's neck.

"*What are you doing?*" Rob screamed, wrenching the weapon from Hollis's hand.

"Knocking him out," Hollis said as Castor slumped

against the desk. "He'll be okay. Help me figure out if this thing still flies."

"I don't care if it still flies!" Rob said, jabbing toward Hollis with the immobilizer as if it were a knife. "Look at him! He looks *dead*."

"I know, but trust me, Delia said—"

"Oh, *Delia* said? One time she told me she had eleven toes."

"Have you ever seen her toes?"

Rob grabbed his father's wrist, checking for a pulse. Hollis moved through a constellation of fireflies into the next room. A single torn chair leaked canary-colored fluff. A table, slanted at an angle toward the chair, had been rigged with a mismatched assortment of levers made out of rifle barrels, lead pipes, baseball bats, scrap metal wrapped in dirty fabric. Fraying rope that had been fortified with twine stretched from the table to an installation of gears housed in a tin box the size of a makeshift shelter. Above the box, an oval window looked out upon a jumble of furniture.

"Dad!" Rob said in the other room. "Wake up!"

A plaid sofa was crushed against the window, a spidery hairline crack where its nubby leg met the glass. Hollis recognized the upholstery: third-class smoking room. He placed his hands on one of the rifle barrels, then changed his mind and selected a baseball bat. He pulled it toward him. One of the ropes stretched taut. The gearbox shook. There was a noise like a frothy waterfall in another part of the ship.

"What did you do?" Rob yelled.

Hollis ignored him and pulled another lever. The ship lurched. The sofa fell away from the window. He pulled two more. Hollow spaces in the hull crawled with activity, as if Samuel's ship was infested with rats and termites. The shuddering sent him into the softness of the chair. Through the window, he watched the wreckage of third class disappear. Floorboards brushed against the glass like the branches of a tree. As if he were riding on an elevator with the doors open, Hollis counted the decks as they went by, quickly noting landmarks among the décor. There was a mechanical horse on its side, a monogrammed tablecloth from Café Pembroke, a lady's hatbox. He kept track of the levers he'd thrown, and when he spotted a smashed crystal decanter set and a rolltop writing desk, he pushed the levers back into place.

Rob appeared next to him. "He's alive."

"Can you hold the ship here? I'm going after my mother."

"She's gotta be on the ground already."

"No." Hollis pushed himself up. Stuffing clung to the seat of his pants. "She'll go down with the ship if I don't drag her off the bridge."

Rob stood in the doorway. His lids were heavy. The cut on his jaw had started to bleed again. "The great uncrashable *Wendell Dakota*," he said.

Hollis shoved past his stepbrother. Jefferson Castor was still propped against the desk, fireflies swarming about his closed eyes.

"Hey," Rob said, "how am I supposed to control this thing?"

"I don't know. If it starts to fly away, pull some levers," Hollis said. "Do whatever you have to do to keep it here until I come back."

Rob was chewing on his lip, watching his slumped, motionless father.

"Look at me, Rob. This whole Castor-Dakota thing can end with us." Hollis stuck out his hand. "Deal?"

After a moment, Rob took it. "I'll be here. Hurry up."

HOLLIS CLIMBED UP out of Samuel's ship on a pile of books. Once he was back in first class, getting to the bridge was a downhill slide. The bow had sunk in the sky, as if the weight of the main propeller had finally become too much for the weary *Wendell Dakota* to bear.

The corridors weren't as empty as Hollis had hoped. Near his own stateroom, he skidded past stragglers, groups of boisterous passengers who refused to believe in the ship's crashability. Or else they were simply accepting their fate with cheery resignation. Either way, this involved hoisting drinks and making toasts.

"Head for the life-ships!" Hollis implored, running past. He was almost to the bridge. Those passengers would just have to take care of themselves. He was done herding people who didn't want to be herded. Maggie's words came to him: *That's how it's gotta be at a time like this.*

As if this thought had summoned her, she came bursting out of a skeletal doorframe, Lucy and Chester in tow.

"Hey!" He waved his arms. The carpet between them was littered with the contents of a wardrobe, gowns and under-garments dragged from a closet, then left behind. He short-ened his steps to keep from pitching forward. With a plaintive wail, the bow creaked lower in the sky. The tormented sound made Hollis feel like the airship was actually in pain. His foot got caught in a lacy slip, and he kicked it free. The electric lanterns blinked once, twice—and stayed lit. Which meant that furnace men were still shoveling coal. *Dead men*, he thought. *Keeping the lights on.*

"Hollis!" cried his mother. She was working her way up the tilted hallway, elbows bent, arms moving like a toy figurine. Chester had a bloody bandage wrapped around his wrist. His sleeve was shredded. Maggie's handkerchief was gone, letting her snarled hair free. Hollis was hurtling toward them so fast he practically bowled them over. He scrambled to change direction, fingertips hitting the floor for balance. Then he was running up the incline alongside them.

"I'm fine," he assured his mother before she could say a word, "and I've got a way out. You're never gonna believe what—"

"I thought I'd lost you!" She reached for his hand and managed to give it a single squeeze.

"I'm sorry, but——"

"There may be a collapsible remaining up top. Find a way to get to the sundeck."

"No, just follow me, forget the sundeck—wait, what about you?"

"My place is here on the airship. There are rules about this sort of thing."

"I found something that changes the rules."

Crazed laughter echoed from a stateroom. A dog howled; another joined in.

"Run faster," Maggie said.

"I told you to get out of here," he said to Maggie. "You should be in a life-ship."

"Margaret and Chester saved my life," his mother said. "Some of the men from this absurd militia refused to stand down."

Hollis glanced at Chester's wrist. A deep laceration snaked out from beneath the bandage. His exposed shoulder was leaking blood from a puncture wound. Hugging them all right now would be a mistake, but Hollis almost couldn't help himself. Chester was wheezing. Hollis caught a glimpse of scar tissue above Chester's wound; an old injury right next to the new one.

"We're not going to the sundeck," Hollis said firmly. "I'm getting us all out of here right now."

A cold gust of air slammed into them. First class had become drafty. When the lanterns finally went out, they were crawling up the steep floor. Ahead, the end of the canted hallway looked like film of a starry night projected on a screen. Hollis couldn't make sense of the angle.

The bow of the ship was plunging downward, faster and faster. They were scrabbling at the carpet, trying to bury their fingers in its plush threads.

Above them was nothing but sky.

They climbed the last few vertical feet and clung to protruding wreckage; nail-studded boards and iron girders, once laid flat supporting the first-class deck, now poking up into the night. Hollis and his mother held on with both hands. Maggie scrambled onto a perch of torn carpet and wood. Chester dangled, his one good arm wrapped around a board. Below their feet, the hallway had become a vertical shaft. Furniture crashed against the stateroom door that had once marked the end of the hall but now served as the floor. Hollis couldn't see very much of this because it was dark at the bottom, but he could hear the tumult of mirrors, paintings, end tables, and ottomans.

The *Wendell Dakota* had cracked like an egg, splitting amidships, and the two halves were floating side by side, upended.

As they peered over the rim, a vast cross-section of the decks lay before them. It was like gazing across the top of a moonlit labyrinth. Hollis picked out the flat line of the second-class deck. If the wind weren't whipping around, he could have walked along the paths created by the exposed, severed interior.

In its death throes, the dark ship was silent.

Hollis searched the skies for shimmering negative space, an impossibly airborne collection of rubble, *anything* that might be Samuel's ship. Even if it had been knocked around by the split, Rob should have figured out a way to keep it hovering nearby. Hollis had made it work, and his stepbrother was even better at things like that. Had he accidentally rehidden the ship when he'd pulled those levers?

"Hollis," his mother said. The rest of her words were lost to the wind. A cloud covered the moon, and her face retreated into shadow.

"It'll be here," Hollis yelled. "It's a ship. Nobody let go."

His body was so heavy. Fatigue was a soothing voice telling him to relax his grip. His toes kept digging into the carpet. The moon came back, and his mother's eyes were spectral pools.

"There!" Maggie yelled.

A creature was picking its way, squidlike, along the decks of the cross-sectioned ship. It was coming toward them. Not really touching the decks, Hollis realized as it approached, but floating, just barely. There was a hitch in its movement, a tremulous hesitation as if it were just learning how to be mobile.

It wasn't until it was almost on top of them that Hollis figured out he was looking at one of the spiders from the lift chambers. The machine was shedding parts, damaged beyond repair, but it was propped up in the air by swarms of beetles. Chester began to cough. Nozzled fingers descended all around them, then legs of wire and wood. Hollis was struck by the pungent gas. The stars were eclipsed by the unwieldy willow-tree of a machine. Back in the chamber Hollis had listened to its rhythmic hisses and clanks. Now it was chirping. His mother, Maggie, and Chester disappeared as it twined around them.

"Get on!" cried a familiar voice.

"Delia?"

He caught a glimpse of her sitting astride one of the legs, just in front of the shattered bubble. Surrounded on all sides by the many-limbed spider teeming with beetles, he let go of the ship one hand at a time and transferred his grip to the machine. He closed his eyes and felt his body ascend.

THE LANDING PLATFORMS at the Washington, D.C. Sky-
dock were tiered gardens bursting with cherry blos-
soms. Rows of tall iron lamps in the shape of trees lit the
docks, painting the undersides of incoming life-ships with a
pale glow. Fifty-three crossed the sky from the floating wreck
of the *Wendell Dakota* to the dock under their own power.
Twenty-six drifted. Four collided in the dark. One crashed
into the Potomac. Emergency crewmen, summoned from
their beds, launched sky-canoes at stranded ships. Hysteria
reigned. It was not a cold night, but rescued passengers huddled under blankets, crowding the cones of light beneath
the lamps. They had had enough of the dark. They sipped
cocoa and coffee and tea until it ran out and more had to be
trucked in from a warehouse in Bethesda. A few glittering

women were laden with as many jewels and family heirlooms as they could fit on their bodies. Lone, furtive men clutched rescued cashboxes. Others smoked cigars and chatted. What a story! Some had escaped in their pajamas. As the night wore on, families were reunited, or they weren't.

A photographer for the *Evening Star* happened to catch the stupendous arrival of what appeared to be a cluster of driftwood and machine parts. By the time his camera was ready, crewmen had aimed the sky-dock's beacons at the ungainly thing. Spotlights played along a thicket of beetles. Someone said it was a spider. The photographer thought it looked more like a family of squid dragging scarves of seaweed and kelp through the air. One man was in favor of shooting it. Crewmen cleared a landing platform as best they could. It was coming in fast. Like a nervous soldier in a trench, the photographer waited until the last possible moment to trigger his flashbulb. The spider was almost upon him, its finger-tubes dragging across the dock, when he captured the image that would win him the 1912 Thayer Prize: a girl in a tattered dress clinging to one of the legs, her hands lost among the beetles, eyes shut tight against the flash. He was so intent on getting another picture of her that he missed the four others disembarking from their hidden berths.

A freelance reporter recognized one of them as Lucy Dakota, and it wasn't long before his colleagues picked up the scent. The night galloped along in a frenzy of questions and photographs. She gave statement after weary statement to reporters. Around four in the morning, when government aviation inspectors finished hauling off hijackers—and a number of steerage passengers who weren't hijackers—she had to tell the whole story again from the beginning. Of the spider's other mysterious passengers, the big lug of a boy was seen to immediately, as his wounds were severe. The red-haired girl stayed by his side. The subject of the photographer's lucky picture prowled the dock, lending a hand here and there, but mostly just walking, until a glass of water was forced upon her by one of the volunteer nurses who had begun to arrive in droves.

When the lamplights began to fade into the breaking dawn, the final passenger from the night's most-talked-about arrival was alone at the edge of the dock, sitting cross-legged in front of a memorial plaque affixed to the reconstructed railing. He was watching the two halves of the great airship. They were drifting very slowly, keeping pace with one another. There was nothing between them but empty sky.

The photographer had already packed away his equipment—he was looking forward to a stiff drink and a long nap. But when he saw the boy, he paused for a moment. There was nothing special about the scene, just another shell-shocked passenger collecting his thoughts, gazing with wonder at the magnificent remains of the greatest airship in the world. And yet something drew him closer. The boy had a heavy reference book in his lap. The photographer watched him move a finger inside the book as if it were a telegraph device. Over and over he tapped out a message, looking up into the sky, then back down at his lap, as if he were waiting for an answer.

EPILOGUE

HOLLIS MADE THE DECISION to move the press conference indoors. It was the end of June, and the shipyard was a sunbaked expanse of dust and heat. He had planned a ceremonial riveting, but a less dramatic unveiling would have to do. When he'd asked his mother if that was okay, she'd told him it was his ship, his decision.

The crowd funneled into the empty hangar and filled the neat rows of folding chairs. Reporters jostled at the edges, and when Hollis took the podium, he was flanked by photographers. High above, the beams of the vaulted ceiling met in a point. He forced himself to look down at his notes. The words jumbled together. He'd practiced a million times in front of the mirror, in front of his mother, in front of Delia, and now he felt unable to string together a single sentence. He took a deep breath. It was just a little speech. He reminded himself that the inquest was over, that Dakota Aeronautics had been absolved of any blame. He wasn't testifying before some grim congressional committee. He was giving people a glimpse into the future.

"Thank you all for coming." His voice sounded squeaky, and he was already talking too fast. He wanted to pull the sheet away from the easel and get it over with. But first, the notes. His speech had been written and revised countless times by the company's advertising team. It was important for him to learn how to sell his ideas to the public.

"I loved my father," he said.

In the front row, his mother, who knew the speech by heart, looked at him curiously. Next to her, Delia sat with her hands folded politely in her lap.

"I miss him every day," Hollis continued to improvise. "So I want to start with a moment of silence for the people who never made it off the airship." He counted to sixty in his head, then resumed. "As much as I want to tell you that when it comes time for me to take my place at the head of the company, I'll keep moving along the path that my father and mother set out, I can't. The *Wendell Dakota* was the last airship of its kind."

He paused for the murmur to ripple through the crowd. Reporters jotted furiously. He tucked the notecards into the pocket of his jacket.

"Let me just say that my mother is still in charge. She decides when I'm ready to take over. I still have a lot to learn before that day."

"Obviously!" someone yelled from the back. Hollis waited for the laughter to die down. He caught his mother's eye, and she gave him a slight nod: *Go on.*

"We've always tried to stick to the rules, to make air travel as comfortable as possible. But I've been thinking a lot about rules lately, and I wanted to give Dakota passengers a chance to break them a little bit."

With that, he whisked the sheet away from the easel with a flourish. He was relieved that he didn't send the blueprints crashing to the ground. He crossed his arms and smiled at the design while the crowd surged forward to get a better look. Flashbulbs popped.

The barrage of questions began, everyone yelling over everyone else. Hollis was forced to point to one reporter at a time.

"You can't seriously intend to put first-class staterooms alongside third-class bunks *on the same deck?*"

"Why not? Next question, please."

"Yeah, where's the steerage hold supposed to be?"

"There is no steerage hold. Everyone gets a bunk."

"Your ship will be the darling of the progressive papers, I'm sure, Mr. Dakota. But how, exactly, does it stay in the air? I only see one lift chamber."

Hollis grinned at Delia. "We've got our best people working on some new ideas."

AFTER HE'D FIELDED the last of the questions and the reporters scurried off to file their stories, his mother took to the podium to reassure some very nervous-looking board members about the profitability of faster, more affordable air travel. Hollis wandered off with Delia, not wanting to listen to another word about budgets or company policy or shareholders. At the edge of the hangar, they paused to watch a stray mutt retrieve sticks tossed by a few off-duty workmen. Across the yard, the framework of a new ship shone like a ruby in the light of the setting sun. *Monster bones*, he thought.

Maggie and Chester came around the corner.

"About time!" Delia said.

"We miss anything good?"

"Unbelievable." Hollis shook his head. "You were supposed to be here."

"Take it easy, Dakota. Chester was getting his cast off."

Chester held up his arm and rotated his wrist.

"Looks like you found time for a haircut, too," Hollis said, rubbing the fuzz of Chester's newly shaved head.

"The nurse did that. She said I had a lice problem."

Hollis pulled his hand away. One of the workmen launched an apple core. The dog loped after it. An airship from Newark was cruising past Manhattan, and the sound of the distant propeller thudded across the yard.

"You think he's still up there?" Hollis asked.

Delia watched the sky, as if Samuel's ship were going to suddenly appear above them. "Well, I don't think they'd risk a landing. Unless they flew somewhere really remote."

"Why doesn't he just come down? We were working things out. We were so close."

"Would you, if it was your dad up there?"

Hollis didn't have an answer for that.

"You know what I been wondering?" Maggie asked. Her eye had healed. She was wearing a brand-new Dakota Aeronautics handkerchief. "What are they eating up there?"

"I really don't want to know." Hollis said, walking toward the low-slung brick building that housed the new design office. Before he got too far away, he turned back and waved. "See you tomorrow, then?"

But they were all watching the airship head out to sea.

ACKNOWLEDGMENTS

Massive airship-sized thanks to Lauren O'Reilly for her unflagging love, support, and encouragement over the years. I'd like to thank my parents for providing constant artistic and personal inspiration.

My deepest thanks to my agent, Elana Roth, for her invaluable guidance and savvy insight into matters both on and off the page.

This book would not exist without the jaw-dropping expertise of my editor, Noa Wheeler, whose wide-ranging intelligence and attention to the oddest little details never ceases to amaze. Thanks also to April Ward for the pitch-perfect cover design, and to Ana Deboo for the wonderfully sharp copyedit.

Along with Lauren, Matt Lambert read the very first draft and helped set this book on the right path.

Finally, very special thanks to Walter Lord, whose *A Night to Remember*—the undisputed classic of *Titanic* books—was both a useful reference and a source of great inspiration.